STUART PAWSON had a career as a mining engineer, followed by a spell working for the probation service, before he became a full-time writer. He lives in Fairburn, Yorkshire, and, when not hunched over the word processor, likes nothing more than tramping across the moors, which often feature in his stories. He is a member of the Murder Squad and Crime Writers' Association.

Also by Stuart Pawson

Last Reminder

Stuart Pawson

This edition published in 2005 by
Allison & Busby Limited
Bon Marche Centre
241-251 Ferndale Road
london SW9 8BJ
http:/www.allisonandbusby.com

First published in 1997 by Headline Book Publishing.

A catalogue record for this book is available from
the British Library.

10 9 8 7 6 5 4 3

ISBN 0 7490 8319 0

Printed and bound in Great Britain by
Bookmarque Ltd, Croydon, Surrey

To Doreen

ACKNOWLEDGEMENTS

Sometimes we forget to thank those to whom we are most indebted. I would therefore like to record my appreciation of the skills and efforts of Teresa Chris and Marion Donaldson.

I am also grateful for the assistance and patience of the following: Hazel Mills, John Crawford, Dennis Marshall, John Mills, Douglas Laycock and several anonymous experts who answered my questions when they no doubt had more important tasks to complete.

Most of the jokes came from the aforementioned too.

Chapter One

I was late, so I indulged myself with a leisurely breakfast. I have a theory about these things. Breezing into the office an hour after everybody else, bristling with energy like a hedgehog on the live rail, creates a better impression amongst the troops than skulking in at ten past, ill shaven and suffering from caffeine deficiency.

The personal radio propped against the window was asking all available cars to go to the by-pass, where a lorry had shed thirty tons of self-raising flour. A lot of other people were going to be late for work this Monday morning. Could be interesting if it rained. I looked out of the window but there wasn't a cloud in the sky, worse luck. I snipped the end off the boil-in-the-bag kippers, guaranteed not to stink out the kitchen, and poured myself another cup of strong, sweet tea.

I was on my way in, personal radio hissing and crackling on the passenger seat, when the message came for Lima Tango to go to the park.

'We've our hands full at the by-pass, skip,' I heard the observer protest. 'Can it wait?'

I reached across and pressed the transmit button.

'Charlie Priest to Heckley control. What's the problem in the park?' I asked.

'Hello, Mr Priest,' came the reply. 'Have you slept in?' Another theory crashed and burned.

'Only exercising my knack for being the right man in the right place. Am just passing park gates. What's the problem?'

'Not sure. Message garbled, caller sounded hysterical. We'd be grateful if you could take it.'

'OK, will be at the keeper's cottage in under two minutes. Out.' I spun the car round and made a left turn through the gates of Heckley municipal park.

I grew up in this park. When I was a toddler my parents would bring me for walks on Sunday afternoons. We'd feed the ducks and I would ride the paddle-boats on the little lake. Later, it was birds' nesting and cowboys and Indians in the woods. As teenagers we would moodily follow the girls around, rarely integrating with them, or maybe use the tennis courts or the putting green to show off our skills with racket and club. Later still, much later, it was moonlit strolls under the chestnut trees, the air heavy with the scents of magnolia, honeysuckle and unrequited lust.

A newspaper headline described the assassination of President Kennedy as the day innocence died. I'd put it about fifteen years later than that. No one in their right mind came into this park at night since that time, unless they were looking to be mugged, stabbed or raped. Teenagers of both sexes roared round on motorbikes or in stolen cars, leaving their jetsam of lager cans, used condoms and burnt-out wrecks in their wakes. Addicts and dealers plied their trade, while others sought comfort and privacy in the cloying darkness.

The leaves across the road told me that I was the first vehicle down the avenue that morning. The rhododendrons had long lost their blooms, but the roses were confused by the late summer and managed a respectable show. The tennis courts were still there, but Tarmac now, and their wire cages hung broken, like wind-blown spiders' webs.

The curtains moved when I drew up outside the keeper's cottage, and he came to the door as I opened his front gate. He was a little man, his face lined and cracked by the drought, or perhaps by the ceaseless battle against impossible odds to keep the park a thing of beauty. He wore a grey jacket over a collarless shirt. Gardeners always wear jackets. Roses grew round the door and his little garden glowed with colourful plants that I couldn't begin to recognise. Clearly, no weed ever made it past infancy there.

I flashed my ID. 'Detective Inspector Priest, Heckley CID,' I told him.

He gestured with a wave of his hand, as if he had difficulty speaking. 'They're ovver 'ere,' he managed to say and, moving past me, he began striding towards the lake. I hadn't expected him to congratulate me for being quick, and he didn't. Two minutes is a long time when you are waiting for the police. I turned, carefully closed the gate, and followed.

There was a muddy patch leading down to the water's edge, puddled by webbed feet and several generations of guano. The mud was criss-crossed with the tracks of mountain bikes.

I stood next to the keeper, surveying the carnage.

'They allus come to t'door to be fed, every mornin'.' I realised he was weeping. 'They din't come this mornin'.'

Well, they wouldn't, would they? After a moment I put my hand on his arm. 'Go put the kettle on,' I suggested.

'I'll see what I can find here.' He sniffed and nodded and shuffled away.

They were floating in the shallows, four of them, their necks abruptly terminated, so the carcasses resembled weird retorts from a Dali-esque chemistry set. There had been nothing graceful about these deaths. No prima ballerina, nudging her sell-by date, had given the performance of her career in this park last night. Deprived of life, of balance, the swans had slumped over, bobbing about with all the elegance of bags of sausages. Their waterlogged wings were extended and black feet reached upwards, like bats taking flight. When I looked into the water, staring through the reflections, I could see blood oozing into the mud. And everywhere, blowing across the grass, into the flower beds and the azalea bushes, was a blizzard of white feathers. Winter had come early, and I could taste kippers.

I hooked a finger into a discarded beer can and studied it. Once it had contained Newcastle Brown, and now it was smeared with gore. I used to be a Newky Brown man myself, a long time ago. We drank it in the back rooms of pubs with flagstone floors, listening to songs about moving on, and the people you saw on the streets of London. Never was a generation so deluded. Now we have people like that in every market town in the country. Back at the car I popped the can into a plastic Sainsbury's bag.

The front room of the keeper's cottage was tiny and cluttered. He and his wife collected toby jugs. And little dolls with crocheted clothes. And plates celebrating various events and places. A coal fire blazed in the hearth and condensation streamed down the windows. The keeper's wife, still in her dressing gown, gave me tea in a china mug with teddy bears on it.

'Don't see many like that, these days,' I said, nodding towards the fire. They mumbled agreement. The morning sun was lancing through the window, and between the runnels of water you could see the mist rising from the dew-sodden grass. 'You'd live in a beautiful place,' I told them, 'if it wasn't for the people.' This time the agreement was more enthusiastic.

They'd seen and heard nothing. On the previous evening they had driven into the estate, to a harvest festival supper, and returned about ten thirty. It was impossible to say if the deed had been done by then. They gave me descriptions of the kids they regarded as the most likely offenders, but they meant nothing to me.

'Do you know who to ring at the council,' I asked, 'to get them to remove the bodies?'

He was a council employee, so he did.

'OK. Well, I suggest you arrange for them to be collected, as soon as possible. Do you have any objections if I ask the *Gazette* to do an article, with photographs? It's very doubtful that we'll catch anybody, but if we create enough fuss we might just tweak their consciences.'

They had no objections, but disagreed with me about the consciences. 'Right. I'll ask them to have a photographer here as soon as possible, and I'll tell our town parks officer to call on you. Thanks for the tea. I'll have another look around, and let you know if we turn anything up.'

Outside, I rang the *Gazette*. The girl on the front desk told me that the photographer was at the accident on the by-pass, but she'd see what they could do. I collected the Sainsbury's carrier bag and wandered back to the water's edge.

The tyre tracks led me through the flower beds, tiptoeing

in the mud and trying to avoid the worst of the wet leaves that soon soaked my trouser legs. I found a plastic bag with evidence of solvent in it and a couple of butane canisters that might have been there for quite a while. Slowly, I worked my way towards the little jetty where the boats are moored.

The boats are intended for children only, and looked just like the ones that were there when I was a kid. I've never seen any similar ones anywhere else. They have paddles, operated by a hand-crank, and large white numbers painted on the side. To protect them from vandals a chain laced them all together, and the whole jetty was fenced off with iron railings that arced down into the water. I dropped the carrier and stared at the railings, hypnotised by the scene. I edged forwards, drawn by disbelief and horror.

Pulled over the tops of the iron spikes, like those socks that golfers use on their clubs, were the necks and heads of the four swans.

The office was unusually full when I arrived. Detective Constable David Sparkington, known as Sparky to cops and crooks alike, except when he's in earshot, looked up from the keyboard he was tapping with all the confidence of a novice bomb disposal expert.

'Morning, boss,' he said. 'Sleep in?'

'No, I've been on a wild goose chase.' It was the first time I'd been late in twenty-odd years, and everybody knew about it. 'Heavy night,' I explained.

'Somebody lie on your shirt flap?'

'Sadly, no. Home-made booze. Sloe gin, to be precise. God knows what they'd put in it, but it was good stuff.'

'They put sloes in it. Otherwise it's solid gin.'

'It didn't taste anything like gin.'

'It doesn't, but it is.'

'That could explain it.'

Nigel Newley, my bright young detective sergeant, was doing his impression of a koi carp, opening and closing his mouth as he tried to interrupt us. 'Thanks for going to the morning assembly, Nigel,' I told him. 'Give me twenty minutes to do a quick report and we'll have a chat, unless there's anything spoiling?'

'OK, boss. There's nothing that won't wait.'

My little world is a partitioned-off corner of the main CID office. I hung my jacket behind the door and typed up the details of the Heckley Park massacre, in rhyming couplets to give it more impact. On the way in I'd left the beer can and other goodies with the scenes of crime boffins. When I'd finished I wandered out into the main office, looking for a cup of something hot and sweet and an update on the morning's proceedings.

Sparky looked at his watch. 'Might as well have one in the canteen in ten minutes, when they do the judging,' he replied when I suggested putting the kettle on.

'Judging? What judging?' I asked, puzzled.

'The silly tie contest. Don't pretend you'd forgotten.'

The silly tie contest was the latest in a series of fund-raising exercises for the local hospital. 'Aw, Carruthers!' I thumped my palm with my fist. 'Completely slipped my mind. What time does it start?'

'Now.'

Nigel caught my attention with a wave. He placed his hand over the mouthpiece of the telephone he was holding and hissed, 'Are you in, Mr Priest?'

I looked down, recognised what I modestly call my body, and nodded to him.

'It's the editor of the *Heckley Gazette*. Says somebody has killed the swans in the park, and that you know all about it.'

I reached over his desk and took the phone. 'Hiya, Scoop. It's Charlie Priest. Did you get a photographer there before the dustbin men took the bodies?'

'We certainly did. Now all I want is a nice juicy quote from you.'

'Right,' I said. 'Is your pencil poised?'

'Yep.'

'Have you licked it?'

'Get on with it!'

'OK, put this. Detective Inspector Priest, that's spelt P-R-I-E-S-T, of Heckley CID, says, "If I catch the sadistic *bastards* who did this I'll personally hang them by their knackers from the town hall clock." Knackers starts with a K. Did you get all that?'

Nigel's mouth dropped open, revealing a set of lower teeth whose gleaming symmetry could have graced a wall chart. Sometimes I hate him.

The editor, who I went to school with, thanked me. 'Put it on the slate,' I replied, handing the phone back to Nigel.

The troops were beginning to drift towards the door, on their way to the silly tie contest, so I stood there, reviewing them as they passed by. 'Good morning, my brave young crime busters,' I enthused, rubbing my hands together. 'Nice to see you have all entered into the spirit of things, or are you just sloppy eaters?'

The canteen was crowded. I queued for a toasted currant teacake and mug of tea and joined two uniformed sergeants at their table. 'Excuse me, is this chair vacant?' I asked, in my best attempt at a Liverpudlian accent.

'No, it's just a bit absent-minded,' one of them responded in a much better one, piling a couple of plates on top of each other to make some room.

I told them about the Heckley Park massacre and they agreed to round up a few glue-sniffers and take their dabs. A prosecution was unlikely, but we like to keep the pressure on them.

'Can I have your attention, please!' Gareth Adey, my uniformed counterpart, was standing up and using the canteen's primitive PA system to bring the room to some semblance of order. After lots of mumblings and another request for silence he said, 'Thank you. This won't take long because some of you...' He repeated himself for effect. '*Some* of you have work to do.' It was a veiled dig at CID and an overt threat to his own men to get their butts out of there as soon as this was over. 'As you know, we are here to announce the winner of the CID silly tie contest. This proved to be very difficult, as the depths of silliness being plumbed were extreme even for our beloved CID. So, without further ado, I announce the winner is...' He pulled an envelope from his pocket and pretended to read the contents. '... the one-and-only Detective Constable Jeffrey Caton.'

Inspector Adey made an expansive gesture towards Jeff, and loud jeering erupted. Jeff strolled to the front of the room and took the microphone from Adey. When it was quiet again he said, 'This is the proudest moment of my life. I'd like to thank the following people from the bottom of my heart: first of all, Mrs Brenda Prawn, who for many years worked the electronic testing machine at the Durex factory. If Brenda hadn't had an off-day in June 1966, and let a faulty batch through, I might not have been here today. I'd also like to thank the midwife for having...'

'Right, Jeff,' Adey interrupted. 'I think we get the message.'

'Oh, OK.' Jeff handed the mike back and whispered something in Adey's ear.

Adey told us, 'Jeff has kindly donated the first prize of ten pounds back to the hospital fund.'

Cheering and clapping all round, but we weren't finished yet. Adey blew in the mike and asked for silence. 'In the runner's-up position,' he said, 'after a very tight contest, was our very own, wait for it, Detective Inspector Charlie Priest!'

The room burst into applause.

'But I . . .' I started, then shut up.

'But you what?' one of the sergeants asked, clapping and grinning like a seal in a salmon farm.

'But never mind,' I said, jumping to my feet. 'I'll take the money,' I shouted, above the commotion.

'Sorry, Charlie,' Adey responded. 'There's no prize for second place. In fact . . .' He looked at his sheet of paper again. 'In fact, we don't seem to have your entry fee. It would appear that you owe us two quid.'

'Get stuffed!' I yelled. I was going to add something else, but behind him I noticed one of the canteen ladies holding up the telephone and gesturing towards me. I sprinted towards Adey, and a look of surprise flickered across his face, but I went straight by him and took the handset from her.

It was the front desk. 'We've had a report of a body in a house out by Sweetwater,' the duty sergeant told me. 'Milkman reported it. Looks like a suspicious death.'

'Have you somebody there?' I asked.

'Mmm. Young lad called Ireland. Only six months

service, but he's sensible enough. He says there's a head wound and a broken plant pot nearby.'

'OK. We'll be with you in a minute.'

I was putting the phone down when I heard him call, 'Charlie?'

'Yes?'

'How did you go on?'

'Useless. Only managed second place.'

'That's not bad.'

'Nah. I could have won it if I'd entered.'

People were drifting away. I put my hand on Dave Sparkington's shoulder and said, 'C'mon, sunshine. We've a suspicious death over in Sweetwater.'

'Ooh, great,' he answered, rising to his feet. As he threaded his arms into his jacket he asked, 'Are we taking the murder bag with us?'

'Might as well,' I told him.

Dave turned to the table where DC Margaret Madison was deep in conversation with three uniformed WPCs. 'Maggie,' he called.

She looked up at us.

'You're wanted.'

Mad Maggie took a final gulp from her mug and joined us. 'What's so funny?' she asked, warily eyeing each of us in turn.

'Dave made a sexist comment,' I told her. 'We've a suspicious death. Let's go.'

'Umph!' she retorted, glowering at him.

A uniformed constable, male, at an adjacent table, was reaching over for the ketchup. Maggie took the opportunity to snaffle the Eccles cake from his sideplate as we passed by.

'That's called theft,' I informed her.

'Then I'm safe as houses. This lot couldn't catch a train.'

I collected all the available information from the duty sergeant while Dave fetched anything we might need from the office upstairs. We piled the stuff in the boot of my car and set off. Sweetwater is an upmarket development on the outskirts of Heckley, encroaching on to the moors like bracken does. I'd considered moving there myself when they started building, until I saw the prices. Maggie knew the area, and gave me directions through a mouthful of crumbs.

'Don't make a mess in my car,' I warned her.

'Soddy, both,' she replied. 'It'th the nexg threet on the lebd.'

It was the last house, separated from its neighbour by about fifty yards of what the estate agent probably referred to as paddock and a thriving hawthorn hedge. It was posh, private and remote. Young Constable Ireland was waiting at the gate.

'Good morning, Graham,' I greeted him, having asked the duty sergeant for his first name. 'What have you got for us, then?'

He gabbled a description of what he'd seen when he entered the house, stressing that he hadn't touched anything and not leaping to any conclusions. Usually they have it solved before I arrive, until the facts emerge.

'Was this door open?' I asked.

'Yes, sir. Well, unlocked.'

'I see. This'll be your first suspicious death?' I surmised.

'Yes, Mr Priest, sir.'

'OK, this is what happens. I take a peek inside, as carefully as possible, to confirm what you've already told us. If I'm satisfied that it looks like murder we send for the duty detective superintendent who takes over as SIO. He will then bring in all the boffins and momentum does the rest. Where's the milkman who reported it?'

'He rang from home, sir. Apparently he'd noticed that Sunday's delivery was still on the doorstep when he came this morning. He finished his round, but was concerned, so he rang us.'

'He delivers on Sundays?'

'He must do, sir.'

'Blimey, the man's a paragon. He'll be winning a good citizen's award if he's not careful.' A fairly new Ford Scorpio stood in the drive. 'Presumably he'd noticed that the car was still here. What's the householder called?'

'He's a Mr Goodrich, sir.'

'Goodrich, right. Now the first thing for you to remember, Graham, is that I don't like being called sir. Use it when somebody of a higher rank is here, if you want, but otherwise, forget it.'

'Oh, right.'

It makes me feel old, and I've never subscribed to all this deference towards rank. That's why my promising career peaked at inspector, and I am now the longest-serving DI in the force. Sometimes I wonder if I'm like one of those women you see at office parties who are the wrong side of middle age, but who wear the shortest skirts and kick their legs higher than their younger rivals. No doubt about it, but at least a man can compete and still retain some of his dignity. Right at that moment I felt anything but dignified as I wriggled into a nifty pale blue overall and drew the hood over my head.

'You don't 'alf look a pillock in one of those,' Sparky confirmed.

I took the disposable paper overboots he was offering

13

and we walked to the front door of the imposing house. A pint of milk, gold top, stood on the step. I slipped the overboots on, and a pair of rubber gloves, then gingerly turned the door handle.

Graham had told me what to expect, but I still felt that familiar, intoxicating cocktail of nerves and curiosity as I edged down the passageway, casting my eyes from side to side, taking in the furniture and bric-à-brac that were like a fingerprint of a person's life. Or of a marriage, perhaps. Poor Graham must have been scared silly when he walked in here. We'd take him for a pint, afterwards.

Goodrich was in the kitchen, slumped in a rocking chair facing the Aga stove. The kitchen was huge, and I could tell that this was the room in which he, or the family, if there was one, spent most of their time. It was a good room, large, but still warm and cosy. Farmhouse, in agent-speak.

The curtains were closed and the television was on. A blond-haired surf-clone was begging a girl in a bikini to come back to him, against a backdrop of the Wallagongawalla hills. Meanwhile, in the house, someone had done the washing-up. One plate, one knife and fork, one coffee mug, one pan. I knew the scene only too well. A glass of whisky – Knockando, according to the bottle – stood on the Aga, and another mug contained the makings for a fresh cup of Nescafé. The kettle was full but cold, and he'd never got round to brewing his drink.

An apparent reason wasn't difficult to deduce. In his bald spot, towards the back of his head, was a gaping gash about an inch long. Lying on the floor, spilling its soil across the carpet, was a plant pot containing what I later discovered was a *Dieffenbachia picta*. I knelt down and saw where the edge of the heavy pot had made contact with skin and skull.

Maggie had armed young Graham with a book to keep a

log of all visitors. They and Sparky gathered round when I emerged.

'Single blow to the head with a plant pot,' I told them. 'Hardly a frenzied attack. Not much blood, possibly not immediately fatal. I get the feeling that he lives alone, but maybe has a cleaner or housekeeper. Rigor mortis, glass of whisky by his side, so he probably died last night. And he must have known his attacker well enough for them to be a visitor to his house.'

Sparky said, 'So we'll see what the neighbours have to say, eh?'

'You and Maggie, yes please. Meanwhile I'll send for the cavalry and get out of this lot. I feel like Woody Allen doing his impersonation of a sperm cell.'

'No, you're much funnier,' Maggie assured me.

There's a buzz in the air at the beginning of a murder enquiry. The adrenaline is pumping and you feel as if you are standing at the brink of some great discovery. Murder is the ultimate crime, with no going back. In the next few hours we would know more about the late Mr Goodrich than his bathroom mirror did. And perhaps we would know who hated him enough to kill him.

Most of all we needed to know who and what the dead man was. How did he earn his living? What was his social life like? More plainly, what did he do for money and sex? Maggie and Dave went knocking on doors. Neighbours can be amazingly forthright when they know that any comebacks are unlikely. The houses were widely spaced, so there weren't too many doors to knock on in the immediate vicinity. In my street the builder would have fitted another three desirable dwellings, ideal for the first-time buyer, between Goodrich's and the house next door. Maggie and Dave would ask the neighbours about

him, his friends, his lifestyle; and about any odd movements, strange cars, et cetera, in the street. Slowly, we
would build up a tapestry, leading us to the point where
the guy in the last panel catches the arrow in his eye.

I took a quick look round the exterior of the house
while waiting for the sub-divisional officer and the scenes
of crime officers to arrive. It was made from fine old
stone, probably reclaimed from some demolished Victorian building in the town, like a workhouse or a mill, or
some other temple to suffering, and the SOCOs would
paint the whole place silver with their aluminium fingerprint powder. There were three or four bedrooms, at a
guess, with a double garage stuck on one side and what
looked like an office extension on the other. The garden
was designed for economy of effort – mainly grass, with a
few shrubs and fruit trees round the edge. Once again I
recognised the style. My ultimate ambition is to replace
my grass with Astroturf. There were no footprints, no
discarded swag bags, no signs of forced entry.

The scenes of crime van arrived and I let the officers in
after a brief discussion. If they decided that the kitchen
was where it all happened – the locus of the crime, to use
the jargon – then I wanted to be let loose in the rest of
the house as soon as possible.

'Start with that,' I suggested, pointing to the bottle of
gold top standing on the step of the side door. 'Let's not
waste time looking for the milkman.'

Next to arrive was Gilbert Wood, my superintendent.
'Hello, Gilbert. What are you doing here?' I asked.

'Les Isles should have come but he can't make it. They
made an arrest yesterday in one of his other cases and
time's running out. He says can we manage and to keep
him informed. So,' he said and rubbed his hands to-

gether, 'here I am to keep a weather eye on my ace detective.'

'Great,' I replied. 'The old firm back together again.'

'The old firm indeed. So what have we got?'

'Male victim, fiftyish,' I told him. 'Killed by a single blow to the head. Broken plant pot, complete with plant, lying on the floor. Not a very determined attack – I've had worse knocks playing football. Possibly he died afterwards; choked or something. Rigor mortis, so he's been dead a while. Maggie and Dave are talking to the neighbours.'

'What about motive?'

'Doesn't look like robbery, at this stage. He's sitting in his chair, with the telly on, so he must have known his assailant. Door not locked, no sign of forced entry. Looks as if they let themselves in, or out, walked up behind him, picked up the plant pot, and *pow*!' I did a little demonstration of bashing someone's skull in with a flower arrangement.

The SOCO came out, a bunch of keys dangling from his hand. He nodded to Mr Wood and turned to me. 'Excuse me, Mr Priest. There's an office at the side of the house. I've unlocked the outside door, so you can be having a look in there, if you want. The internal door was locked, so there's probably nothing in it for us.'

'Great. Thanks.' I led Gilbert round the side and we let ourselves in.

The room was L-shaped, a single storey extension with lots of windows. It looked as if clients called on him, for the bottom bit of the L was a waiting area, with four chairs and a coffee table with magazines. *Executive Car*, *What Boat?* and *Investment Monthly* should have given me a clue to how Goodrich earned his crust, but they didn't.

He had the biggest leather chair I'd ever seen, looking out of place behind the type of desk you can buy flat-packed in any office furniture store. On other desks there were two PCs, with VDUs, keyboards and a shared printer; fax machine, duplicator and shredder; and two walls were lined with filing cabinets. Between all these was an assortment of stacks of trays in coloured plastic, all flooding over with paperwork.

I didn't know where to start, and Mr Wood didn't offer any help. The blotter pad on Goodrich's desk was from the Prudential and his walls bore calendars from Norwich Union and Sun Alliance. His diary had the Eagle Star logo embossed on the front and alongside it was a jotter pad from Scottish Widows.

'He's an insurance man,' I concluded. They pay me a lot of money to arrive at conclusions like that.

Gilbert studied the diary while I riffled through a few drawers of files. Some were filled with glossy leaflets and presentations from various companies, but I soon found the ones filled with his clients' files, all in neat alphabetical order. There were eight cabinets of them, each with four stuffed drawers. They started at Aaron and went right through to Mr and Mrs Zwendsloot. Somebody had some work to do.

Sparky poked his head round the door. 'Morning, Mr Wood,' he said.

'Good morning, David. Glad to see we've got some brains on the job.'

'She did it,' I told them, holding up Mrs Zwendsloot's file. 'It's bound to be the last one we look at.'

'Thought you might like to know – he was a financial adviser,' Sparky announced.

'A financial adviser?' we echoed in unison.

'That's right. The neighbour told me.'

'Just what I thought,' Gilbert claimed.

'Well, if you're going to *ask*,' I protested. 'Anybody can *ask*.'

'The neighbour's called Eastwood,' Sparky said. 'Might be a good idea if you had a word with him, Charlie. He seems to know a bit about the victim.'

'Right. Will do.' Sparky might still be a constable after serving as long as me, but I always do as he says.

Gilbert said, 'I'll get back to the factory, start things at that end. Incident room over there?'

'Mmm.'

'Want me to drag the HOLMES team in?'

I nodded my head. 'Yeah, but only one of them. I can't see us needing it. I haven't heard of any other financial advisers being bumped off.'

'OK. What help do you need?'

I threw a desperate glance at the rows of filing cabinets. 'What's the chances of getting someone from the Fraud Squad to have a look at these? He might even be known to them already.'

'Will do. I'll see you when you get back.'

Dave led me round to the neighbour's house. It was in the same style as Goodrich's, but smaller and the garden was well kept. Eastwood was as tidy as the garden. He was late middle-aged, with neat grey hair and one of those scrubbed complexions that looks as if it belongs on a baby. He wore a patterned cardigan that might have been a Christmas present from an aunt who thought he was still a teenager, and a striped tie. And shiny shoes. People who wear a tie and leather shoes in their own homes disconcert me.

Sparky introduced us. 'I wonder if you could repeat to

19

Inspector Priest what you have already told me about Mr Goodrich.' With a conspiratorial wink he added, 'Then I don't have to write it down.'

'Ah, I see,' Eastwood replied with a smile. He didn't seem perturbed by the fact that his next-door neighbour was lying, or more precisely, sitting, with his head bashed in.

He gave us the general background that we needed.

Goodrich was single and lived alone. He had been a financial adviser, dealing with clients all over the East Pennine region and was famous for his involvement with a variety of worthy causes. He had a reputation for supporting local charities and for an ability to commute modest savings into serious wealth.

'You sound sceptical,' I interrupted.

'Do I?' Eastwood replied, with exaggerated surprise.

'So what was the secret of his success?'

'Well, for a start, he was a master of self-publicity. And he'd made a few good investments, but he didn't realise that it was just good luck. He thought he was clever. Infallible. Believed his own publicity. There's only one way to make a lot of money on the markets, Inspector, and it's the same as the way for losing a lot of money.'

I leaned forward, waiting for the secret to be revealed. This could be useful.

'Gambling,' he explained.

'Gambling?'

'That's right. Going for the big-interest investments. Trouble is, this year's top earner is often next year's disaster. Goodrich thought he could pick them out, but he just had a little luck. He only advertised his successes, nobody knows about the fortunes he lost.'

'So you weren't one of his clients?'

'No chance, thank God. I am assistant manager of the Heckley branch of the York and Durham, so all my investments are through them.'

'Lucky you. What else can you tell us about him?' I'd let him volunteer what he could, then ask the searching questions. Like: did you kill him?

'Well,' he continued, 'six months ago, his luck ran out. He was declared bankrupt. Apparently it was the talk of the neighbourhood, but unfortunately I was away on holiday; missed all the gossip. Since then he's lived like a recluse.'

Sparky said, 'So what will have happened to all his clients?'

Eastwood shrugged. 'Nobody knows. It's all up in the air. Some will have lost their money, others will have had their investments frozen. Either way, there's a lot of angry people after Hartley's hide. Apparently,' he added with relish, 'quite a few of them are retired police officers.'

Hartley. Hartley Goodrich. A fine name for a whizz-kid. I wondered if growing up with a name like Goodrich had made it inevitable that he would drift into the world of high finance. As soon as he learned the meanings of the components of his name, did the cells down one side of his body grow larger, subtly bending him towards anything that smelled of money? There used to be a dentist in Halifax called I. Pullem, and I remember marvelling at such an incredible coincidence, but it wasn't. Long before the poor kid had cut his own first tooth his relatives would bounce him on their knees, saying, 'By 'eck, our Ian, tha'll make a reet good dentist when tha grows up.' It wasn't a coincidence, it was inevitable.

And then there's me. Priest. I was never ordained – didn't like the uniform – but I do take confessions.

'When did you last see him?' I asked.

After some thought he said, 'Last Wednesday.' They'd crossed paths in the doorway of the newsagent's shop, about a quarter of a mile away, and exchanged good mornings.

'And you haven't seen or heard of him since?'

'No, I'm afraid not, Inspector.'

'Did you notice any comings and goings over the weekend?'

He shook his head. 'Sorry, but no. You see, the two houses are separated by the hedge and are almost invisible to each other. Also, I spend a lot of time in my little workshop, at the other side. At the moment I'm constructing a model of the *Temeraire*.'

'The *Fighting Temeraire*?' I wondered.

'Yes. Are you familiar with her?'

'Only from the painting.' I did a thesis on it at college. Turner, the painter, was the true father of impressionism, but he doesn't get the credit.

'She was second in the line at Trafalgar. Avenged Nelson's death. It's said that . . .'

'Is there a Mrs Eastwood, sir?' Sparky interrupted.

'Oh, er, no. Well, yes there is, but not here. We were divorced not long ago.'

'Pardon me for asking,' Sparky told him, 'but women are often more observant about these things than we mere males.'

'Yes. Yes, I can understand that, but I'm afraid I live quite alone.'

I said, 'Have you ever heard anything about any particular dealings he made that might have brought about his downfall? Anything at all? And if it was other people's money he was losing, why has he been declared bankrupt?'

He shook his head. 'I really don't know, Inspector, but he had his fingers into all sorts of schemes. I don't envy you, having to unravel the mess he's in. It's true about the bankruptcy, though. It was in the papers, and he had a brief mention on the consumer programme on Radio Four.'

I'd been hoping that Eastwood might have pointed us in the right direction, or any direction. Now we'd have to rely on the Fraud Squad, and they could take months. Unless, of course, one of the names in the filing cabinets could help us.

I thanked Mr Eastwood for his cooperation and said we'd no doubt have to consult him again. He seemed quite pleased at the prospect. Funny how the right choice of words can create a favourable impression. If I'd suggested that we'd like him to help us with our enquiries he'd have been scared witless.

The photographers had finished and the SOCOs had moved to other parts of the house, so we had the run of the kitchen. The pathologist was informed and the police surgeon came to confirm that life was extinct.

We have a new lady pathologist. When she arrived we shook hands and I told her my name. 'DI Charlie Priest,' I said.

'Professor Simms,' she replied.

Sometimes, I prefer working with the opposite sex, although my reasons aren't anything to do with their competence, efficiency, or anything else revolving around ability. That's evenly shared between the genders. It's because usually they have softer voices. This is a grubby job, and a gentle voice, at the right time, might be all that makes it bearable.

She had a quick look at the overall attitude of the body, then knelt on the floor to see up at his face.

'Handsome enough, for his age,' she said, pulling at an eyelid with her thumb.

'The sort of face you'd trust?' I wondered aloud.

'Mmm. Why do you ask?'

'Apparently he was some sort of financial adviser.'

She took his temperature with a thermometer in his mouth and used another for the room temperature. When they had him on the slab they'd stick one up his bottom. The doc examined all his limbs, loosened his shirt to look at his torso, smelled where his breath would have been, if he'd had any.

I needed confirmation of cause of death, and a rough estimate of its time, quick as possible. The prof looked puzzled, and kept returning to the wound on Goodrich's head. I knew she wouldn't be hurried, so I left her to it.

Maggie was still out talking to neighbours, while Sparky and Jeff Caton, who'd just arrived, were looking at files in the office. I studied the place, taking in the machinery and devices of modern-day commerce. However did we manage without them all? This office had everything. Until it all went wrong. He'd filed for bankruptcy six months ago, and that was the last filing he'd attempted. Since then all the paperwork that came into the office had been piled on the desks and in the brightly coloured trays. The reason was obvious.

'He had a secretary,' I announced.

The two of them turned to me.

'He had a secretary until he went bankrupt, then she had to go. Find her, then maybe she can help us with this lot. Failing that, we'll have to bring Luke in to crack his computer.' Luke was a civilian nerd who talks to computers like some people talk to their hairdressers. 'We need a complete list of his clients. That should give us something to start on.'

'Just sorting a few out to be going on with, boss,' Sparky told me.

'Good. Find a couple of local ones for me to visit. Jeff, you have a look at his diary, and see if you can find an address book. We need his secretary, pronto. Not to mention next of kin.'

'Inspector?'

I turned round to find the professor looking round the door. She said, 'Time of death, late yesterday. Say between four and midnight. Can't be more precise than that, I'm afraid.'

'And the cause?' I asked.

She gave me a weak smile. 'Contradictory indications. For the time being let's say it was the blow on the head. There are no other marks on the body. Sorry, but we'll know better when we open him up. I've finished with him here, so you can arrange for his removal.'

'Right, Professor. Thank you.'

'There is one thing I'd like to show you. It might be interesting, but on the other hand it might be nothing.'

I followed her through into the kitchen. Goodrich was still more or less as I'd seen him earlier, slumped forward with one hand on the chair arm, the other in his lap, fist clenched.

'Look here,' the professor said, taking his fist. She pointed with the tip of her pen into the circle made by his thumb and first finger. 'He's holding something.'

I could see the end of a piece of clear plastic, or maybe Cellophane.

'Do you want to retrieve it now?' she asked.

I nodded. 'Yes, please. Might as well.'

I held the rigid arm while she prised his fingers open. Slowly a piece of plastic, a couple of inches long by half-an-inch wide was revealed. It fell into my gloved hand and I peered at it.

'How about that?' I said after a few seconds, holding it towards the doctor.

'Wowee!' she gasped, under her breath. 'Is it real?'

'I wouldn't know,' I confessed. I'd only ever bought one, and that ended in disaster.

It was a little transparent package, thermo-sealed to avoid tampering. At one end was what looked like a frame of microfilm, and at the other a piece of paper with some numbers and letters on it.

In the middle was the biggest diamond I'd ever seen.

Chapter Two

Colonel Bartlett was a wiry little man with a wiry moustache and a grizzled wire-haired terrier following him around, as if attached to his ankle by a very short lead. Sparky had found the colonel's file in Goodrich's cabinets and, as he lived less than a mile away, I'd come round to see what he could tell me. His wife, who I felt an overwhelming urge to call Lady Bartlett, although I suppose she was a mere Mrs, placed a delicate tea-cup and saucer on the table alongside me, with a matching plate holding a couple of pieces of that cake that looks like a chequered flag with marzipan round the edge. If he was wiry, you could have cut cheese with her.

'Thank you. That's most welcome,' I said.

'Dead, did you say?' the colonel asked. The dog had left his ankle and come to sniff at mine. We were sitting in flowery easy chairs in their pleasant front room. A large regimental photograph hung above the fireplace, and on the sideboard was one of Bartlett himself, looking remarkably Errol Flynnish. Mrs Bartlett, the niceties of hospitality accomplished, perched on his chair arm.

'Yes, sir. I'm afraid so. You weren't close to him in any way, were you?'

'No. Not at all. Business only. And bad bladdy business at that, if you ask me.'

'That's exactly what I do want to ask you about. First of all, though, can I ask you to treat this conversation as confidential, as we haven't found any next of kin yet?'

'Of course, Inspector. Mum's the word.'

Mrs Bartlett nodded her agreement. The dog was definitely interested in my left ankle. I noticed that it had grown an erection, so I pulled my feet against the chair. It's difficult to conduct a serious interview with a terrier shagging your leg.

'At the moment,' I began, 'we're treating his death as suspicious.'

'You mean . . . murder?'

'Possibly, although not necessarily.'

'Oh my God!' Mrs Bartlett wailed. I'd have thought army wives were made of sterner stuff.

'Can't say I'm surprised,' Bartlett declared. 'Might have done it myself, a few years ago.'

She was ahead of him. 'Does this mean,' she asked, 'that we are . . . suspects?'

'Please,' I said, holding my hands up in a gesture of appeasement. 'We have no suspects, so, in a way, everybody is a suspect. At the moment I am only interested in investigating Goodrich's affairs. All I know about him is that he was some sort of financial adviser. I plucked your name from the files because you are nearby, and I hoped you might be able to fill me in with some details about his business dealings.'

'Oh, we can do that,' Bartlett declared, unable to hide the bitterness that my visit had resurrected. 'We can certainly do that.'

They had £70,000 invested with Goodrich – most of their life savings. Someone at the golf club had introduced him, and at first things had gone fairly well.

28

'To be fair to him, it was a bad time,' Bartlett said. 'The recession, you know.'

I nodded sympathetically, although I've never understood how the whole world could be in recession at the same time. Unless recession is a virus, like Asian flu.

He continued. 'He put our money in various bonds, PEPs, stuff like that. All High Street names, and we had steady returns, although they were quite small. Then, one evening, he came round on his regular visit and suggested it was time we made our portfolio work for us. He was a dynamic bugger, I'll say that for him. Would've made a bladdy good colour sergeant.'

'So what did he suggest?' I asked.

'Diamonds,' he growled.

'Diamonds?' This was what I was looking for.

'Investment diamonds, to be precise,' Mrs Bartlett informed us.

'So you transferred your savings into these diamonds, on his suggestion?'

'Yes, but not all of it, thank God,' the colonel replied. He anticipated the next question. 'We bought three, at just over one carat each. Cost us thirty thousand altogether.'

'So what went wrong? Didn't they exist?'

'Oh, they existed all right. They did quite nicely to start with – looked as if they'd double their value in about five or six years. Then one day, completely out of the blue, a letter came from a firm of lawyers acting on behalf of the official receiver. It said that the company who supplied the diamonds, called IGI – International Gem Investments – were bankrupt, and we qualified as creditors. Eighteen months later all we've found out is that our diamonds are worth approximately one tenth of what we paid for them.'

I took a sip of tea and, trying not to attract the dog's attention, stretched out my legs. I had cramp in them. 'So what went wrong?' I asked. 'Were they selling the stones to more than one person?' That's a well-tried scam, used with everything from armaments to ... Zimmer frames. You prove you possess something, maybe a boatload of Italian wine that is going cheap because your brother-in-law works in the excise office, show the punters round it, supply them with samples and all the paperwork, but do the same thing with ten other people.

Bartlett rose to his feet. 'I'll fetch the bumf, let you see for yourself.'

When he'd gone I asked Mrs Bartlett if the rest of their money was safe.

'Yes, thank God,' she told me, 'but we're not receiving any income from it. Low interest rates sound a good idea, until you're depending on your savings. Poor Gerald's taken it badly. Blames himself. Always thought he was a good judge of a man's character. Now he works three days a week as a groundsman at the golf club. We should have been ...' She produced a tissue from within the folds of her dress and blew her nose. 'I'm sorry, forgive me.'

'It's all right,' I murmured, awkwardly.

Bartlett returned and handed me a sheaf of documents, some glossy, some photocopied. 'Here we are,' he said. 'Have a look at that lot. Some from Goodrich, saying what a fine deal they were, some copied from various financial magazines, whose advice was bordering on the criminal, and some nice glossy brochures from IGI.'

I pulled out a glossy and started reading. In times of recession, it said, people the world over looked for more traditional investments to safeguard their wealth. Like gold, or, it suggested, diamonds. In a typical year enough diamonds were mined to fill an average-size skip. Ninety per cent of these would be industrial grade, used for making machine tools. Eight per cent would be gemstones, used in the jewellery trade, and the remaining few, the very best, would be snapped up by investors.

My left leg felt warm. I lowered the papers and looked down. The dog had jumped it while I wasn't looking. Rover didn't know what danger he was in – I used to take penalties with my left foot. I snatched it back, placed it hard against the front of my chair and pressed my feet together for mutual protection. The stones in this two per cent, the leaflet continued, would be measured for weight, colour, clarity and cut, and then each one sealed in a package with a piece of microfilm containing its exact description. That sounded like what Goodrich was clutching when he died. The price of diamonds, it assured the reader, had not gone down in sixty years.

As I finished the brochure and put it to the back of the bundle I was holding, Bartlett said, 'Except, it's all bladdy balderdash.'

'Can I borrow these?' I asked.

'Of course. Anything to help.'

'Thanks. So what's balderdash?'

'All that about investment diamonds. There's no such thing. It's nonsense. IGI dreamed up the whole scheme. While they were selling plenty everything appeared pukka gen, but as soon as a few people tried to cash in, the whole damn plot fell through. We were investing in IGI, not in diamonds.'

'But you're happy that they exist?' I queried.

'Oh yes, but what we paid ten grand each for could have been bought for less than one in any bladdy souk in the world.'

'Do you still hold them?'

'No, we never held them. They're all in a bank on the Isle of Man.'

'So you've never even seen them?'

'No, but the diamonds are there. The receiver is trying to allocate them to the various investors at the moment. Only problem is, their value is as what they call collectibles. You know, jewellery. Might make a decent pair of earrings for her and a tie pin for me. If I could get my hands on the scoundrels, I'd . . . I'd . . .'

His face started to glow like my ceramic hob does when I forget to turn it off. Mrs Bartlett put her hand on his shoulder and he covered it with his own. 'Don't upset yourself, Gerald,' she murmured to him.

'No, try not to upset yourself. And for what it's worth, it looks as if someone did get their hands on Goodrich. What about safeguards?' I asked. 'Didn't you make sure he was a member of the appropriate governing bodies?'

'Of course we did,' Bartlett replied indignantly. 'He was a member of everything. More bladdy initials after his name than Saddam Hussein. And all as bladdy worthless. Washed their hands of us. Said we should have read the small print.'

I offered words of sympathy and stood up to leave, thanking them for their assistance and Mrs Bartlett for the tea. I hadn't touched the cake. 'One last thing,' I said. 'Could you let me have the name of the receiver who's handling the bankruptcy? It might be useful to have a word with him. If I find anything, I'll let you know.'

While I waited for the colonel to fetch the information the dog leapt up into the chair I'd vacated, rolled on to one side and started licking its cock. They do it because they can.

The next couple Sparky had found for me were an even sadder story. He'd worked as a window cleaner all his life and was now an invalid, crippled with arthritis and emphysema. They'd had twelve thousand pounds invested with Goodrich, doing reasonably well in General Accident, but he'd persuaded them to buy a couple of small diamonds with it and they were now poorer and wiser. Thirty English winters of climbing ladders and squeezing a washleather, with nothing to show for it but ill health. There was no doubt about it, Goodrich had left a long wide trail of heartbreak and anger in his wake. The enquiry was four hours old, and we had enough genuine suspects to crew a quinquereme of Nineveh.

I needed a break, so I fished the mobile out of the glove box and dialled my favourite number. After three rings a soft, warm voice confirmed that I'd got it right.

'It's Charlie,' I said, 'desperately in need of a friend. Any idea where I might find one?'

'Sorry,' she replied in a comic voice, 'we're not doing friends today. Today, friends is off.'

Annabelle Wilberforce is built like a beanpole, with short fair hair and a smile that flakes granite. Once, she lived in Africa, where she witnessed the atrocities of the civil war in Biafra. From there she moved to Kenya and married a man who became a bishop. He died of cancer, and now she hangs about with me.

'Oh, that's a shame,' I said, lamely. I wasn't really in the mood to be half of a comedy double act.

'We can do fish fingers,' she declared, in the same silly voice. 'Or even fish arms, fish legs, or a nice piece of rump fish. Fish is definitely on.'

'Wait!' I shouted into the phone. 'What's got into you? Can a man find a sensible conversation round here?'

'Sorry, Charles,' she said in her normal voice. 'I thought you said you wanted cheering up.'

'No, I said I needed a friend.'

'Oh, well, I'm the one you want. My middle name is Abacus.'

'Abacus?'

'That's right – you can count on me.'

I put my hand over the mouthpiece so she couldn't hear me chuckling. When I'd recovered I said, 'Is it possible for us to have a normal man-to-man talk without all these silly comments and second-rate impersonations?'

'You have a hangover!' she announced with obvious glee.

'No I haven't.'

'Yes you have. I can tell. The hard-boiled, hard-drinking detective has a hangover after too much sloe gin.'

'I thought religious people didn't drink.'

'You choose your religious friends and I'll choose mine. If you don't mind me saying so, you were drinking it as if it were lemonade.'

'I didn't realise it was so strong. I'll know better the next time.'

'We won't be invited again!' she exclaimed. 'Not after you . . . after you . . . Well, you know.'

'Now you *are* having me on. Listen, Annabelle. Something's cropped up. A suspicious death. I doubt if I'll be able to see you for the next two or three nights. OK?'

'You mean a murder?' Now she sounded anxious.

'I didn't say that. Can't say much on the phone; I'll tell you all about it when I see you.'

'How about popping round for lunch? Surely you are allowed a lunch break.'

'That sounds a good idea. Tomorrow, about one.'

'Let me know if you can't make it. And Charles?'

'Mmm?'

'Be careful.'

'Don't worry. It's not very heavy. Just routine.'

Except it's never just routine. I put the phone in my pocket and drove back to Goodrich's house.

The body had gone, replaced by a couple of marginally healthier ones from Fraud Squad.

'Not . . . Maud and Claud, from Fraud?' I asked when I saw them.

'Not . . . Defective Inspector Priest?' the female DS responded. I'd worked with them once or twice before; been for a drink with them a few more times; seen them in the canteen several times a day for the last five years. 'Where do you want us to start?' she asked.

'That lot,' I said, waving expansively at the rows of filing cabinets. 'Find out what he was up to. Oh, and who killed him.'

'It's gonna be a long night,' she sighed.

I had a wander round the house. If fingerprint experts found a tenth as much evidence as they leave behind we would eliminate crime. Every surface in the place was coated with their powders, creating an impression of neglect. His sitting room was all black leather and stripes. He must have read somewhere that stripes were sophisticated, so he'd gone overboard with them. Or perhaps he had a contact in a deckchair factory. Everything looked expensive and tasteless. A couple of heavy table lamps were held aloft by naked nymphettes, at odds with the large hunting scene above the fireplace. I looked at it more closely. Original, about three thousand quid at a guess, by an unknown artist whose credibility would die with him.

35

Upstairs were a junk room, a gymnasium of sorts, a study-cum-library and his bedroom. The gym had an exercise bike, a jogging machine and one of those multi-purpose machines of torture that they threatened Galileo with. The speedo on the bike told me he'd cycled eighteen miles on it, and the jogger had done forty-five. Arnie Schwarzenneger was safe.

The books were unedifying. Mainly thrillers, at the more violent end of the spectrum. He was a Jackie Collins fan. Some Wilbur Smith and John Grisham, lots of book club editions. One cabinet was filled with military histories.

In the bedroom, above the double bed and on the facing wall, were arty photographs of young men flexing their pecs. Black and white, so the sweat showed. The duvet cover was chequered, almost Black Watch tartan, with matching pillow cases. Two pillows, one on top of the other, sat in the middle of the bed.

It was the pillows that brought it home to me; pulled me up with a start. It was a human being we were dealing with. No matter what his tastes were, how he lived his life and earned his money, we had a duty to him. I looked through the drawers where he kept his socks and underpants, ran my hand across the shoulders of the suits in his wardrobe. He had more suits than I have bad habits. As I left the room I glanced at the pillows again. I pile mine up like that, except that he made his bed after he got out of it, while I make mine when I climb in.

I rejoined Maud and Claud, who are actually Maud and Brian, downstairs. Brian was looking at a file, trying to compile a table of basic information from it. Maud was on the phone. She is Afro-Caribbean, and joined the police when, midway through an accountancy course, after they'd sent her abseiling in Borrowdale, she decided she needed more action in her life. She made sergeant, but one night a gang of skinheads cornered her and left her for crippled. When she recovered she was determined that they wouldn't drive her from the job. She did a spell back in uniform, then Fraud learned of her background in accountancy and snatched her up.

'He's known to us, Mr Priest,' she said, clicking the phone off.

'Like how?' I asked.

'Allegations of fraud resulting from his bankruptcy. Nothing concrete. We're waiting for something more specific from the receiver.'

'He went bankrupt six months ago,' I protested. 'How long does it take?'

Maud shrugged her shoulders. 'Solicitors,' she stated, explaining everything.

Sparky popped his head round the door. 'Hi, boss. There you are. How's it going?'

'Slowly, David,' I replied. 'But hopefully you are now going to give us the breakthrough we've been waiting for.'

He came in and sat in a typist's chair that looked as if it might collapse under him. 'Hardly that,' he said. 'Talk about keeping yourself to yourself. It's a wonder this lot round here ever get round to breeding. Mr Goodrich's neighbours lead very discreet lives. Never look through their lace curtains, never take their eyes from the road ahead when they are forced to leave their desirable little castles. I've had more cooperation on the Sylvan Fields estate.'

'But . . .' I said.

'Whaddya mean, but?'

'But you wouldn't have come back if you didn't have something to tell me.'

'We've been working together too long,' he grumbled. 'But there was just one thing. Young girl at the end of the street. Works shifts at some fast-food joint. She says there are sometimes posh cars in Goodrich's drive as she passes in her car. All times of night and day.'

'So what? He's a businessman. Works from home. It would have been odder if there hadn't been.'

'She particularly noted one about a month ago, in the afternoon.' He glanced awkwardly at Maud, who was standing next to me, part of the conversation.

'Go on.'

'He parked in the road, so she noticed his number plate as she drove by. She says it was a BMW, a big one. They were playing a George Michael song on Radio Two, and the registration number stuck in her mind. It was W-A-M, WAM.'

'Wham?' I repeated.

Maud said, 'They were a pop duo. Not your type. George Michael was the leading light until he went solo.'

'I'm not totally decrepit, Maud,' I stated. 'But shouldn't there be an aitch in there, somewhere.'

'Christ, Charlie,' Sparky retorted. 'She remembered part of his number. Give her some credit for that, don't criticise her spelling!'

'OK, I'm sorry. W-A-M. Any idea where that might be from?'

'No.'

'Did she notice anything else about the car? Or him?'

Sparky looked embarrassed, something I'd never seen before. 'There was one thing,' he said.

'Go on.'

'According to her . . . He, er, was a black guy.'

The best way to meet any sort of a problem is to charge at it, headlong. I turned to the DS from Fraud Squad and said, 'Sounds highly suspicious to me, Maud. What do you reckon?'

Expressionless, she replied, 'No doubt about it. With a car and a complexion like that he must have been a drugs dealer. Let's try to find this BMW, top priority.'

It was ten o'clock when I arrived home. The fish and chip shop was closed, I was out of cornflakes and the bread needed defrosting, so I went upstairs to have a quick shower and then crash. I needed a good night's sleep more than food. Tomorrow's big meeting wasn't scheduled until nine thirty, so I'd have time for a full English in the canteen, first thing. You could lubricate a JCB with a canteen breakfast, but to hell with the risk.

I was sitting on the end of the bed taking my trousers off when the phone rang.

'Priest,' I intoned, rather pleasantly, in the hope that it was Annabelle.

'This is Inspector Lockett from Lingwell. Is that DI Priest?'

'The one and only, Mr Lockett. How can I help you?'

'Ah, good. Good evening.'

'Good evening.'

'We have a problem with a hostage situation, and I've found your name on the list of trained negotiators. Could you possibly come and take over?'

'A hostage?' I queried, adding, 'I didn't know I was on any list of negotiators.'

'Well, you are. Once every three months, for a week.'

'I took the course, about five years ago. I always

imagined I'd failed it. I wasn't exactly a natural.' I only signed on because I'd approved a uniformed WPC called Kim Limbert for it and I was crazy about her at the time. Kim was our first black WPC, and she made Naomi Campbell look plain. The thought of three days sitting in the next desk to her was more than I could resist. I took her for a drink once or twice, but it was strictly business, dammit.

'Will you help us, please? I've been ringing round for nearly half an hour.'

It's difficult to turn them down when you are their last hope. 'Who's he holding hostage?' I asked with a sudden burst of interest.

'Well, actually, it's a dog.'

'A dog! Are you winding me up?'

'No, Mr Priest. Let me tell you the story.'

'I think you'd better.'

'It's a youth. Don't know who he is, yet. He was disturbed at the top of a ladder, as he came out of a second-floor flat that he was burgling. He grabbed the dog and now he's at the top of the ladder, threatening to throw the dog and himself down. A bit of a crowd has gathered, so we want to play it by the book.'

'What is it, a Rottweiler?'

'No, thank goodness. A Chihuahua.'

'When you say second floor, do you mean second floor?'

'That's right. It's a long ladder. He's about thirty feet from the ground.'

Dogs and people don't bounce from that height. I said, 'OK, give me the address.' I wrote it down. 'Be with you in about twenty minutes. Try to keep the ghouls back and don't harass him – he might come down on his own. Oh, and one other thing . . .'

'Yes?'

'Order some sandwiches and a flask of coffee, please. It might be a long night.'

'Will do, Mr Priest. And thank you.'

I swapped my decent trousers for jeans and drank half of the mug of tea I'd taken up with me. Then I put my trainers and leather jacket on, swapped the contents of my pockets round and went outside. The car interior was still nice and warm.

On the way over I tried to remember what I'd learned on the course, apart from the fact that Kim thought I was a schmuck. A likeable schmuck, but still a schmuck. One, create a safe environment. That was it. Five, try to build a rapport with the hostage-taker. In between was something about empathy. Like I said, I wasn't a natural. The overriding memory was of having to suppress your instincts and do nothing. Enforced inactivity, like lying in a hospital bed with your legs in traction while all the other patients partied with the nurses. Be calm, and let nature take its course. Time heals everything. Well, stuff that for a box of soldiers.

He was right – it was a long ladder. Three extensions, fully out. The crowd was growing all the time, their faces, yellow in the glow of the sodium lights, turned up towards the unfortunate youth. One or two shouted for him to jump, trying to build up the rhythm of a chant. They'd do better in about half an hour, when the pubs turned out.

'Charlie Priest,' I said, identifying myself to Inspector Lockett.

'Inspector Lockett,' he replied, giving me a limp handshake. He looked younger than I was when I made inspector. Bet he wouldn't break my long service record, though.

41

The youth was sitting a couple of rungs from the top, facing outwards. That was a feat in itself. Don't think I'd have dared do it. He was level with the street lamps, and they cast shadows either side of him, like the floodlights at a football match.

'Where's the dog?' I asked.

'He's got it down the front of his bomber jacket.'

'Anyone from the RSPCA here?'

'No. Do you want me to call them?'

'Er, no. Not yet.' Definitely not yet.

The window he'd come out of was open, and a couple of policemen were inside, but they'd stopped trying to persuade him to surrender.

'Tell them to close the window and stay away from it,' I told Lockett, pointing upwards.

'Right,' he said, and started giving orders on his portable.

'Where are the sandwiches?' I asked when he finished.

'Oh,' he replied brightly, 'we shouted up to him, asked him what he wanted, and he declined.'

'He declined! *He* declined!'

'Well, told us to go and, er, eff ourselves, actually.' He dropped his voice as he said 'Eff', presumably so God couldn't hear.

'Sod him!' I gasped. 'They were for me. I haven't eaten for fourteen hours!'

'Oh, sorry, Mr Priest. I must have misunderstood. I'll arrange some now. In fact, maybe I should order the mobile canteen?'

'Just a couple of ham sandwiches will do.'

We were in a parking area in front of the block of flats. Nearby were several builders' huts and skips of rubbish. The youth must have found the ladder there. These flats are under a constant renovation programme, starving the rest of the housing of funds. Three police cars were parked, their flashing lights reflecting off the front of the building. I studied the situation and tried to remember Isaac Newton's first law of ladders. My memory wasn't much use to me tonight. I was tired, shouldn't have taken this on. Never did learn how to say no. Didn't he say something about a ladder being exactly the same length upright as it was when lying on the ground? Sounded reasonable to me. I did some elementary geometry in my mind, and when Lockett finished on the radio I asked him to move the crowd another fifteen feet back.

He had about six uniformed PCs with him, and they pushed and jostled until I was satisfied. The crowd were good natured, some of them on personal terms with the bobbies, but the mood could soon change. A fire engine with a turntable ladder came warbling down the road.

'Right,' I said. 'Now turn those blues off and tell Thomas the Turntable to go hide somewhere. We'll let him know if we need him.'

When it was quieter, the environment as reassuring as I thought I could make it, I strolled towards the foot of the ladder. The crowd stopped jeering.

'Gerraway!' the youth yelled at me. 'I'll chuck fuckin' dog darn if tha comes any closer.' He pulled the terrified hound from within his jacket to reinforce his words.

I took an extra couple of strides and stopped. 'Hi!' I shouted up to him, with all the sincerity of a reluctant recruit at the Mormon training academy. 'My name's Charlie.'

'I'll jump!' he yelled back, rising to his feet. 'I'll chuck me-fuckin-sen off.'

He was leaning against the wall. 'Please, be calm,' I pleaded. 'We don't want to hurt you. Can we just talk?'

'Warrabout?'

'Well, I'm called Charlie. What are you called?'

'Joe Fuck!'

'Do you live round here?' I asked, adding, 'Mr Fuck,' under my breath.

He didn't bother answering, but he put the wriggling dog back inside his jacket. It was calmer in there.

I was about six feet from the foot of the ladder. I shuffled forward, my hands in my pockets. 'Is it your dog?' I called out. I'm usually reasonable at interviews, but this was different. The spectators had brought their video cameras along, and tomorrow I could be on the news. He ignored my question.

'Do you like dogs?' I tried.

'They're all right.' That was an improvement.

'I expect you prefer bigger ones?'

'Yeah.'

'What sort's that one?'

'How the fuck do I know?'

He was an articulate so-and-so. I was at the foot of the ladder now.

'Don't come any fuckin' closer,' he warned.

'No, I won't,' I assured him, taking my hands from my pockets.

He was agitated. 'I'll fuckin' jump. I'm warnin' thi.'

They say a drowning man clutches at straws. I wondered if a falling one would cling on to a dog. It was worth the risk – it wasn't my dog. With one easy movement I placed my right foot on the bottom rung of the ladder, grasped the fifth rung in both hands and heaved. As the foot of the ladder came off the ground it started to accelerate away from the wall with a velocity that shocked me. I jumped aboard, and was propelled backwards towards the hushed crowd, like a surfboard rider, my arms flailing wildly. He scraped down the wall at exactly the same speed, emitting a long wail of fear and surprise.

My end stopped, and I fell backwards into a mess of arms that pushed me upright again. His end bounced a yard into the air, ejecting him like water off a sheepdog's back. The Chihuahua scampered away, between the legs of the cheering crowd, and into the open doorway of the flats. He'd had enough excitement for tonight.

I drew a breath and turned to Inspector Lockett. His eyes were wide and his mouth gaping, but he couldn't form any words.

'Cancel the sandwiches,' I said.

The youth could have had a gun or a knife, or even a fractured spine, so I approached him warily. He was about nineteen, undernourished and under average. On drugs at a guess. He had landed in a sprawled position, his shoulders against the wall, the residual fear still pulling at his face. Or maybe it was a new fear.

'Are you hurt?' I asked.

He didn't answer but his unblinking eyes tried to focus on me. I moved one of his feet with the toe of my trainer, and he snatched it away. Same with the other – he'd survive.

'OK, son,' I said, grasping the collar of his jacket. 'On your feet.' He resisted for a few seconds, then allowed me to haul him upright. 'You won't believe this,' I told him, 'but I've just done you a favour.'

Lockett took him away and most of the crowd wandered off, wondering if whatever was on satellite TV would be as good as this. A couple of grinning youths invited me in for a beer and a woman with an anorak over a housecoat told me that it was no thanks to me that the dog hadn't been hurt. I chatted with one of the PCs for a few minutes – he'd had a spell at Heckley a couple of years ago – and went home.

Two minutes in the microwave at number four warmed up the half a mug of tea I'd left on the worktop. Upstairs, I cleaned my teeth, stripped off all my clothes and crept into a nice warm bed. Just as I'd arrived at Lingwell I'd remembered that I'd left the electric blanket on. I reached out for the alarm clock and set it for fifteen minutes earlier than usual, to give me time for a shower in the morning. It was two minutes past midnight. It had been quite a Monday.

Chapter Three

There was a message on my desk next morning to ring a PC in Traffic. I did it straight away, in case it was anything I might need in the meeting.

'It doesn't matter, Mr Priest,' he replied. 'I didn't realise you were tied up with a big case. It'll do some other time.'

'Go on, you might as well tell me,' I said.

'It's OK. I was just going to ask you to do a poster for us.'

I went to art college before I became a policeman. It's an unusual route into the force, but it can be surprisingly useful. Any of them could have told me about the *Fighting Temeraire*, but how many knew that Wham! took their name from a Roy Lichtenstein painting? It doesn't help solve cases, but I pick up a few useful points at Trivial Pursuit. The drawback is that I get asked to do all the posters for police dances.

'No problem,' I told him. 'Send me the details and I'll do it when I can.' Actually, I find it quite relaxing, enjoy doing them.

'It's about bullbars,' he said.

'Bullbars?'

'Yeah, you know, on the front of off-road vehicles. The van that hit that little boy in town last week was fitted with one. We've just received the pathologist's report and it says that they made a significant contribution to his injuries. In other words, if it hadn't been for them, he'd be alive today.'

'Mmm, it's sad,' I said. 'So what do you want? A little poster that you can stick up all over town?'

'That's right, Mr Priest. And maybe we can go round putting them behind their wipers while they're in the supermarket, that sort of thing.'

'Right, I'll see what I can come up with. Have you managed to find some money in the budget for them?'

'No, sir. We've decided to pay for them ourselves.'

'Out of your own pockets?'

'That's right.'

'OK, well, put me down for a couple of quid. Give me a few days – as you said, we're a bit busy at the moment.'

'Thanks a lot.'

The phone was halfway back to its cradle when I heard him calling me.

'Mr Priest!'

'Yes?'

'Sergeant Smedley would like a word with you.'

He came on after a couple of seconds. 'Hello, Charlie,' he said.

'Hi, George. What can I do for you?'

'Do you still have that old E-type Jaguar?'

'You mean thirty thousand quids' worth of desirable motor car; the pinnacle of auto engineering, never approached before or since?'

'That's the one.'

'Yes, I still have it. Want to buy it?'

'No. I'll stick with my Morris Eight. More my image. Can I put you down for the cavalcade at the Lord Mayor's parade?'

'Oh, I should think so. I enjoyed it last year. Will you send me the details?'

'Will do. Cheers.'

'No problem.'

I inherited the Jag when my father died. It was a wreck, but I restored it, more or less in his memory. Then I sold it and bought it back again. It's fun to drive, but I'm not an enthusiast. Annabelle likes it, which is all the reason I need for keeping it.

Upstairs, I had another coffee with Gilbert. 'Hobnob?' he asked, pushing the packet towards me.

'Not for me,' I replied with a grimace. 'I've just finished a piece of chipboard.'

I brought him up-to-date with the case and Gilbert filled me in with a few titbits that he'd gleaned. Goodrich was a member of the Rotary club, Neighbourhood Watch, the Road Safety Committee and several other worthy organisations; all of which, no doubt, brought him many openings through which to ply his trade. Nothing illegal in that.

'Let's have this one sewn up, Charlie,' Gilbert said. 'Then we can get the strength back on the streets, where they belong. I'm catching hell from the Chamber of Commerce.'

'My heart bleeds for you,' I told him, looking at my watch. 'I bet some of those shopkeepers can be really nasty. C'mon, let's see what Fraud Squad have found for us.'

There were twenty-five assorted policemen and women waiting in the conference room, talking noisily, reading newspapers – all, depressingly, tabloids – and sitting on the desks.

'Quiet!' I shouted, trying to hush them. Slowly, they turned their attentions our way. 'We don't expect you to leap to your feet when we come in,' I railed, 'but it would be nice if you could tear yourselves away from the football pages.'

'It's the financial news,' the worst offender answered, turning a picture of a blonde bimbo towards me.

'OK. Settle down. Before we begin Mr Wood has an urgent message.'

'That's right,' he said. 'Very urgent. Next week I am on holiday, so it would be nice if we could wind this up before then.'

'Skiing in Aspen, Mr Wood?' Sparky wondered aloud.

'No, David, we're going to our cottage in Cornwall. The phone number is ex-directory and sorry, but you can't have it. The next piece of good news I have for you concerns overtime.'

'All unpaid,' somebody called out.

'I didn't say that,' Gilbert told him. 'We might manage to squeeze something from the budget, but no promises. Now let's get on with this enquiry. DS Newley is at the PM, so hopefully he'll have some news for us soon. Meanwhile, we'll treat it as murder, committed some time on Sunday evening. Over to you, Mr Priest.'

'I'll assume you all know the background,' I told them, 'so let's fill in the details. Jeff, what can you tell us?'

DS Caton placed his notebook on the desk in front of him. 'Not a great deal, I'm afraid,' was the answer. 'First of all, Goodrich doesn't appear to have any next of kin. He never married and his parents are dead. An older sister died a couple of years ago, and so far we've not found a will. Various solicitors he did business with are being contacted with a view to finding this. We have managed to track down his secretary. In Scotland.'

'Day out for you there, Jeff,' someone said.

'Don't think I'll bother,' he responded. 'She's a middle-aged widow and only worked for him for two years, before he went bankrupt. Now she's returned home to look after her elderly parents. We've asked the local CID to have a word with her.'

Funny how these youngsters thought 'middle-aged widow' was a pejorative. I knew one that any of them would have climbed a hot lava flow for, except that they'd have been in my footsteps.

'Anything else?' I asked.

'Not really. Young Luke has found something, on Goodrich's computer, but I'll let Maud tell you that.'

'Thanks, Jeff. The stage is yours, Maud.'

She stood up. 'Can I come to the front?' she wondered.

'Course you can.' I jumped to my feet. 'Here, use my chair.'

'It's OK, Mr Priest. I prefer to stand.' She shuffled the sheaf of papers she was holding and addressed the room. There were four women in it, and the only other non-white was Shaheed, an Asian PC. 'First of all, I'll tell you about Luke's success.' Because he was a civilian he wasn't at the meeting to speak for himself. 'He found Goodrich's data-base in about thirty seconds. "What do you want to know?" he asked, before we'd turned round, so we told him to bring up the client list. He tapped two keys and there it was. All I ever get is "Message error, bring me someone who knows what they're doing".' She said the last bit in a tinny robot voice.

I glanced at her audience. Most of them were smiling, but one or two weren't impressed. I suspected that she was nearly as good as Luke on the computer, but was deliberately demeaning herself. To survive in the job she needed the full cooperation of her colleagues, and that meant not being a smart arse or a threat to their promotion prospects. It shouldn't be necessary, and it made me angry.

Maud continued. 'So, I told him to print us a list and left him to it. He ran one off and realised that all the entries were in chronological order, by the dates that they signed on as clients. That's OK on a computer – you just tap in a name and it finds it for you. Luke thought that perhaps we'd prefer alphabetical hard copies, so he asked the machine to sort the names and print another list. While he was browsing through he noticed that it contained a disproportionate number of people called Jones. He did some quick calculations with the phone book and reckoned that Goodrich should have had about four Joneses among his seventeen hundred clients. In fact, he had eleven. Then Luke noticed that seven of them were called A. Jones, B. Jones, C. Jones, right through to G. Jones.'

People shuffled in their seats, wondering if this was relevant. If there was a fraud, they just wanted to know the basic details.

I said, 'So he had files for seven people called A., B., C., D., E., F. and G. Jones.'

'Not files as such, Mr Priest. They were on his list of clients, but the information was incomplete. There are no addresses and no amounts of money against them. It rather looks as if someone entered the names but didn't know how to set up a file. Like as if he did it himself, without his secretary's knowledge. Instead, he started using . . . this.' Maud held aloft a plastic bag. Inside it we could see what looked like an exercise book.

'This is a cash book; available at any good stationer's or newsagent's. We found it in the back of the file – the filing cabinet file – for a Mr and Mrs W. F. Jones, who appear to be a perfectly respectable retired greengrocer and his wife. Goodrich evidently just put it there for safe-keeping. It was his secret account book. Inside are pages for each of our seven Mr Joneses, with long lists of amounts of money against them. Two to three thousand pounds at a time, once a week, for the seven of them. In other words, about twenty thousand pounds a week, for over two years, ceasing just before last Christmas.'

'So if these were some sort of payment,' someone asked, 'which way were they going? In or out?'

'It's not clear,' Maud told him. 'There are other figures and dates, but we haven't cracked what they mean, yet.'

'Was he being blackmailed?' a voice at the back wondered.

'We don't know. But we've found something else. As you already know from the handouts, we were investigating him for possible fraud, at the request of his clients' solicitors. However, we have another piece of information about him which has just come to light. Two years ago, just about when he set up the file for A. Jones, we were notified by N-CIS about an SCT against him.'

I sat up. 'Money laundering?' I wondered aloud.

Maud nodded in my direction. 'Possibly.'

'Er, explain SCTs to us,' I suggested.

'OK,' she said. 'An SCT is a suspicious cash transaction. If you go into a bank to deposit a large amount of cash, currently three thousand or over, you will be asked where it came from. If the bank manager is not satisfied, the law requires him to report it. The National Criminal Intelligence Service correlate the reports and let us know about any coming from our patch. It's a bit of a dodgy area, so we keep mum about them until we are sure that the money comes from criminal activities.'

A bit dodgy was putting it mildly. Over eighty per cent of SCTs were quite legitimate, and the civil liberties people would have a field day if we acted on them all. A handful lead to convictions and the rest fall into a grey area. Lawyers are the best people to launder money. They are protected by rules of confidentiality that priests and doctors can only envy. Second-hand car dealers come next on the list. A financial adviser, calling into his bank every week with a couple of thousand pounds in grubby notes that his clients have handed to him, might just about get away with it. Except that he would be doing it in every bank in town.

Gilbert grunted and shuffled around. 'Do you think we're talking drugs money?' he asked, peering at Maud over his new half-spectacles.

'Early days, Mr Wood. Let's see what we find.'

Hartley Goodrich was beginning to look interesting. Maud answered a few more questions before I invited the SOCO to spellbind us all with his revelations.

'Fingerprints,' he announced, briskly. 'First of all, to eliminate the milkman who started the whole thing off, we checked the bottle on the doorstep. It had been wiped clean. We asked him if he wore gloves and he said not. We also checked next door's bottles and they bore his prints. The plant pot that hit Goodrich had also been wiped clean, most likely with a tea-towel that was hanging in one of those pull-out rails, under his worktop. His assailant had put it back, but it bore dirty marks similar to the soil from the pot. We've sent it to the lab. On the table was a bowl, or a planter, that the plant pot has stood in at some time. We found plenty of Goodrich's prints and one or two other marks, probably old ones. I'm not hopeful of them being of interest. For what it's worth, the plant was a

Dieffenbachia picta. It would have been less messy to have poisoned him with it.'

I said, 'Let's not explore that avenue. This isn't St Mary Mead and Mr Wood isn't Miss Marple.' I couldn't resist adding, 'In spite of the spectacles. Anything else?'

'We've taken the usual fibre samples and found a couple of hairs that we haven't identified yet, but they are almost certainly his own. Oh, and a few flakes of dandruff.' He turned to me, saying, 'We'd like a word with you about that, Mr Priest,' which earned him a cheap laugh from the audience.

'I see,' I replied through gritted teeth. 'Is that all you could find? You were there long enough.'

'One little thing,' the SOCO said. 'When I lifted the milk bottle to dust it, there was a wet ring of condensation on the step, where it had been. Next to it was what might have been the remnants of a similar ring, as if one bottle had been taken away, or the one present had been moved. Unfortunately, the mark dried out and vanished as we were looking at it.'

I wasn't sure if this was interesting or confusing. We all want to be detectives, follow the trail, make sweeping deductions, but mostly it's easier than that. Look for the woman or the money; find the blunt object; match them together. End of story. This was going to be one of those, I hoped. I'd had enough revelations for one day, but I was reckoning without Nigel's phone call.

We held a questions and answers session and doled out the various jobs. I asked Jeff Caton to take over the list of clients that Claud – Brian – had started and try to develop some sort of profile of each one that would eliminate most of them and leave us with a few possible suspects. Criminal Records would be a useful starting point. Maud and

Brian were visiting local bank managers. One or two of them were going to have a nice day. Hopefully they'd be able to match the dates and amounts in the cash book to transactions over the counter.

The phone rang just as we were winding up. It had to be Nigel because we'd arranged to be undisturbed except for his call.

'Have you met the new pathologist, boss?' he enthused in my left ear.

'Professor Simms. Yes, I've met her.'

'Heather,' he announced, with barely disguised triumph. 'She's ever so attractive, isn't she?'

'Er, yes. Very pleasant. What did she say.'

'I've never seen anything like it,' he gushed. 'She just pulled the sheet back, looked at his hands and then at his face and said, "Sedentary work. Very trustworthy looking. Meets lots of people. Self-employed, possibly in the financial sector." She's brilliant!'

I said, 'No, Nigel. She just has a reasonable memory. I told her all that, yesterday.'

'Honest?' His voice had lost its enthusiasm.

''Fraid so.'

'Bloody hell!'

'Come on, Nigel,' I urged. 'There's a room full of people here, hanging on your every word, so hide your disappointment and tell me what she had to say about the stiff.'

'Right, boss. But you're not going to like it.'

He was right, I didn't. And when he'd finished I wished I hadn't asked.

The troops were all on their feet, waiting to disperse. I turned to them and said, 'Just as we thought: time of death sometime Sunday evening. Ring in with anything interesting; otherwise, same time tomorrow. Go to it, my bonny boys and girls, and make sure to put it all down on paper, tagged for the computer. Remember, reports mean arrests. What do reports mean?' But nobody answered. I turned to the super. 'Can we have a word in your office, Gilbert?' I asked.

Trudging up the stairs, Gilbert said, 'Well?'

'In your office,' I replied. 'I'm playing for time.'

We need major enquiries. If we didn't have one, every once in a while, it would be necessary to invent them. A murder investigation opens doors, and we often solve several other, less serious crimes, on the way to catching the killer. During the hunt for the Ripper the crime rate in West Yorkshire fell dramatically. That was because anybody out late at night became accustomed to being stopped by the police.

'Do you mind if we have a look in your boot, sir?' we'd say. 'Oh. And could you explain what these forty-eight turkeys are doing in here?' Or these silver chalices, or this jemmy and balaclava.

'Coffee?' Gilbert asked, closing the door behind us.

'You've just had one,' I protested.

'Well, I'm having another. I've a feeling I'm going to need it.'

I sat down and looked at the pictures on his walls while he prepared a brew. Most officers of his rank have framed photographs of themselves adorning their offices, taken at peak moments in their careers. Yours truly meeting the Princess Royal; the class of '82 at Bramshill; me, when I won the Silver Truncheon at Hendon.

Gilbert collects pictures of fish. I was studying an evil brute called a thornback ray when he flopped into his chair.

'Can you eat those?' I asked, nodding towards it.

'Mmm, delicious. Caught two last year. Go on then, break my heart.'

I said, 'According to the post mortem, Hartley Goodrich died of a cardiac arrest while seated in his favourite chair, sometime Sunday evening. He was hit on the head by the plant pot about twelve hours later – Monday morning. Somebody wasted their energy.'

Gilbert took a sip of coffee, grimaced and produced a dispenser of sweeteners from his drawer. He clicked one into his cup and gave it a perfunctory stir. Now he was playing for time. 'Is that an offence?' he wondered, although he knew the answer.

'Depends on what the intention was,' I confirmed.

'And that's nearly impossible to prove.'

'Mmm.'

He did the routine with the sweeteners again, complete with grimace.

'Why don't you use sugar?' I suggested.

'Empty calories.'

'You could always eat one less biscuit.'

'Don't be so bloody self-righteous. So I can tell Les Isles that we don't need his help and we can wind up the enquiry and put the troops back where they belong – keeping the streets tidy, eh?'

I shook my head. 'I want to keep on with it,' I declared. 'Tell Mr Isles that it's not murder, but Goodrich is – was – up to his neck in something, and I want to find out what it was. A murder enquiry gives me the licence I need to knock on doors. Doors that otherwise would be slammed in my face.'

Gilbert said, 'And where does the coroner fit in with this little scheme of yours?'

'You have a word with him. Don't you have a lodge meeting, or something, where you could collar him?'

Gilbert rolled his eyes. 'We're in the same bloody golf club,' he stated.

'You don't play golf,' I reminded him.

'I'm a social member, same as he is. They have the best selection of whiskies in the county. If I have a word with him it will be in office hours, not over the Macallan.'

'OK. Thanks.'

'I said "if."'

'We need the inquest adjourning, indefinitely,' I said. 'If no next of kin turn up it shouldn't be a problem. I want to find out who the Jones boys are, and where all that money came from.'

'Right, but I want DS Newley back, running operations, and most of the staff.'

'No problem, but I'll need Sparky, Maggie, young Caton, and Maud at least.'

'It's a deal. We'll start winding down tomorrow, and you can have until the end of the week.'

'The end of the week!' I gasped, dismayed. 'That's not long enough!'

Gilbert held his arms out, like John the Baptist on the banks of the Jordan. 'I'm on holiday next week,' he announced. 'You'll be in charge. What more can I say?'

'Right,' I said, nodding and smiling. 'Right.'

I had an hour at the keyboard, typing my own version of events, and read a financial magazine that I'd bought on the way in, swotting up the difference between a PEP and a TESSA, in case anybody asked me. Fraud Squad was still working through the files when I called at Goodrich's house. We'd decided it would be easier to work from there, rather than hump all the files to the nick, where we didn't have room for them. I noticed that they'd commandeered a kettle and his tea-bags.

The rest of the house already smelled of disuse – death, even – or was my imagination playing games with me? I wandered through the rooms, trying to read the mind of a man I'd never met. He was obviously well off. The pans in the kitchen were by Le Creuset. I'd heard of them because Annabelle told me that she'd just bought one, and he had a full set. I put the *Dieffenbachia* back in its bowl and ran some water into it. The curtains in the other rooms were made of a heavy silken material, elaborately ruffled and brocaded, with ropes to open and close them. The dining room seated eight around a polished mahogany table, with a captain's chair for the head of the household. It all looked unused under a thin patina of dust, as if the place had been sealed until the master came home from the war. The decor throughout was by Barratt, out of Harewood House. Upstairs the slim-hipped slack-lipped young men still held their poses, and a red admiral had died of exhaustion against a window. I opened drawers, felt down the back, found an unopened packet of twelve condoms, long past their use-by date, and gave an uneasy nod of recognition.

Sparky came looking for me. Maud and Brian had identified the banks that Goodrich used, and went off to put the willies up the managers. It's a stiff sentence for not reporting suspicious cash transactions.

As soon as they'd gone I asked, 'Anything on the WAM number?'

'No, but we're in with a chance,' he replied. 'AM is a Swindon registration mark, so there shouldn't be too many around here. I've asked Swansea for a printout of any BMWs with those letters kept in Heckley to begin with. No point in overdoing it just yet.'

'Good. Now let me tell you something.'

Sparky listened as I related the pathologist's findings, a big grin splitting his face when I'd finished. 'You crafty sod,' he said. 'Trust you to make a convenience out of a midden. So we're after wheeler-dealers, eh, and not really bothered who biffed him on the bonce?'

'That's about the size of it.'

'Right. Well, I think we need to know who was in that car, whoever we upset. I'll get back to the station and do some chasing.'

'You do that,' I told him. 'And find me the addresses of the directors of the diamond company, IGI, if you have the time. Maybe we should pay them a visit. I'd, er, buy you some lunch, but I have an appointment. See you later.'

'I noticed you'd washed your neck,' he replied.

First thing I saw outside Annabelle's back door was a pair of wellington boots that were far too large and definitely not her colour. I knocked and went in. Seated in the kitchen was a young man, several inches of sock wriggling off the end of his toes, as if his feet desperately needed circumcising.

'Hello,' I said. It seemed as good as anything.

'Hello,' he repeated nervously. He had a long face that was slightly askew, and nursed an empty coffee mug.

'I'm Charlie,' I told him. 'And you must be Annabelle's gardener.'

He nodded and examined the coffee mug. His trousers were too long for him and his jacket sleeves too short, and they looked as if they'd been machine-washed at regular intervals. The poor lad obviously wasn't quite all there. ESN, we used to call it – educationally sub-normal – but that was now considered politically incorrect and I couldn't remember the new term.

'You've certainly done a good job,' I admitted. 'Annabelle's garden has looked smashing all summer.' I gave him a grin. 'I hope you charge her the proper rate for the job.'

'Sh-she pays m-me three pounds f-fifty an hour,' he declared in a burst of verbosity.

I was suggesting that he demand four quid when Annabelle strode in, looking all the things that reduce me to the state of the young man who did her borders, and gave me a peck on the cheek.

'Sorry about that, I was on the phone,' she explained. 'I thought I heard you. Have you met Donald, the person who works wonders in my garden?' She was wearing a striped butcher's apron over a skirt and bright red blouse, and I noticed the makings of lunch at the far end of the work surface.

'Yes,' I said. 'I've just remarked what a good job he does. I was wondering about making him a better offer to come and do mine.'

All the praise was making him blush. He rose to his feet, slouching, and put his mug in the sink. 'I'll go n-now,' he announced.

'But your bus isn't for another fifteen minutes,' Annabelle told him. Turning to me she said, 'He missed the one he usually catches.'

'Where do you live?' I asked.

'Oates S-S-Square,' he informed me.

I briefly wondered if it was named after Titus or Captain. 'Where's that?'

'N-near the p-park.'

'Heckley park?' I wondered with sudden interest.

'Y-yes.'

'Do you go in the park much?'

'S-sometimes.'

I said, 'Look, it's trying to rain outside. I could easily run you home. It wouldn't take ten minutes.'

'N-no, I'll walk to the n-next stop.'

'Are you sure?' Annabelle asked. 'Charles could easily give you a lift.'

'N-no thanks. Is it all r-right if I come W-Wednesday?'

'Tomorrow? Instead of Thursday? Of course it is, if you prefer it. Have you put your money somewhere safe?'

'It's in my p-pocket. 'Bye.'

'Goodbye, Donald.'

'S'long, Donald. Nice to meet you.'

As the door closed behind him the smile slipped from Annabelle's face. 'He'll go straight to the pub,' she said.

I shrugged my shoulders. 'If it makes him happy . . .'

She came to me and we hugged each other. 'This is nice,' I told her. 'I think I could get used to it. Trouble is, I won't want to go back to work.'

She leaned back from my embrace. 'I was ringing Marie and Toby to thank them for the meal on Sunday. They are coming to stay for a couple of days at half-term. They haven't got a car, so I'll have to run them around, show them the sights. You don't mind, do you?'

Toby and Marie were the manufacturers of the sloe gin that had laid me low. 'Of course not. They're good company. Tell them to bring some home-brew with them.'

'I doubt if they have any left,' she reproached, breaking from my grasp.

'Oh. So when is half-term?'

'Three weeks. Right. Food. How does trout in almonds, with vegetables, sound?'

'Dee-licious. With Annabelle surprise for pudding?'

'Oh, I don't know about that. I thought you only had an hour for lunch.' She removed something from the refrigerator and busied herself with the cooking. 'It was good of you to offer to run Donald home,' she said, over her shoulder.

No it wasn't. There was nothing good at all about it. I wanted a talk with him, ask him if he'd killed the swans in the park. But you are beautiful and naive, I thought. A summer's breeze blowing through my corrupt and jaundiced life, and I don't deserve you.

Sparky was replacing the phone as I walked in. 'Appointment go well?' he casually asked.

'Yeah, not bad,' I told him, sitting in the chair opposite.

He leaned across and brushed my lapel. 'Bit of seafood sauce on your collar,' he said.

I looked down and pretended to wipe some more off. 'It's probably *crème brûlée*,' I replied. 'It gets everywhere.'

'I bet it does. There are no WAM Bee-Emms in Heckley, but two in Halifax. Unfortunately the owners don't fit our description.'

'Like, they're white.'

'Exactly.'

I thought about it for a few seconds. 'They've got a point, you know,' I said.

'Who has?'

'We're only tracing this car because it was driven by a black person.'

Sparky turned on me. 'No we're not. We're trying to trace it because it's the only bloody lead we have.'

'Yeah, maybe. But it looks bad.'

'I don't give a toss how it looks.'

'That's my boy. Anything on the diamond merchants, IGI?'

He turned over a sheet on his pad and read off it. 'Head office, Park Square, Leeds. Three directors. One is the Right Honourable Lord Onchan, who lives on the Isle of Man. He was a professional figurehead, but he lives in a nursing home now. He won't tell us anything because apparently he's ga-ga. A man called Rockliffe was the money behind the venture. He went for a long drive without opening his garage doors, shortly after the whole thing went pear-shaped. Carbon-monoxide poisoning. Don't let anybody tell you it doesn't work when you've a catalyser fitted.'

'And the third?'

'A man named . . .' He ran the pencil down his list of notes. 'Here we are – K. Tom Davis.'

'K. Tom Davis? What sort of a name's that?'

'A fine name. At least, I bet he thinks so.'

'And he lives in the Outer Hebrides, no doubt.'

'No, Wakefield.'

'Wakefield . . . New Zealand?'

'Uh-uh. Wakefield, capital of the old West Riding.'

'Right then. Grab your coat and the *A to Z*. Let's see what K. Tom Davis can tell us.'

Chapter Four

One would have been desirable, but K. Tom had a terrace of three, knocked through to make a single big house. It was a stone building with a stone-flagged roof, black with age and surrounded by farmland. At one time they had probably been tied cottages, inhabited by the estate's various managers. Now it was a bijou residence for a crook. I knew what to expect inside – the usual catalogue of naff statuary and crap paintings, with eighteen hours of pan pipes dribbling out of the Bang and Olufsen – and my heart sank at the thought of it.

Nobody answered the door. I pressed the bell, Sparky hammered. We regarded two unsuccessful attempts as a licence to wander round the back, see if anyone was there.

'This is how the other half live,' I said as the conservatory came into view.

Sparky whistled through his teeth, saying, 'I wouldn't mind some of this bankruptcy myself.'

It stretched the full length of the back of the building, housing a full suite of wicker furniture, several sun-loungers, a forest of hibiscus and a modest swimming pool. A woman was reclining in one of the loungers, dark glasses hiding her eyes.

Sparky's knock rattled the ice in her glass and she jerked awake, startled and alarmed. We held our warrant cards against the double glazing, and after peering at them she slid open the door that led in from the garden.

'Yes?' she asked, already on the defensive. In the lexicon of barmy questions, that must be the daftest.

Sparky said, 'This is DI Priest from Heckley CID, and I'm DC Sparkington. Is Mr Davis in?'

'Er, no, I'm afraid he isn't.' She was about forty-five, sharp featured, wearing what I suppose is called a sun-suit – baggy shorts with a matching top – in a bright flowery material. It, and her legs, gave her age away.

'Are you Mrs Davis?'

'Yes, I am.'

'May we come in?'

It was like stepping off the plane in Brazil. Although it was a dull day the temperature leapt fifteen degrees as we crossed the threshold, and the heavy smell of the flowers, mixed with swimming pool, hit you like a whore's hand-bag. I was wrong about the music – it was 'Lady in Red', giving way to Radio Two's fanfare – but I awarded myself a near miss.

'This is very pleasant,' I enthused, looking around. Mrs Davis eyed me as if I was a bailiff, making a quick assessment.

'Could you tell me where Mr Davis is?' Sparky asked. He's better at keeping his mind on the job than I am.

'Er, no, I'm not sure.'

'When did you last see him?'

'Just before lunchtime, this morning.'

He'd left, she told us, saying he was off to see their son, Justin.

'And when are you expecting him back?'

'I'm afraid I don't know.'

'But some time today?'

'He said he might be gone a day or two.'

I butted into their conversation. 'Does he often go away without telling you when he's coming back?'

'Yes, he does,' she replied, defiantly.

'Where does Justin live?'

She gave us an address and directions. He lived in a house called Broadside, up on the moors, not too far from Heckley. 'But they might not be there,' she added.

'So where might they be?'

'Justin races motorcycles, he's a speedway rider, and races on the Continent once or twice a week. Tom acts as his manager-cum-mechanic. Travels all over the place with him. They might be abroad. I think he said something about a big meeting in Gothenberg, but I may be mistaken.'

'Justin Davis?' Sparky asked.

'Yes. Have you heard of him?'

'Mmm. Seen his picture on the sports pages.'

'Could you tell me what it's all about? Why do you want to speak to my husband?'

It had taken her a long time to come round to asking that, almost as if she'd been expecting us. She had been living on a knife edge since the business went bust, but my heart wasn't bleeding for her. 'Did you know a man called Hartley Goodrich?' I asked.

She nodded. 'Yes,' she whispered. 'He was a business acquaintance of Tom's. We heard about his death on local radio over breakfast. It said you were treating it as suspicious.'

'For the time being,' I told her. 'But at the moment we're just trying to build up a picture of his movements.' I took a CID card from my wallet and signed it. 'When Mr

Davis comes back will you tell him to get in touch with me as soon as possible?'

'Turn left,' I told Sparky as we drove off.

'This is not the way we came.'

'I know. I want to look at something.' I'd seen a sign at the side of the road that interested me. 'So what do you think?'

He shrugged. 'Dunno. Too suspicious to be true. He's in the frame, though.'

'Next right. I've never been to the speedway, have you?'

'Took the kids about three years ago. Just the once. Sophie enjoyed it more than Daniel did. When I was a nipper we'd go to Odsal nearly every Saturday. It was fun.' I could see him smiling to himself at the memory. He went on, 'My favourite rider was a bloke called Eddie Rigg. And Arthur Forrest. We used to chant, "Two, four, six, eight; Eddie's at the starting gate. Will he win? We don't know. Come on, Eddie, have a go."'

'So what did you shout for Arthur Forrest?'

'Two, four, six, eight, Arthur's at the starting . . .'

'Not very original,' I declared.

'I was only nine!' he protested.

We'd arrived at the gate of the Yorkshire Sculpture Park, at Bretton Hall. 'So this is where it is,' I said.

Sparky turned the car round in the gateway. 'Is this what we're looking for?'

'Yeah, I saw the signs on the main road. Might bring Annabelle at the weekend. It's been on my list of places to visit since it opened.'

'So what's inside?'

'Oh, just a big park, with about forty-eight million pounds worth of Henry Moore bronzes lying around.'

'And they're still there?'

'One or two have gone walkies, I believe, but they're only good for scrap value. It would be like stealing the *Mona Lisa* and getting eight quid for the frame at the risk of twenty years in the slammer for services to art.'

Dave glanced round, working out his bearings. 'I reckon our elusive friend K. Tom must live just over the other side,' he said.

I pushed the passenger seat back and reclined it a couple of notches. 'Let's see if he's with his son,' I suggested. 'What was the house called?'

'Broadside.'

'That's it. Drive slowly and wake me up when we arrive.'

Tiredness was catching up with me, but I only dozed. I opened my eyes as Sparky killed the engine twenty-five minutes later, and stepped out into a different weather zone. Broadside was a long, low bungalow, high on the moors, with views down towards the Peak District and huge picture windows to make the best of them. The big garden was contained by a stone wall and the nearest neighbour was two miles away.

I nodded in appreciation, gulping in the cool air and enjoying the wind tugging at my hair. 'This is the one for me,' I said.

'What, no swimming pool?' Sparky wondered.

We left the car on the road and crunched up the gravel drive, noting the sophisticated security system and hoping there wasn't a dog. A triple garage stuck out to one side, or maybe it was a row of stables, and a satellite dish hung on a wall. Neither K. Tom or his son was there and I was beginning to feel more like an estate agent than a detective.

'Should get decent TV reception,' Sparky noted, nodding towards the Holme Moss and Emley Moor transmitter masts that dominated the skyline.

We didn't nose around too much in case we triggered the alarm. Once we were sure the place was deserted we crunched back down the drive and carefully closed the big wooden five-bar gate behind us.

I looked at my watch. 'Fancy a snifter?' I asked. The snooze in the car had left me with a mouth like a rabbit's nest. 'The pub down the road had an open-all-day sign outside.'

'Not while I'm on duty,' Sparky replied, making something of a production out of it.

'OK,' I said. 'You can sit in the car while I nip in for a quick one.'

He condescended to come in with me, agreeing that perhaps he could manage a pint of low-alcohol beer.

'Yak! What's this?' he gasped, after the first sip.

'It's called I Can't Believe It's Not Dog Wee,' I told him. My pint of Black Sheep was first class. After further grumbling from Sparky I took his glass back to the bar and had ten shots of lime juice put into it to mask the taste, and borrowed a menu.

'Hey, this sounds good,' I announced, flicking through the pages. It was all home-made, and they did Barnsley chops and rhubarb crumble. My mouth started to water.

'I thought you'd eaten once, today,' he protested.

'It's not for now,' I said. 'Maybe one evening. It looks a good place for a meal.'

We were nearly in Heckley when an ambulance came towards us, blue light flashing. Sparky held up the traffic to allow it to make a right turn across our bows. The word 'Ambulance' was emblazoned in back-to-front letters across its front. The sign writers must love doing that. I'd been thinking about the BMW the girl had seen outside Goodrich's, wondering how far to take it. If it was a standard registration mark in Swindon there could be several thousand cars carrying it, hundreds of them BMWs. Tracing the car we wanted would be a lot of effort for a doubtful cause.

I said, 'Do you think the WAM number is a no-no?'

Sparky nodded. 'Looks like it. It was worth a shot. How far do you want us to go with it?'

'Tell me what the girl said, the one who saw it.'

A youth in a Fiesta came tearing past us, realised he was running out of room, and hit the brakes. 'Prat!' Sparky cursed. 'Sorry, what about the girl?'

'Tell me exactly what she said.'

'Right. She was going to work. She started at seven so it would have been about twenty to.'

'So it was light.'

'Correct. She noticed that there was another posh car outside Goodrich's house, although she didn't know his name.'

'Had she ever met him?'

'No. Never even seen him, that she knows of, but was intrigued by the fancy cars that called on him. I think it set her imagination wandering. The driver of this one, the BMW, was getting out, and she noticed that he was a black man. Be honest, Charlie – Sweetwater isn't exactly Heckley's answer to Harlem.'

'OK. He was black. He was the wrong side of the tracks. Anything else? How come she didn't get a description if she was so interested?'

'Rasta haircut, and he took a briefcase out of the boot of the BMW, which she thought was odd. That's all.'

'Except she noticed the registration letters, and they struck a chord with her because she's a George Michael fan.'

'That's about it.'

I half turned in the passenger seat, so I was facing him. 'How does this sound?' I asked. 'If she saw him, watched him take his briefcase out of the boot, perhaps she was already past him when she took his number.'

'You mean, in her mirror?'

'Mmm.'

'So it would be M-A-W, not W-A-M.'

'It's worth a try.'

He nodded his approval. 'Sounds possible. She could have been watching in her mirror and WAM on his number plate caught her attention. Do you want me to have another talk with her?'

'No. Just give it a whirl.'

I looked at my watch as we were swinging into the nick car park. 'Half six,' I said. 'You might as well have a reasonably early finish.'

'What about you?'

'I'll just see if I can catch Nigel.'

He parked and released his seatbelt. 'In that case, I'll just try the DVLC with this number.'

I got out and spoke to him across the roof of the car. 'OK, you win,' I said. 'We'll both have an early night. See you in the morning.'

I called in at the supermarket on the way home and stocked up on frozen meals for slimmers. They're the last thing I need, but they're tastier than the regular ones. If you're trying to encourage people to eat less, I'd have thought it would make more sense if they tasted like reconstituted tennis balls, but their loss is my gain, so to speak.

After I'd eaten I had a look at the E-type in the garage, sitting in it and running my fingertips round the wooden rim of the steering wheel. It smelled of leather, with perhaps a hint of Annabelle's perfume, or maybe that was just my imagination. We'd had some adventures together, and some fun. The car didn't need anything doing to it before the Lord Mayor's parade, just a quick hose down and twenty gallons of petrol putting in. I wished Dad could see it now. I wished Mum could have met Annabelle, known I was doing all right.

I found my drawing board and a pad of 140 lb paper and did some sketches for the bullbars poster. Computers have taken all the skill out of lettering. I typed the words 'Bullbars Kill Kids' in forty point Optimum, with 'Take them off, NOW!' in smaller letters underneath it and ran off a copy. After a few adjustments it looked good. I watercoloured the sketch and superimposed the wording. When I was happy I did a final version. As an afterthought, in small letters across the bottom, I wrote that further information could be obtained from East Pennine Police Traffic Division, to make it look official without actually saying so.

There were only six of us at the morning meeting, including Nigel, who wasn't in the team any more, and Brian from Fraud, who'd just called in to give us the latest findings. Maud was staying with us, and Jeff Caton. Sparky was barely able to contain himself, struggling to stifle a smile, like a scrap-dealer at a disaster. I deliberately ignored him.

'First of all,' I told them, 'keep calling it a murder enquiry. Or at least, a suspicious death. We don't want it leaking to the press that Goodrich died of natural causes.

Mind you, they all reported his murder, so it's unlikely that they'll retract the story and apologise. The main problem is Wednesday's *Heckley Gazette*. We could ask them not to print the truth, but it might be easier just to keep them in the dark, so watch what you say. Right, Maud, what have you got for us?'

'The credit's Brian's,' she said. 'So I'll let him tell you.'

'Right, ta,' he said. 'Well, I started ringing banks, partly armed with information from Goodrich's files, partly cold calling, trying to pin down his clients' accounts. In the end I had to start counting them on my toes – I'd run out of fingers. His main accounts seem to be here in Heckley, with First National, but he has other accounts in Bradford, Leeds and Halifax. None of the managers were willing to talk without consulting a higher authority, in fact they were all bloody cagey. Except one.' He awarded himself a little smile of satisfaction. 'Last year I was at Bradford, and we uncovered a potential fraud at a branch of the Consolidated that could have cost them millions. A young girl, a graduate recruit, had worked out a scam that was near foolproof. We saved the manager's skin, so yesterday I decided it was time to call in the favour. He couldn't have been more helpful: spent half an hour on the computer, with me looking over his shoulder, and tracked down an account at their Oldfield branch where the amounts coincided with those in the book for Mr D. Jones. I have a printout here.' He waved a sheet of paper at us.

'Well done,' I said. 'Tell us more.'

'Right, ta. Well, all the money was moved on fairly quickly, to other accounts and various other places, but the two largest payments were made to someone called International Gem Investments, whose head office is in

Leeds. Then we found something similar with his E account, which is with their Huddersfield branch.'

I must have shuffled or something, because Brian hesitated and looked at me. 'Sorry, Brian,' I said, 'but maybe I can interrupt to explain something. When we interviewed the people who lost money through Goodrich, most of it went down the tube with something called investment diamonds, bought from this company called IGI. Apparently the intrinsic value of the diamonds they bought is only about a tenth of what they paid. And now IGI have conveniently gone bankrupt and the MD is playing hide-and-seek with us. Anything else?'

'No, Mr Priest. That's it.'

'Thanks. OK, Dave,' I said, turning to Sparky. 'You need keep us in suspenders no longer. What have you got for us?'

He pushed his chair back on two legs and launched straight into his disclosure. 'The registration number of the BMW seen outside Goodrich's house would now appear to have the letters M-A-W, not W-A-M as we were first led to believe. A BMW of that mark is registered in the name of a citizen of Heckley called Michael Angelo Watts, who has numerous motoring convictions, all fairly trivial, and two for possession of a class B substance.'

We couldn't confirm that he was black, but knowing smiles broke out here and there in our little group. They'd fall flat on their prejudices if we discovered that Watts' ancestors came over with William the Conqueror, or the Bastard of Normandy, as we prefer to call him in these parts. It wasn't much, but at least we now had something to follow that had the right feel about it.

'Good,' I said. 'We'd better have a closer look at Mr Watts. Anybody want to say anything else?'

There were a couple of questions, before I asked Maud and Jeff if they knew what they were doing next.

'Bacon sandwich first priority for me,' Maud said. 'I'm famished.'

Why is it that the words bacon sandwich are guaranteed to start the saliva flowing? Pavlov must have wasted years messing about with dogs – he could have arrived at his conclusions after five minutes with a policeman and a bacon sandwich. 'Good idea,' I declared. 'Let's all have a bacon sandwich in the canteen, then you won't need to stop for lunch.'

As we skipped downstairs I caught up with Sparky and said, 'It might be useful to have a word with Drugs about Michaelangelo. Perhaps they'll have something on him.'

'We'll look pillocks if he's white,' he whispered in reply.

It was between-times in the canteen, so it was deserted and the staff were cleaning the place. My order of six bacon sandwiches and six mugs of tea earned me a look similar to the one God threw at Moses when he was asked to part the Red Sea. I placed my arm round the manageress's shoulders. 'And put them on a chitty for me please, Elsie,' I said. 'We've been working all night.'

She gave me a more-than-my-job's-worth scowl and went behind the counter.

Nigel was already sitting at a table with Maud. I pushed another table up to theirs and sat opposite them. I insisted that a puzzled Jeff join them, which left two places at my side for Brian and Sparky.

'Right,' I said brightly. 'It's role-play time. Just what you've all been waiting for. You three, at that side of the table, are a heap-big drugs dealer, and us at this side are an extremely clever financial adviser. Let's have a talk.'

Five blank faces turned to me.

'Go on, then,' I urged, flapping my hands.

'Go on what?'

'Talk. What would we have to say to each other?'

'What about?'

'That's what I'm trying to find out. What would a drugs dealer and a financial adviser have to say to each other?'

'Which are we again?' Jeff asked.

'The dealers.'

'Right. OK.' He licked his lips while gathering his thoughts. Eventually he said, 'Hullooo,' in a perfect impression of Eccles. I didn't think he was old enough.

Sparky responded, *à la* Bluebottle. 'Hello, my little curly-nosed friend,' he mimicked.

'Hulloo, Bluebottle, what have you got there, my hairy-legged master of disguises and funny voices?'

'Sweeties.'

'Sweeties? What sort of sweeties?'

'Oooh! Make you fly in the sky sweeties. Want to buy any?'

'OK, OK,' I interrupted. 'Stop messing about. We'll just imagine the *Goon Show* voices from now on. Jeff, you were asking Dave if he wanted to buy any sweeties.'

'Right.' He coughed to clear his throat, as if ridding himself of the funny character. In his normal voice he said, 'Wanna buy any drugs, Dave?'

Sparky replied, 'No,' but couldn't resist embellishing it with Neddy Seagoon's famous, 'I'm trying to give them up, sapristi yackle!' before adding; 'do you want to buy an insurance policy? Probably could use one in your line of work.'

'We have our own insurance. Why would I want some more?'

Brian chipped in with, 'To get rid of some of that cash you're swimming around in.'

Maud wasn't to be outdone. She said, 'You mean, if I came to you with a few thou in grubby fivers you could, sort of, put it somewhere more convenient for me?'

'Oh, I would think so, if the price was right.'

After a pause Maud said, 'We wouldn't want it anywhere with our label on it, and I think we'd prefer something more substantial than an endowment policy. It'd be out of our hands, easy to seize.'

The teas had appeared on the counter and Nigel jumped up to fetch them. Sparky leaned forward, elbows on the Formica, saying, 'We could do you a nice little line in diamonds.'

'Diamonds?' Jeff responded. 'We don't not know nuffink about no diamonds. Gold would be better.'

'We 'aven't got no gold, only diamonds.'

'Diamonds is nice,' Jeff told us, 'but who can value them for us? Everybody knows the price of gold.'

Sparky thumped the table. 'We 'aven't got no effin' gold!' he yelled. 'Just diamonds, cloth ears!'

Nigel appeared with the teas while we were having a giggle break. 'What have I missed?' he asked.

'Just a Sparkington tantrum,' I told him.

He went back for the sandwiches, and Maud rose to help him. When we all had a mouthful I said, 'So far, Nigel, we have the situation where the financial adviser is wanting to convert some of the dealers' cash into diamonds. Now does that sound likely?'

He nodded, chewing and swallowing. 'Remember that fire in Leeds – Harehills – last year? The local force found nearly three-quarters of a million in a suitcase in the basement. Not bad for a back-to-back terrace in a run-down area.'

We all remembered it. The fire had been started deliberately in what was known as a safe house. Safe for the drugs dealers who lived there. It had steel grilles over the windows and a lions' cage gate over the door to foil any sudden raid by the Drugs Squad. Before they could gain an entrance all the evidence would be down the loo. Somebody poured petrol through the letterbox and ignited it. The residents escaped via holes conveniently knocked through into the adjoining properties, and when the fire brigade arrived they were stoned by a rapidly organised mob of local youths. Some of them were as local as Manchester. The riot team was called in, and next morning the money was found.

Jeff said, 'Tell us more about these diamonds, then.'

'No problem,' I replied. 'You pay me what you can, in cash, and I create a client account, just for you. Then I invest that money in diamonds with International Gem Investments. You can either leave them in the vault on the Isle of Man, or keep them yourself. Diamonds haven't gone down in value since Pontius was a pilate – I'll show you the bumf.'

'And presumably you receive a nice commission for every diamond sold,' Maud said.

'That's right, plus a small percentage from you to pay the cleaning bill.'

'Makes sense,' she conceded, 'but I'm still not convinced.'

Nigel stirred a spoonful of sugar into his tea. 'In America,' he told us, 'the drugs barons have so much cash stashed away that the administration has seriously considered changing the colour of the dollar bills just to foil them.'

'It can't be easy, buying a new Mercedes with a suitcase full of grubby fivers,' I suggested.

'Wouldn't mind giving it a try,' Sparky replied, adding, 'I can't really see us changing the colour of the fiver to fool the drugs boys. This lot can't agree on when to change their underwear.'

Nigel leaned forward. 'No,' he asserted, 'but in three or four years we might all be spending Ecus, or Euro dollars.'

'Euros,' Maud told us.

'That's right, Euros. Where will that leave you, Mr Drugs Dealer? I think you'd be better off investing in my lovely diamonds. They're a much more flexible currency, accepted all round the world.'

'You're supposed to be a drugs dealer,' Jeff told him.

'Oh, am I? Sorry, I wasn't listening when you picked the teams.'

'That's all right,' I said. 'It's a good point, but I think we've milked this for all we can. The conclusion is that if these Jones boys are one or more drugs dealers it would make a lot of sense for them to convert their money into diamonds. Or it would have done, before the diamond market crashed.'

Everybody agreed, except Jeff, aka Bluebottle, who said, 'I told you I'd rather have gold.'

I thanked Brian for his contribution and he went back to his cosy office at headquarters with a coathanger behind the door. Nigel had a query about priorities on the outstanding crimes printout I'd passed over to him and Sparky rang our friends in Drugs Squad. I was halfway up the stairs when Elsie caught me, waving the chitty for the sandwiches.

A couple of Goodrich's clients looked interesting. One was the husband of the landlady of a town-centre pub, with convictions for handling stolen property. He was known to our intelligence officer because of the shady characters who drank with him. Goodrich had invested forty thousand of his hard-earned smackeroos, fifteen of it in diamonds, and he looked the sort of person who might bear a grudge.

The other was a retired rugby player with a conviction for violence, and his benefit money was now helping to heat K. Tom's swimming pool. Wouldn't like to be on the wrong side of him. They both sounded dangerous, so I gratefully agreed when Sparky and Jeff volunteered to interview them.

It was nearly lunchtime when the call from Mike Freer of the Drug Squad came. 'Shagnasty!' he boomed in my ear. 'What's this about you playing snakes and ladders, with real ladders?'

'Hiya, Catfish,' I replied. 'I thought I told Sparky to ring you.'

'I'm returning his call. From home – I'm having a day off. In fact we were thinking of having a ride out your way for a bite of lunch. Can you recommend anywhere?'

'I can, as a matter of fact. Yesterday we called in a pub called the Eagle, up on the back road to Oldfield, just before the tops. Menu looked good, can't speak for the food. Oh, and they serve hand-pulled Black Sheep.'

'I would say that clinches it, my little crime-buster. The Eagle it is.'

'What's the celebration?'

'Good grief, Sherlock! It's no wonder you're in the detectives. Actually it's our wedding anniversary, but we don't make a song and dance about it. What did you want me for?'

'It was you that rang me.'

'Ah yes, but I rang you because David Sparkington,

whom God preserve, and may his offspring be as numerous as the stars in the sky, rang me. And he rang me because you asked him to. Therefore, I deduce that it is really you that wants to talk to me.'

'Right. OK. Here it comes: does the name Michael Angelo Watts mean anything to you?'

I heard him exclaim: 'Waah!' and the phone went dead.

'Hello?' I said.

'Sorry, Charlie. Just crossing myself. Michael Angelo does voodoo, he's not one to tangle with.'

'How's that?'

'Tell you what,' he said. 'If you can get away why not join us, about one o' clock?'

'Would discussing him over lunch spoil the meal?'

'No, not at all. I could pretend I was eating him.'

'And I wouldn't be in the way?'

'Don't be silly – it's our twenty-third!'

'Right. Thanks for the invite. I'll see you at one.'

I don't normally give myself extended lunch hours in the middle of a case. Mostly, I don't have a break at all. But I had an excuse. I rang K. Tom Davis's number to no avail, so I typed a letter to Justin Davis, asking him to contact me. I could drop it in at Broadside while I was up there. He might even be in. I sealed the envelope and drummed my fingers on the telephone. After a moment's hesitation I picked it up and dialled Annabelle's number.

She answered, breathless, after the fortieth ring, just as I was considering putting it down.

'I've been out,' she puffed. 'Heard the phone as I unlocked the door.'

'Morning drinky-poos with the neighbours?' I teased. She'd told me about the social scene in Kenya, and the difficulties of escaping the endless alcoholic circus of entertaining that the ex-pats created to alleviate the boredom of their lives.

'No. I've just been to the churchyard.'

'So you haven't eaten?'

'Not yet. Are you coming over?'

'No. Today lunch is on me. Can you be ready in about half an hour?'

'Oh, er, yes, I suppose so,' she replied, without enthusiasm.

'You don't sound sure. If there's a problem it's OK.'

'No, er, thank you. I think I'd like that, Charles. About half an hour, did you say?'

Annabelle still has lots of connections with the church. She fundraises and sits on committees, but I get the impression that she's more concerned with temporal than spiritual matters. She met her husband in Biafra, at the height of the famine, but what they saw there cemented his faith and nearly destroyed hers. I wasn't surprised when she said she'd been to church, except that she'd said churchyard, and it never registered with me.

Before leaving the office I put the keys to Goodrich's house in my pocket. Maud had finished there, but I'd have another look round after lunch.

I parked in the turnaround at the end of Annabelle's cul-de-sac and walked along her drive to the kitchen door. Donald was at the bottom of the garden, behind the compost heap, deep in concentration. I paused with my hand on the door knob, watching him.

He was poised, like a heron waiting to pounce, one leg slightly raised and a garden fork held level with his chest, the tines pointing at the ground.

Suddenly he struck. The fork plunged forward, again and again, until Donald straightened up, triumphant, and held the implement aloft. Impaled on it, squirming in its death throes, was a rat.

He gazed at it, grinning, until his eyes re-focused and he saw me, fifty yards away, watching him. He lowered the fork, and I turned the door handle.

Annabelle met me in the kitchen and gave me my customary peck. 'I'll just get my coat and some money for Donald,' she said. As she disappeared I saw his be-dribbled coffee mug on the draining board.

'I'll be in the car,' I shouted through to her, and picked up the mug between my finger and thumb, holding the edges. I went to the car, placed the mug in the glove box and waited.

'So what's the celebration?' she asked as she slid into the passenger seat.

I told her about ringing Mike for some information, and it just happening to be his wedding anniversary.

'Super,' she replied. 'Do you often break off for parties in the middle of the day?'

'It's not a party, it's a working lunch.'

Annabelle insisted on stopping at a corner shop for a bunch of flowers for Susie, although I warned her that this might create some disharmony in the Freer household.

'You buy me flowers,' she stated. 'If this Mike doesn't, then it is on his own head.'

'Ah, but I'm a new man,' I replied with all the in-genuousness I could muster, only to be rewarded with an 'Hurrumph!' and a scowl as she slipped out of the seat belt.

Buying the occasional bunch of flowers for a lady is one of the few lessons I've learned about relationships. Probably the only one. A couple of quid for a bunch of daffs, every two or three weeks, is the best investment it is possible to make. The rewards are a thousandfold the expenditure. The secret is to make them intermittent, without apparent reason. That has the additional benefit of giving you an excuse if you forget a special date in the calendar. You just loftily state that you buy her flowers when you decide to, not as and when dictated by convention and commercialism.

Annabelle came back carrying a bunch of roses and the new issue of the *Heckley Gazette*. I pulled out into the traffic as she scanned the front page. After a few seconds she said, 'Did you know you are in the paper?'

I remembered the quote I'd given the editor, and a little wave of panic swept over me, like when the dentist's receptionist calls your name. 'Er, no. What's it say?'

'It's on the front page. You didn't tell me about the swans in the park.'

'No. It's not a very pleasant topic of conversation.'

'It says: "Inspector Priest of Heckley CID told us that they were treating it as a very serious crime."'

I heaved a sigh of relief – that didn't sound too bad. But my contentment was premature.

We travelled the rest of the way in silence, Annabelle reading the rest of the paper, then watching the fields go by, as they gradually changed from handkerchiefs of grass to blankets of moorland, divided by drystone walls.

'The heather's starting to turn purple,' I said.

'Yes,' she replied, her face turned away from me.

Susie was delighted with the flowers, blushing and saying she shouldn't have bothered. I was right – Mike wasn't a great flower buyer. I'd have to have a word with him.

The girls had lasagne, while I chose a steak – 'Just for a change' – and Mike tackled a Barnsley chop. Annabelle couldn't believe her eyes when she saw it. Later, halfway through my rhubarb crumble, I said to him, 'So what's special about this Watts?'

Mike paused, spoonful of cheesecake in mid-air. 'Michael ... Angelo ... Watts,' he enunciated, chewing each word as thoroughly as the rack of ten lamb chops he'd just devoured. 'Drugs dealer extraordinaire. On his own, we could probably handle him. Unfortunately he's under the protection of his father, the one and only Dominic Watts.'

'Never heard of him,' I admitted.

Mike finished off his pudding. 'Haven't you? I'm surprised. Mr Wood knows all about him – they've had several dust-ups.'

'Gilbert? How come?' I asked, puzzled.

'Because Dominic Watts is president of some association of local traders – he invented the position himself – and sits on the local Community Forum.'

'Oh, them,' I said, intending to add, 'wankers,' but deciding it was more grammatical to leave it out.

'Don't you read the minutes?'

'No. Gilbert's good about things like that. As long as we produce results he does his best to shield us from the flak. They only sit every three months, don't they?'

'Three years would be too soon. Twice we've done Michael for possession, twice I've been hauled before a disciplinary panel. Racial harassment. He just smokes a little ganja now and again for his migraine, or his MS, or in honour of Haile Selassie. You know the picture.'

I went to the bar for some more drinks. Community Forums were set up by the local Police Authorities in the wake of the Bristol riots. They're comprised of various dignitaries and businessmen, who grill and generally slag-off the poor senior officer who has been delegated to attend. In theory they make suggestions about police activities, priorities, that sort of stuff, but they usually degenerate into chronic moaning sessions. We need them desperately, and the intentions are noble enough, but recording them in the minutes is no substitute for action on the streets. And then there are the members, like Watts, with their own private agendas.

When I was seated again Mike told me that Michael lived in the middle of a block of three ex-council houses on the edge of the Sylvan Fields estate. His father, Dominic, who owned the whole block, lived in an end one. 'Claims it's some sort of housing cooperative,' he said, 'but it's just a safe house for dealing drugs.'

'A safe house, on my patch?' I replied.

"Fraid so, Charlie.'

'Like, fortified?'

'Yep. The middle house for sure. We call on him now and again but there's steel bars across the door. We never get in.'

I said, 'We could spin him, if you wanted. No need for you to be involved.'

Mike shook his head. 'Good of you to offer, but you'd be wasting your time. If you did find a magistrate willing to sign a warrant, by the time you'd battered the door down all the evidence would be on its way to the local sewage works, via the toilet.'

I explained to Annabelle and Susie how a safe house, imported from Los Angeles, worked, but I don't think they believed me. Things like that didn't happen in Heckley.

We left Mike and Susie in the pub and drove the couple of miles to Broadside. I parked outside the gate and reached into my pocket for the letter I'd written.

'I think I could live here,' I declared.

Annabelle turned to look at the house. 'Mmm, it is lovely,' she agreed, without conviction.

'I won't be a minute. I'll just pop this through the letterbox,' I told her, waving the envelope.

This time they were in. A face at the window saw me approach and a young man opened the door as I reached it.

'Mr Davis?' I asked.

'Justin Davis,' he replied, pleasantly. 'What can I do for you?'

He was in his late twenties at a guess, small and wiry, with fair hair tied back in a ponytail.

'Detective Inspector Charlie Priest, from Heckley CID,' I replied. 'I was wondering if I could have a chat with you some time?'

'Who is it, darling?' a female voice asked, moments before a willowy blonde swayed into view. She was the type that knows they look good in jeans and a navy-blue sweater, so that's what they wear. Only the cream-coloured labrador was missing.

He half turned to her. 'A policeman,' he said, followed by, 'Now?' to me.

'Er, well, actually, I'm off duty at the moment. I was just passing and intended leaving a note for you. We called yesterday, but you weren't in.'

'It's now or never,' he stated. 'I'm off to Australia tomorrow. What's it about?'

'Do you know a man called Hartley Goodrich?' I asked. He shook his head. 'No. Should I?'

'He was a business acquaintance of your father's. Unfortunately he was found dead Monday morning.'

'I think you'd better come in,' the woman said.

'Thanks, but first I'll pop to my car and tell my girl-friend that I'll be five minutes, if you don't mind. We've just had lunch at the Eagle.'

As I turned to leave she said, 'It's all right, I'll fetch her,' and sidled past me in the doorway, adding, 'I'm Lisa Davis, by the way.'

Her husband took me inside, past a heap of designer luggage in assorted shapes, sizes and colours. The room was bright and airy, furnished with light woods and lots of chrome. On a stand, in a corner of the room, was the biggest parrot I'd ever seen.

'Good grief, what's he called?' I asked, warily, as the bird bobbed up and down as if about to launch an attack.

'Oh, that's Joey. He's a scarlet macaw,' Davis junior replied.

The ultimate executive toy, I thought. An endangered species. His beak looked as if it could slacken the wheel-nuts on an Eddie Stobart articulated lorry.

'Does he bite?' I asked.

'No, he's an old softie.' He walked over to the bird, which lowered its head, expecting a tickle. 'Have you ever been bitten by a parrot?'

'Er, no,' I admitted. 'That pleasure has never fallen within the, er, ambit of my experiences.'

'Ha! You don't know what you've missed. Come and look.' He prised open the bird's beak for me to study from a safe distance. 'You get three bites for the price of one, and it hurts three times as much. I've broken my arm, ankle and collar bones, but nothing's ever hurt me as much as a bite from a parrot.'

'I thought you said he was an old softie?' I commented.

'No, not from Joey,' Justin replied. 'Lisa's parents have

a pet shop. I've been bitten there, when we've been looking after it for them.'

'Right, well, I'll take your word for it.'

'Please, sit down,' he said.

I chose a seat a long way from the bird, but where I could keep a wary eye on it. 'Are you racing in Australia?' I asked, sinking so far into an easy chair that I briefly wondered if I'd be joining him. A photograph of Justin and Lisa, him dressed like a knight at a tournament in his speedway leathers and clutching a huge cut-glass vase, hung over the fireplace. It was the only clue to how he earned his living, but I knew that somewhere there would be a special room stuffed to the Artex with his trophies. I have three football medals in a Zubes tin.

'Yeah. The season's ended here,' he replied, 'so it's three months over there, every winter. It's a hard life.' He was grinning as he said it.

'You're not doing too badly out of it,' I reminded him, with a wave of a hand.

'We're all adrenaline junkies,' he explained. 'The money helps, but nobody goes into speedway for the money. It's the travelling that gets you down.'

I'd have liked to have heard all about it. As a failed sportsman, they've always fascinated me. I didn't know anything about speedway, but it was a Cinderella sport, and I'd bet pain and sacrifice were a commoner story than fame and riches.

Justin was polite and friendly, but I was there to quiz him about his father's involvement in a scam.

'We met your mother yesterday,' I explained. 'She said your father was possibly over here, or maybe he'd gone to a race meeting with you. I'm trying to piece together Mr Goodrich's movements, and I'd like a word with your father. Have you any idea where he might be?'

'You said ... dead. Was this guy murdered?' he asked. At the mention of his father he looked worried, or angry. His face was pale and he fidgeted with his fingers. Maybe he was ready for another fix of adrenaline.

'At the moment it's just a suspicious death,' I lied.

Voices came from the hallway as Lisa and Annabelle came in, then faded into another room.

I opened my mouth to ask, 'When did you last see your father?' but choked it off. We'd had too many paintings in this enquiry. 'Have you seen your dad recently?' is what came out.

'No,' he whispered, his brow creased in thought.

'So when did you last see him?'

'In the summer, when I went round to see Mum. He was there. July. I don't think I've seen him since then.'

'He doesn't go to meetings with you?'

'No.'

'Never?'

He gave a little smile. 'Sometimes I wonder if he's there in the crowd, watching me, but it's a dream, I know he's not. We fell out. They sent me to a good school, wanted me to go on to university, be a lawyer, help him in the business. Thought I should be grateful. I bunked off to go racing.' He paused, wondering how much to confide in this stranger. 'Truth is,' he said, 'K. Tom is only my stepfather. I was about six or seven when he married my mother. Let's just say we don't get on. He came to see me race once, about two years ago, in Gothenberg. Came up to me in the paddock, right out of the blue, saying he'd brought me my spare bike, just in case I needed it.'

'And had he?'

'Yeah. He'd collected it from here and taken it over to the Continent. Said he'd had a premonition that I'd need it, wanted to be involved, let bygones by bygones, all that crap. I said "OK," but he never came again.'

Lisa appeared and placed two coffees on a low table. 'We're in the kitchen, talking seriously,' she said, walking out with an exaggerated wiggle and a backward glance.

I shouted a thank you after her, and when she'd gone I asked Justin, 'How much do you know about K. Tom's business?'

'Nothing. He's into all sorts of wheeling and dealing, all over my head.'

'What about International Gem Investments? Have you heard of them?'

'Was that the diamonds racket?'

'Mmm.'

'In that case, I've heard of them. He sent me a load of information about it and rang me up, said he'd double my money in two shakes of a cat's tail. I showed it to my manager, who said, "No way." Then I read that they'd gone bust and a lot of people had been hurt. Since then I've had nothing to do with him. Bad for my image, I'm told, as if that mattered.'

'Sounds as if you have a good manager.'

'The best. She's called Lisa.'

I shook his hand and thanked him for being candid with me. He told me that he didn't like K. Tom, but was convinced that he couldn't kill anyone. 'Oh, he's not a suspect,' I reassured him. They both walked to the gate with us, and as I got into the car Lisa said goodbye to me across the roof, her eyes lingering just a little longer than was necessary.

I broke the silence a mile down the road. 'They're a pleasant couple,' I said.

'Yes.'

'They have a parrot.'

'Really?'

'A scarlet macaw.'

'Mmm.'

I looked across at Annabelle. She was staring straight forward, her face pale, hands in her lap. I felt I was with a stranger. As soon as a lay-by appeared I swung into it and stopped, switching off the engine to indicate the seriousness of the situation. Annabelle took a deep breath and bit her lip.

I said, 'All the way up here you were quiet. In the pub with Mike and Susie you were the old charming Annabelle, a delight to be with. The same, no doubt, with Lisa Davis. Now, alone with me, you've gone quiet again. It's obviously something I've done or said that's upsetting you. For that, whatever it is, I apologise. If I've inadvertently hurt you, then I've hurt myself a hundred times more. But if I don't know what it is, how can I make amends?'

She turned to face me, and I looked into those light-blue eyes that can look like cornflowers in June but now shone like glaciers. Something gripped me that I'd last experienced when I'd looked down the barrel of a twelve-bore held by a madman. It was called fear, but this time it was desolation, not death, that I was risking.

'You think Donald did it, don't you?' she said.

So that was it. 'Oh,' I replied.

'You think Donald killed the swans in the park. You offered to take him home so you could quiz him. I'm surprised you didn't ask him for his fingerprints.'

My eyes flicked towards the glove box that held his coffee mug. 'It's a possibility,' I told her, lamely.

'But Donald's parents are friends of mine, Charles. Donald is a friend of mine. He wouldn't hurt a fly. Can you imagine what it must be like for him? He was brain damaged at birth, and he knows it. He knows what he is like, and if that isn't enough he has to fight prejudice, too. It makes me so angry.'

She was close to tears, and she doesn't cry easily. I risked reaching out and holding her hand, and she placed her other one over mine. The best thing to say when you don't know what to say is nothing.

I could go so far towards imagining what it must be like for Donald. Willing to work, but no proper job. No chance of ever driving a car or enjoying himself on equal terms with other young people. And then there was sex. Every time he looked at a newspaper or the TV he'd hear about couples bonking, or have some bimbo's breasts thrust towards him. This mysterious activity was being used to sell everything from cars and coffee to walnut whips, but at twenty-eight he'd never had a nibble of it. The nearest he ever got was to dig the garden of the beautiful lady who was a friend of his parents. We're told that it's themselves that the mentally handicapped usually hurt, not other people. If that's true, and it is, then they must have the forbearance of the angels.

After a few minutes I said, 'I've been a policeman for a long time. Maybe too long. Sometimes I wonder if I've lost sight of how normal people behave. But I'm a good cop and I enjoy what I do. I've tried to share as much of it with you as I can, Annabelle, to involve you as much as possible. I've tried, love, believe me, I've tried.'

She squeezed my hand and said, 'I know you have,

Charles – that's why you brought me here today. It's not all your fault. I've been feeling a little low since the weekend, perhaps I'm over-reacting.'

I placed my hands back on the wheel and shook my head. 'No, you're not over-reacting. You're dead right. I've let my prejudices show, and it hurts.'

Annabelle started to speak, but I interrupted her with the words, 'Look in the glove box.'

Puzzled, she moved the catch and the lid fell open, revealing Donald's coffee-stained mug. 'Oh, Charles,' she sighed, lifting it out. 'You are impossible.'

The intention was to take Annabelle home and then visit Goodrich's house for a last look. Maud had confiscated what documents she needed, so we'd vacated the place. It was now standing empty, but under regular surveillance from the mobiles to discourage ghouls and souvenir hunters. As we drove into town I said, 'Goodrich – the dead man – lived alone. I'm going there next for a look round. Maybe you could come and give me a woman's perspective on him, eh?'

She smiled indulgently. 'You don't have to, Charles,' she replied. 'What would your superiors say if they discovered that you were in the habit of taking your ladyfriends on investigations?'

'I don't have ladyfriends,' I protested. 'I have you. And we don't have superior officers, we have senior officers. Have you ever studied psychology?'

'Only for a year.'

'Good, you're hired – consultant psychologist. Hold tight, we're back on duty.' I flicked the Cavalier down a gear and stepped on the accelerator.

Let's face it, anybody would grasp the opportunity to rummage round somebody else's home. When it had belonged to a murder victim, and Annabelle still thought it was murder, you'd have to be moribund not to be intrigued. I parked on the drive and unlocked the door to the house.

'This doesn't feel right,' she whispered, glancing round the kitchen. It smelled like the inside of my washing basket at the end of the week – what my mother would have described as foisty – and the dust from the fingerprint team had redistributed itself evenly over every surface. We'd turned the power off, and it was much colder than on my previous visits.

'Why?' I whispered back to her.

'I don't know.'

'Why are we whispering?' I whispered.

I steered her through the kitchen and gave her a quick tour of the place. 'Ooh!' she said, when she saw the photos in the bedroom.

'First question, Madame Psychologist, is: "Was he gay?"'

'I'd need more evidence before I could give a diagnosis, Mr Policeman,' she replied.

'You psychologists are all the goddamn same,' I railed. 'Where would *we* be if we asked for evidence every time we needed to make a decision?'

'So what are you looking for?' Annabelle wondered.

'Well, we've had a good search of the place, but we don't seem to have discovered much about the man himself. We know quite a bit about his business, but nothing about his social life. Maybe he was gay, maybe not. Most of all we'd like some names and addresses, or telephone numbers, apart from the ones in his diary. Otherwise, anything that might be of interest.'

'And where do you want me to look?'

'I'll rummage in the pockets of his suits, see what I can find there. How about if you had a good fossick through his bookshelves; see what that tells you about the man. You're better read than me,' I added.

'Mmm. Right.'

I could see that she was apprehensive about being left alone. 'C'mon, I'll show you his library,' I said, giving her a squeeze.

There were fifteen suits in the wardrobe. I found cinema tickets in the more casual pockets, a menu for a Rotary Club bash in a dinner jacket. It would be interesting to know what films he liked, but hardly productive. The odd fiver and a tenner were stuffed into top pockets, as if he'd been given them in change at the bar and not bothered to put them in his wallet. There was a membership card for a dining club and another condom. He had more ties than a lottery winner has relatives, and amongst his highly polished shoe collection I found a pair of tooled leather cowboy boots that he must have bought in a moment of weakness and never worn. I'd have loved them.

I lifted drawers out and looked into the bare cabinets. His nooks and crannies were a lot cleaner than mine. Nothing in his luggage – matching Vuitton – but the name tickets were from the Caribbean Queen Cruise Line. So he'd been on a cruise. Lucky him.

I wandered in to see Annabelle. 'How's it going?' I asked.

'His reading tastes are about as dismal as yours.' Pulling a volume out she said, 'Look at this.'

It was *The Illustrated Kama Sutra*. I extended an arm towards the bedroom, saying, 'We could always ... no better not. It might confuse the SOCO.'

We'd already seen the *Kama Sutra*, and a catalogue of ladies' underwear of the type that a lady would never wear. It wasn't enough to typecast him. I told her that I was going downstairs, to investigate the lounge, and a patrol car called while I was there. I thought about making some tea, but decided it might look callous. His drinks cabinet was well stocked, mainly whisky, and he had all the *Mad Max* and *Lethal Weapon* videos. In a display cabinet were some Lladró figures, several pieces of Caithness glass – how do they do that? – and three cheap little trophies announcing that he'd been Salesman of the Year. Personally, I'd have taken the GTX with wide wheels and go-faster stripes. It's easy to knock – I've never made Cop of the Year. All I found down the back of the settee was a paperclip and a button.

'Charles?' I heard, followed by footfalls on the stairs.

'In here.'

Annabelle came through the doorway, doing her best to stifle a smile. '*Cherchez la femme*,' she said, holding a dark brown folder towards me.

'What have you there?' I asked.

'Photographs.' She placed the folder on the table and pulled a sheaf of glossy prints from it, blown up to about ten by eight. The logo on the folder was the same as on his luggage labels – wavy lines, surmounted by a crown.

In the first photograph, which was in a cardboard mount so you could stand it on the sideboard, Goodrich had his arm round an attractive woman and they were gazing into each other's eyes. He was wearing a flowered shirt and they both had chains of blooms draped around their necks. Behind them was a lifebuoy with the name *Caribbean Queen* emblazoned on it.

'Do you know her?' Annabelle asked.

'No. Never seen her before. Let's look at the others.'

The next one showed him resplendent in white tuxedo, shaking hands with a ship's officer, presumably the captain. I had the impression that it was part of a ritual: shake hands with the skipper as you go in to dinner, then buy the photo at an inflated price while you're feeling replete. A nice little earner, as they say.

'Sadly, I've never met him, either,' I declared, pointing at the captain. 'Next please.'

There were five of them on this one. Two pirates were standing behind three paying customers, making sure they had a good time by threatening them with plastic cutlasses and leering at the camera. Goodrich and the woman we'd seen earlier were laughing, but the other man with them looked embarrassed.

It's hard to tell with photographs. They're not the definitive evidence that you are led to believe by films and books, but I was fairly sure I knew who this third person was.

'But I have met him,' I said, pointing.

'Ooh, good. Who is he?'

'He's called Eastwood. I think I'd better have another word with him.'

'Does he live nearby?'

'Fairly near. Like, next door.'

'Right, boss. Let's go.'

'Uh uh. The only place you are going is home. I don't want you solving my most difficult case single-handed. Besides, he'll be at work.'

Driving to Annabelle's, I told her that it wasn't murder, but that we were using the enquiry to look into Goodrich's business dealings, which looked shady. I left it at that and she didn't ask any questions, although I'd gamble that she had plenty.

'The Davises were a decent couple,' I said. 'Very pleasant.'

'I suppose so.'

'You don't sound sure.'

'She fancied you. Don't tell me you did not notice.'

'Er, no. Can't say I did.'

'Well, I noticed.'

'Really? She is rather attractive, so maybe it's as well they're going away tomorrow,' I said, smiling.

'She's not going with him. Not for a couple of weeks. So I don't want you making any follow-up enquiries.'

'Oh, er, right.'

At her gate I thanked her for her assistance, and told her I meant it. I wasn't being patronising. 'You never told me where you found the pictures,' I added.

'They were just inside a book.'

'*The Kama Sutra*?'

'*Mechanised Warfare on the Eastern Front*.'

'No wonder we missed them.'

As she opened the car door I said, 'Am I forgiven, then?'

Annabelle closed the door again. 'Not completely,' she answered, looking at me but not smiling. 'But perhaps in a day or two.'

'OK. I'll settle for that.'

She heaved a big sigh and fidgeted with the collar of her jacket. 'It's not your fault, Charles,' she confessed. 'It's me. Next Saturday would have been mine and Peter's wedding anniversary. I've been trying to push it out of my mind, but when you said it was Mike and Susie's . . .'

She shrugged her shoulders and left the rest of it unsaid.

'I'm sorry, I never realised,' I told her.

'You weren't to know.'

'Look,' I started, not really knowing what I was going to say. 'I'm not sure what I'm supposed to do. I can either smother you with attention, take your mind off things, or maybe you'd prefer some time to yourself?'

'I thought you were busy, with this enquiry.'

'Priorities. I can make time.'

She was quiet for a moment, then said, 'I think I'd like a few days to myself, if you don't mind, Charles.'

'OK,' I mumbled.

There are two roundabouts, three sets of traffic lights and about eight junctions between Annabelle's house and mine, but I don't remember negotiating any of them. It had to happen, but I couldn't help feeling that something was slipping away. I expect too much from relationships, invest everything I have in them, but it's me that hurts when they fall through. I'd never felt like this before about anyone, and knew I never would again. There'd been an awful lot of before, but there could never be another again. I yanked the handbrake on outside the place I call home, then realised I was supposed to have gone to the police station. I cursed and restarted the engine.

The office was deserted, which was fine by me. I typed my reports and read some others. Eastwood would be busy assistant-managing at the York and Durham. I'd assume he worked normal office hours and hit him at about six, after he'd eaten but before he started on the *Temeraire*.

Maggie and Sparky came in with long faces. They'd plenty of misery to report, but no confessions.

Eastwood was leathering his Audi when I arrived, still wearing his suit and tie. Some office types can't wait to get out of a suit when they go home, but he wasn't one of them.

At the back of his house I noticed a brand new greenhouse standing on a concrete base. It must have been new because there was nothing in it. Eastwood apologised for the non-existent mess and showed me inside.

'How can I help you, Inspector?' he asked.

I didn't prat about. I just laid the photo of the pirate attack on the table and said, 'Do you recognise this lady?'

He swallowed and placed two manicured fingers over his lips, as if a great gob of bile had just made a bid for freedom. 'Y-Yes,' he stuttered, stifling a burp. 'It's m-my ex-wife.'

'Oh, could you explain?'

'Well, er, yes. Did you find this at Hartley's?'

'Mmm.'

'Well, er, 1993 I think it was. Joan and I had booked to go on a cruise, and Hartley remarked that he hadn't had a holiday for years. We saw quite a bit of him in those days – he used to make up a bridge foursome, twice a week. So, Joan and I discussed it between ourselves and suggested he come on the cruise with us. He leapt at the idea.'

I bet he did. 'So why did you stop seeing so much of him?' I asked.

He shrugged his shoulders. 'Just one of those things. We grew bored with him. All he ever talked about was work, kept trying to involve me in his schemes, pump me for information, that sort of thing.'

'And you like to leave it all behind you in the office,' I suggested. 'Work on your models.'

'Quite, Inspector.'

'Pardon my asking, Mr Eastwood, but was your divorce anything to do with Goodrich?'

The bile was still causing him a problem. 'No,' he replied, swallowing and grimacing at the same time.

'Mrs Eastwood wasn't having an affair with him?'

'No, certainly not.'

He'd replied just a little too quickly, so I waited for him to enlarge.

'She ... he ... She went through a bad patch – nerves, you know. Then decided she wanted a completely fresh start. I think he influenced her, made her feel dissatisfied, but no more than that. We quarrelled a lot. She didn't appreciate the pressures I was under.'

No, it must be difficult trying to make all those little figures with peg-legs and eye-patches and parrots on their shoulders. 'So where is she now?' I asked.

'I don't know.'

'Well, where did she go?'

'To a flat in Heckley, but she's moved since then.'

'And you don't know where?'

'No.'

'Where would you look if you needed to find her?'

'I really don't know.'

'Think, Mr Eastwood. Has she any relatives?'

'Oh, yes. A sister in Bradford. They were fairly close, she might know where Joan is.'

'Do you have the sister's address?'

'I suppose so, somewhere.'

'In that case, I'd be very grateful if you could find it for me.'

On the way out I cast a backward glance at the concrete pad under the greenhouse, and wondered how thick it was.

Chapter Five

I stopped at a corner shop and bought an *A to Z*. The sister, Dorothy, lived somewhere off the Haworth Road, on the far side of the town, and Eastwood didn't know her phone number. Some enquiries are like pushing a Tesco's trolley up the down escalator. Bradford has developed a system of by-passes, but I wanted to go through the city centre. There was gridlock at Forster Square, caused by a broken-down bus. Just after the buses were de-regulated the ones in Bradford carried the message: Privately run for the benefit of the customer, or something similar. Immediately underneath were the words: No change given. I noted that they'd had the decency to remove the benefit of the customer bit. A young girl in a sari and a Nissan let me filter on to the roundabout and I gave her a wave. We were off again.

I drove through the Land of a Thousand Curries, past cinemas converted into mosques or carpet warehouses, and halal butchers that had been Co-ops and Thrifts when I was a kid. Old men in pyjama trousers, sticking out from under Umbro anoraks, strolled the pavements, followed by women who might have been sixteen or sixty, ravishing or dog-ugly. The veil is a great equaliser. I felt uncomfortable. I think I subscribe to the melting pot theory of integration. If we have to have ghettos, let them be multi-

107

national. The Romans knew a thing or two. When they conquered a country they adopted the local gods. It must have saved them a lot of hassle.

Dorothy opened the door as far as a chain would allow and a cat shot out through the gap. It was a bow-fronted terrace house in a street that was running to seed but not quite decay. I'd had to park three doors away, and a couple of cars standing on blocks told me that the rot was starting.

'I'm DI Priest from Heckley CID,' I told the pale face that peered at my warrant card through the gap, almost level with my own. 'I'm trying to trace your sister, Joan Eastwood. I wonder if I could come in and have a word with you?'

She took the chain off and let me in. The front room was barely furnished, with unframed prints by Klimt and Modigliani on the emulsioned walls, and I had the choice of sitting either on an upright chair or something between a futon and a palliasse. I chose the upright and Dorothy dossed on the floor, next to her coffee mug and ashtray. She was wearing jeans and a baggy sweater that was perpetually falling off one shoulder, revealing a pale-blue bra strap.

'Sorry,' she said, waving the mug at me and removing the fag from her lips to have a drink. 'Can I offer you a coffee?'

'Thanks all the same, but no. Can you tell me if you know where Joan is?'

'Is this to do with Hartley Goodrich?' she asked.

'Yes. We believe your sister was friendly with him and may be able to tell us something about his lifestyle.'

She smiled and took a drag of her cigarette, which brought on a coughing fit. For a few seconds I thought she was going to choke, but another swig and a puff restored her equilibrium. Sometimes I think there must be a link between smoking and coughing. Perhaps it's something the medical profession should look into. 'Ambleside Road,' she said. 'Number twenty-three. That's Leeds, Alwoodley. A nice area. And, boy, will she be able to tell you about Hartley's lifestyle.'

'Go on.'

'No, I'm only guessing about them. You'd better ask her yourself.'

'So you think they were having an affair?'

She nipped the butt of her cigarette into the ashtray and reached out for the packet of Benson and Hedges that was nearby. 'More than likely, in my opinion.'

'Have you ever met Goodrich?'

She nodded and smiled, dabbing the end of a fresh cigarette against a five-for-a-pound plastic lighter.

'When was this?' I asked.

''Bout four, five years ago. Maybe longer. They used to play bridge on Saturday evenings and tried to fix me up with him. Joan was full of how wonderful he was. Hartley this, Hartley that. In fact, he was a slimy little toad, except that he wasn't little, apart from his intellect. I couldn't stand the guy, but for a couple of weeks I had a certain sadistic pleasure in pandering to his political views. Then I exploded and told him what a fascist shite he was.' She turned her hands palms upwards. 'That was the end of my journey into suburbia.'

I laughed, conscious that she probably regarded me as a fascist shite, too. 'I bet that was worth seeing,' I said.

'I enjoyed it, but I've a feeling I may have driven Joan into his arms. Have you met her ex, Derek?'

'Yes. He gave me your address.'

'Has he finished the *Temeraire*, yet?'

'No, not yet,' I chuckled.

She heaved a big sigh and put the cigarette between her

lips. I rose to leave, thanking her for her assistance. The fug in the room was like it used to be in pubs twenty years ago.

She hauled herself upright, saying, 'You're a man of the world, Inspector, so you probably recognise the types. I'm the bright sister who made a mess of things; Joan was the dumb one who made good. *C'est la vie.*'

'Oh, I suspect you have your moments,' I told her.

'Moments,' she agreed, nodding wistfully.

'One more thing – when did you last see Joan?'

'It'd be about six weeks ago. Met her for lunch in Leeds. But we talk on the phone every fortnight or so.'

'And did she seem just the same as always?'

'Yes, as far as I could tell.'

'Does she work?'

'Yes, as a nursing auxiliary at the local hospital. She moved there to be near the job. Perhaps that's something you should ask her about, too.'

'I'm afraid you've lost me.'

'She worked for York and Durham, like Derek. Pension plan, key to the executive toilets, the full package. Left in an unseemly hurry and was unemployed for a while, after their marriage collapsed. I'd have thought she could have wangled herself a transfer to another branch. Something happened, but I don't know what.'

'I see. Thanks. So when I've gone, presumably you'll give her a sisterly ring and tell her I'm looking for her.'

'Yes, presumably I will.'

'In that case, maybe we could ring her now and make me an appointment, if you don't mind?'

Joan worked shifts and wasn't answering, so I rang her from the station the following morning and then hot-wheeled it over to Leeds. She was probably about five years older than her sister and a good six inches shorter. She had a round face compared with Dorothy's long Virginia Woolf countenance, and dressed differently – mohair twinset against denim and Aran. As far as I knew they were full sisters, but it didn't look as if they shared the same gene pool. Perhaps their mother had been susceptible to the odd smooth-talking insurance man, too. The permissive society didn't really begin in the sixties, we just started talking about it then.

She had the upstairs flat in a rather swish maisonette. Rented furnished, I presumed, although her stamp was on the place: lots of artificial flowers and the dreaded Lladró. Her hand shook as she poured me a cup of tea.

'Mmm, I needed that,' I told her, taking a sip. When she was settled I asked her how well she knew Mr Goodrich.

'Fairly well, I suppose,' she replied.

'I believe you held bridge evenings,' I prompted.

'Y-yes, that's right. For a while.'

'Was he any good?'

'Quite good. Very competitive – he tried harder than we did. He liked to win.'

'Did he bring his own partner?' I asked. I'd heard about bridge evenings. Sometimes they didn't even bring a pack of cards.

'No. We always had a problem finding a fourth. The lady on the other side of us liked a game, but she had to go into a home. Alzheimer's disease. Then Dorothy made the numbers up for a while, but it wasn't really her thing. So eventually they fizzled out.'

'And how many times did you go on holiday together?'

She'd put her cup down, then picked it up again to keep

her fingers occupied. Now she placed it back on the table to avoid spilling the contents. I obviously knew a lot more than she expected.

'Just the once, a Caribbean cruise.'

'Mrs Eastwood, was Goodrich one of the reasons for the failure of your marriage?'

She shook her head defiantly. 'No, not at all.'

I asked her all the routine stuff about when she'd last seen him, finishing off with a query about investments.

'After the divorce,' she said, 'Derek had to buy my half of the house. Hartley offered to invest the money for me.'

'And did you let him?'

She nodded and sniffed.

'Have you lost your money?'

Another nod and sniff. 'It's looking like it. Well, twenty thousand pounds.'

'In diamonds?'

'Diamond. Singular.'

I asked her if she could tell me anything about his business acquaintances, but she had nothing to volunteer.

'Have you ever heard of K. Tom Davis?' I asked.

She looked up, startled. 'Yes, but I never met him. He was behind the diamonds. It was his fault that it all went wrong. Hartley was duped just as much as anybody else.'

She couldn't expand on her theory, so I invited her to ring me if she thought of anything else and left. I picked up a beef sandwich and a curd tart, carefully avoiding the spoonerism, at a local bakery and made my way back to Heckley. Waiting on my desk was a brown envelope, bursting at the seams. It contained a thick wad of coloured photocopies of the poster I'd done for the bullbars campaign. That was quick, for Traffic, I thought. I put a small pile on everybody's desk and pinned a couple on notice boards. Then I went to the loo.

Nigel was washing his hands. 'Hi, boss,' he greeted me. 'I've a message for you.'

There was the sound of a toilet flushing, and a huge PC came out of a cubicle, tucking his shirt flap into his waistband.

'Hello, George,' I said. 'Successful?'

'Grand, Mr Priest,' he replied. 'Like a flock o' pigeons landin' on a wet roof.'

Nigel's gaze switched from the PC to me and back again, his jaw hanging slack, like a moose with a gumboil. He's from Berkshire, and lies awake at night wondering if he'd be more at home in Ulan Bator.

'What was it?' I asked him.

'What was what?'

'The message.'

'Oh, yes. Two things, actually. First of all the Dean brothers are in the court lists for Monday, so I may be out of circulation for a couple of days. And a chap called Davis just rang. Said you'd been chasing him. He left his number.'

'Justin Davis?'

'No, Tom something-or-other.'

'K. Tom. Great.'

Walking back to the office Nigel said, 'I've been wondering about inviting Heather – Professor Simms – out for dinner. She's frightfully attractive, don't you think?'

'Our new pathologist? Mmm, yes, she is.'

'She doesn't wear a wedding ring, but I don't suppose you know if she has a boyfriend or anything?'

We were back at Nigel's desk and he tore the top page

off his notepad and handed it to me. 'No idea,' I told him. 'Met her for the first time myself on Monday. Just go for it, Nigel. She can only say no. Defeat is no disgrace, to quote Idi Amin's chiropodist.'

Now he looked more puzzled than ever. 'Just one thing,' I confided, lowering my voice. 'If she offers to cook for you, don't touch the liver.'

K. Tom Davis's wife answered the phone. 'Hello, Mrs Davis,' I said. 'This is Inspector Priest. I have a message to ring your husband at this number.'

He was there, so I drove straight over to see him. The obligatory Range Rover stood in front of the garages and I wished I'd brought the bullbars leaflets with me, but as I walked past the car I was pleasantly surprised to see it didn't have them fitted. I thumbed the bell-push and heard the first four bars of *Canon in D* from deep within. Or maybe it was the last four bars. Or any combination of bars in between.

This time we didn't sit in the glorified greenhouse. I slithered about on a chesterfield that was as comfortable as a piano lid and they accompanied me on the matching easy chairs. More depressing hunting scenes adorned the walls – horses frozen in mid-leap against backgrounds straight out of *How to Paint Trees*.

K. Tom was a big man, impressive, but his beer gut was winning the weight war and his nose had dipped into too many whisky glasses. The gold cufflinks would have paid off my one and only creditor, leaving the sovereign rings – one on each hand – to put a new set of tyres on the cause of same debt.

'I was scared,' he explained, when I asked him the reason for his disappearance. 'I read about Goodrich's murder and I suppose I panicked. Thought I'd be next on

114

the list, maybe. I told Ruth I was going to see Justin, but I booked into the Devonshire Hotel, in Wharfedale, for a couple of nights.' At the mention of his wife's name he broke off rolling the bottom of his tie and gestured towards her. 'I rang her last night,' he continued, 'and she told me of your visit. It's a terrible business, Inspector. If I can help in any way you have only to ask.'

'Well, first of all, we're not sure that it was murder, but somebody did hit him over the head. At the moment we're calling it a suspicious death.' Might as well clarify that right from the beginning. 'When did you last see Goodrich?'

'Good grief, let me see. Must be over six months ago. I've only seen him once since we . . . since . . .'

'Since you went bankrupt?'

'Since we called the receiver in.'

'So what made you think you might be next on the list?'

The bottom of his tie looked like a spring roll and I felt hungry. He realised what he was doing and flattened it against his stomach. 'Well,' he began, 'I, er, assumed it was a mad creditor, out for revenge because he'd lost a few quid. They should see what we've lost. They all think that we're the villains of the piece, but we've been hurt most of all. The blame really lies with the banks. If they hadn't pulled the plug on us, nobody would have been hurt.'

And Robert Maxwell was a big cuddly teddy bear. I asked them where they were on Sunday night, Monday morning – not because I cared but because that was what they expected me to ask. They never left the house.

'Are there any creditors who have been particularly hostile, or threatened violence?' I asked.

'Yes,' he replied. 'In fact, I've a file of letters you can take with you. Nearly binned them all. Glad I didn't, now.'

Mrs Davis pulled herself upright and volunteered to fetch the letters.

'Thanks. So what are your immediate plans? Are you staying here?'

'Not sure, Inspector. I have a couple of business trips scheduled, trying to sort out a few things – you know how it is. But it's good to be home again. Don't see why the buggers should drive me away. What do you think?'

I thought it was complicated, trying to solve a crime you didn't know about while pretending to investigate one that hadn't happened. 'We're not expecting him to strike again,' I assured him, and immediately wondered if this was misleading advice. Ah well, never mind, I thought.

He walked out with me. 'One last thing,' I said as I opened the car door. 'If it was the diamonds that collapsed, why did Goodrich go bankrupt?'

'Because, underneath, he was a foolish man,' Davis replied. 'I'm in this business to make money, and don't deny it. I'm proud of it. As long as it's legal, I'll consider anything. But that wasn't enough for Goodrich. He wanted to be popular too. Looked up to. A valuable member of the community. When the banks foreclosed on us he thought he could come out of it smelling of roses without any of his punters losing, so he did what all desperate men do: he gambled. Bought shares in uranium mines in godforsaken holes in the Kalahari desert; thought he could find another Poseidon; that sort of thing, instead of facing them and saying: "Sorry, I've lost your money." In the end he lost everything.'

'Right,' I said, nodding as if I understood. 'Thanks for your help. Oh, and I'd be grateful if you could leave word of your whereabouts if you go away for more than a couple of days. Something else might crop up that we need your help with.'

'I'll do that, Inspector,' he replied with a smile that would have melted the heart of a traffic warden.

Maggie was in the office when I trudged through the door twenty minutes later. 'Hi, boss,' she greeted me. 'Where've you been skiving all day?'

'Oh, you know. A little shopping, weeded a couple of herbaceous borders, took in a show.' I plonked K. Tom Davis's file of poison pen letters on her desk. 'Take a look at those when you have a minute, but not as bedtime reading.'

'What are they?'

'Customer reaction, after losing their life savings. Oh, and when you have a chance have a word with the Devonshire Hotel, please, find out who's been staying there the last couple of nights. Anything for me?'

'No. The couple of villains among the creditors had alibis that you could have lined a nuclear reactor with. I suppose it would have been less suspicious if they hadn't.'

'You mean they could have taken a contract out on Goodrich?'

'It's possible?'

'I don't know. It wasn't exactly an IRA job, and I can't see the Mafia sentencing anyone to death by blow to the head with a flower pot, can you?'

'Unless they realised he was already dead.'

'Mmm. Could be.'

'Mike Freer rang,' she told me. 'Said you'd offered to do a bust for him. Wants a word with you about it.

117

Apparently a load of heroin from the Continent has suddenly started appearing on the streets.'

'Great.' I tried his number but he wasn't in.

'How's Annabelle keeping?' Margaret enquired as I replaced the phone. She's kept a weather eye on my love-life ever since my divorce.

'Huh, don't ask,' I snorted.

'Oh no,' she sighed. 'What have you done now?'

I told her about the swans in the park, about Donald and the episode with the rat, and how I had purloined his coffee mug for a sample of his prints.

She shook her head with disbelief. 'This is serious, Charlie,' she declared.

'You think so?'

'You let her down and I bet that's a big sin in the eyes of someone like Annabelle. This is going to take more than a bunch of flowers.'

I was saved from further depression by the phone. 'What's the difference between an astronaut and constipation?' Mike Freer's voice intoned in my ear.

'I'm . . . longing to hear,' I told him.

'An astronaut goes to Mars but constipation mars your goes.'

'Gosh, yes. What else did it say on your cornflakes packet?'

'It said that we'd be very grateful if you could hit Michael Angelo. We picked somebody up who'd just made a collection from him, at his home. It's the same stuff that we're finding all over the place. From the Continent, and we think he's the major distributor.'

'How do you know it's all the same stuff?'

'Analysis – gas chromatography, mass spectrometers, all that gizmology. Far too complicated for you, Charlie.

Basically, what it tells us is that if it grew in yak shit, it comes from Tibet. We can nearly describe which field.'

'Right. Let me give it some thought. Pencil us in for the middle of next week.'

'Will do. Oh, and Charlie ...'

'What?'

'Remember, possession might be nine points of the law, but it's twelve at Scrabble.'

'Definitely, and there's many a true word spoken in Chester. S'long. I've work to do.'

I replaced the phone before he could come back to me and gave my brow a mock wipe.

'Freer, at a guess,' Maggie said.

'The one and only.'

'No, he's not – I know where there's a big houseful like him. So what are we doing next week?'

I rocked back on my chair and tried to grip my pen between my nose and top lip, but I couldn't manage it. Outside, the sun was shining, and a couple of jet fighters streaked by, a long way off, looking for defenceless sheep to fire pretend missiles at. I might have been a fighter pilot, if you didn't have to wear those overalls with pockets down below the knees.

'Maggie,' I said.

'Yes, Charles.'

'What would happen ... just supposing ... if I did something really stupid? I mean ... *stupid*. Would they retire me early, do you think?'

'How stupid do you mean?'

'*Stupid* stupid.'

'*That* stupid?'

'Yeah.'

'Nobody would notice.'

'C'mon, Maggie. I'm being serious.'

'OK. What you're saying is, if you did something that was an embarrassment to the force, would they retire you early on full pension?'

'Exactly,' I declared, giving her a thumbs-up.

'No.'

'No?'

'No.'

'Shit. Why not?'

'Times are changing. They won't let you out on ill health these days if you still have one of all the things God gave us two of.'

'Mmm, that's a disappointment. Never mind, we'll do it just the same.'

'Do what, Charlie? Trying to hold a conversation with you is worse than talking to Freer.'

'Right. I've just invented something called a rhubarb run, and we hold the first one next week, against Michael Angelo Watts. Pass the telephone directory across, please. I'll just make a phone call and then explain it to you. Do you think they still have a sewage department at City Hall?'

They did, but it wasn't called that. Maggie and I drove over to talk to the people who ran it and spent half an hour poring over street plans of the Sylvan Fields estate. It's unbelievable what's going off under our feet.

'It's no wonder the roads are so bumpy,' I said, in a spirit of understanding of their problems. The surveyor who was helping us nodded his agreement and smiled happily.

'They're not bumpy in Bourton-on-the-Water,' Maggie reminded him.

We explained what we were trying to do, and made a firm arrangement to meet two of their staff at six thirty on the following Wednesday morning. We would be paying their overtime. Gilbert would love this, but I decided not to spoil his holiday by telling him before he went. On the way out we had a little explore, wandering along corridors that had coloured arrows on the floor and lighting that didn't cast shadows. The signs and furniture were a cross between Habitat and the Early Learning Centre.

'It makes Heckley nick look like a squat,' Maggie remarked.

Back at the nick I said, 'Put the kettle on, Maggie,' as we strode into the office, adding, 'Bet they're not allowed their own kettles at City Hall.' The young constable who'd discovered Goodrich's body was standing near my desk, helmet under his arm like a guardsman at a court martial. 'Hello, Graham,' I greeted him, hoping I'd remembered the name correctly. 'Come to ask for a transfer to CID?'

'No, sir. I was wondering if I could have a word with you in private.' He sounded worried.

'Sure,' I replied, adjusting to serious mode. 'Come into the inner sanctum.' I turned and raised my eyebrows at Maggie and led him into my little partitioned-off office space.

'Sit down, Graham. Now, what can I do for you?'

'I've come to apologise, sir, for the hair.'

'I thought I'd told you to stop calling me sir.'

'Sorry, Mr Priest.'

'That's better. What hair are you talking about?'

'The hair that the SOCO found at the scene of the crime. Mr Goodrich's, that is.'

Realisation crept over me like when you stand under the heater in Marks and Spencer's doorway on a frosty morning.

'Oh, *that* hair!' I exclaimed, clenching my teeth tight together to immobilise my face.

'Yes. I'd just like to say that I'm sorry for the trouble it caused and I hope that it didn't impede the enquiry too much. Oh, and it won't happen again.'

Nice little speech. 'Was it your hair?' I asked, almost choking with the effort.

'No, sir, Mr Priest. My girlfriend's.'

'I see. Presumably you got it on your collar when she kissed you goodbye.'

'Something like that, Mr Priest,' he blushed.

'OK. Well I'm afraid it's gone away for analysis. From that we will be able to tell all sorts of things about her: what medication she's taking... hormone levels... Ooh, all sorts of things.'

'Oh.'

'And then there's the cost. Fifty-two quid.'

'I don't mind paying,' he blurted out, half reaching for his cheque book.

'No, that won't be necessary,' I told him. 'We'll manage to lose it somewhere. So, apart from this little hiccup, Graham, how are you settling in?'

'Fine, Mr Priest,' he replied, almost smiling.

'No problems?'

'Mmm, I found it hard, at first. But it's getting better. I suppose if you could manage it on your first day, the job wouldn't be worth having.'

'That's the attitude, Graham,' I said. 'Give it a couple of years at least. Anything you need to know, don't be afraid to ask.'

He was still thanking me as I saw him out of the door. Maggie placed a steaming mug on my desk and asked, 'What was that all about?'

'Problems with his sex life,' I replied. 'He just needed some advice.'

'And he came to *you*!' she exclaimed. It's the casual remarks of friends that hurt most of all.

There was a football match on television that night, so I collected a frozen Chinese banquet and four cans of Sam Smith's proper beer from the supermarket and had a quiet night at home. Can't say I enjoyed myself, but I was doing what was expected of me.

While I was in the Friday morning meeting, listening to Gilbert's long list of dos and don'ts, Joan Eastwood left a message to say she had some information I might be interested in. I picked up the phone, then decided to drive to Leeds instead.

Mrs Eastwood poured me a tea, barely avoiding spilling it into my china saucer. Everybody I spoke to on this case was nervous, as if they were hiding something. Even K. Tom Davis's natural arrogance barely concealed the underlying fear, and now Mrs Eastwood was fussing around like a mother hen with a fox at the gate.

'Can I offer you a biscuit, Inspector?' she asked.

'No thank you, Mrs Eastwood,' I replied. 'What exactly is it you wanted to tell me?'

She perched herself on the edge of a chintz-covered chair that might have shot out from under her had it not been so solid. 'It's about . . . Mr Goodrich,' she admitted.

I peered at her over the rim of my cup and invited her to continue.

'You said to ring you if I thought of anything else.'

'Mmm.'

'Well, it may be nothing, but on the other hand . . .'

'Just tell me all about it, Mrs Eastwood. Anything you want.'

'Very well. Er, I don't know where to begin. Hartley – Mr Goodrich – and I were . . . close, if you know what I mean. We didn't have an affair, but we were ... I'm not sure what you'd call it.'

'Let's just say that you were very good friends.'

'Yes. Very dear friends. I suppose it all sounds foolish to you, Inspector.'

'No, Mrs Eastwood. It sounds the most natural thing in the world.'

'Does it? Well, Hartley liked to talk about his work. Most of it was beyond me, but he was filled with all sorts of schemes. After he met K. Tom Davis he was convinced that they would both become millionaires. He was terribly impressed by Mr Davis, thought he could do no wrong. It was Davis who influenced him, got him into trouble.'

She was straying off the point, defending her boy-friend.

'What was it you wanted to tell me?' I asked again.

Her hands were in her lap, fingers intertwined and thumbs rotating around each other. 'One night,' she began, 'two years ago, I was pulling Hartley's leg about K. Tom, saying he thought more about him than he did me. He'd had a little too much to drink. We both had. There'd been a bullion robbery about seven years earlier, over six million pounds in gold bars stolen while on its way to a place in Sheffield ...'

Suddenly, this was interesting. 'The assayers' offices,' I said. 'The Prat something robbery.'

'Hartog-Praat, that's right.'

'Go on.'

'Well, apparently a few people were arrested but none of the gold has ever been recovered. Hartley boasted that Davis knew all about it. Next day he came to see me at work. He looked dreadful. Scared. Told me to completely forget what he'd said; never mention a word to anyone. So I didn't, until now. With Hartley being killed in that horrible way, I wondered if . . . if . . .'

'If maybe he'd spoken to anyone else?'

'Yes, something like that.'

She sniffed and blew her nose on a tissue which she proceeded to twist into a passable origami corkscrew. My impression was that she had a lot more invested in this piece of information than she was claiming. I sipped my tea and waited for her to tell me more while giving her the once-over, the way we men are supposed to do. She was a little overweight, but it was evenly distributed. She carried it well – there was a Rubens model underneath that blouse and skirt, and two or three years ago she'd have been in her prime. I suppressed the improper thoughts, placing my cup on the table. If she had been having an affair with Goodrich, but didn't want it to be public knowledge, that was fine with me. Adultery is still a sin, or at least an admission of failure, to most people, pop stars and Royal Family excepted, but why was she so nervous about it?

'Is – is that of any use to you, Inspector?' she wondered.

I stroked my lips with the knuckle of my first finger. 'Nothing else?' I asked. 'Did he ever mention it again?'

'No, never.'

'Try to think.'

'I've been thinking about it since your first visit. There's nothing else. How close are you to finding Hartley's . . . the person who attacked him?'

I uncrossed my legs and pushed myself more upright in the chair. 'I thought we were fairly close,' I told her, grateful that she hadn't referred to his killer. 'But this new information widens the field. Now there are a lot more people "in the frame", as we say.' I like to throw in some jargon, people expect it from a cop.

'So you have . . . You are, er, following certain lines of enquiry?'

She was better at it than me. 'Well, I shouldn't really be telling you this,' I said, picking my cup up again, 'but we've found a hair at the scene of the crime. As soon as we have a suspect we'll see if it matches. If it does, they have some explaining to do.'

The tissue fell to pieces in her grasp. It wasn't Kleenex's fault, she'd have done the same with a piece of corrugated iron.

'A hair?' she whispered.

'Yes.' I finished my tea and leaned forward. 'Let me explain how we work, these days,' I confided. 'Off the record, of course. We don't just gather obvious clues, like hairs and fingerprints. We try to analyse the behaviour of the criminal, from all the little, apparently inconsequential things that he does, and from this we build up a portrait of the person we are looking for. In theory we could take a hair sample from everyone in the country, but this way we'll narrow it down, eventually, to just the one we want.'

'H-how can you be so sure?' she asked, white faced.

I wasn't enjoying this, but I waved a hand expansively, as if I was being matey, revealing little titbits to a friend. 'We can't,' I admitted, 'but I'll tell you what we have so far. This is the picture, as I see it. The attacker arrives Monday morning, say about eight thirty. Picks up a bottle of milk from the doorstep and enters. Either the door is unlocked or he has a key. Mr Goodrich is apparently watching TV, glass of whisky by his side. The attacker hits him on the head with a handy pot plant, Goodrich slumps forward, dead. Fingerprints! thinks our assailant. He then fetches the tea-towel, which he knows is concealed under the work surface, wipes the plant pot clean and replaces the tea towel where it belongs. He is a very tidy person. On the way out he remembers the milk bottle and puts it back on the doorstep, after wiping that, too. I keep saying "he". It could, of course, be a she. When we find someone who was sufficiently familiar with him and his home to fit in with that little scenario, we'll just use the hair for confirmation.'

'I see,' she said in a very tiny voice, her expression somewhere far away, like Holloway.

I jumped up, looking at my watch, and made a hurried goodbye. 'Anything else you want to tell me?' was my parting invitation, but she shook her head. As I left she closed the door behind me and I heard the click of the latch.

I sat in the car for several minutes, wondering and worrying about her. It would have been easy to go back, tell her that Goodrich died of a heart attack twelve hours before he was hit on the head, but I didn't. I just placed the key in the ignition and turned it. Nobody had wired half a kilogram of Semtex across the terminals, so the engine started and I drove back to Heckley.

Chapter Six

Roland Fearnside is a commander with the National Criminal Intelligence Service. We've worked together on a few cases, and I was probably instrumental in giving him a leg-up from being a mere chief superintendent. I normally try to avoid him, because he usually has a dirty job in mind for me, but this time I rang him.

'I'm afraid Mr Fearnside is busy,' a plummy voice told me. 'Please leave me your number and I'll ask him to contact you.'

'Convenience busy or really busy?' I asked.

'I beg your pardon?'

'Tell him you have Charlie Priest on the line and I'd like an urgent word with him. *Please.*' No point in admitting to being a lowly inspector.

Twenty seconds later he was booming in my ear. 'Charlie! How are you?'

'Fine, Mr Fearnside. And you?'

'Oh, so-so. And Annabelle?'

'She's fine, too.'

'Still got the E-type?'

'Sure have.'

'Bloody hell! You're a lucky bugger, Charlie. To tell the truth, I'd thought about giving you a bell.'

This was what I'd dreaded. 'Oh, that usually means bad news,' I declared.

'No, not at all. I need a joke for an after-dinner speech I'm giving tonight. Thought you might be able to help.'

Typical. I cultivate a contact in N-CIS and he regards me as the force comedian. He probably believed I did the northern club circuit in my spare time. 'Who's it to?' I asked.

'Accountants. City types. Bunch of bloody dead-beats. Keeping them sweet is all part of the job, I'm afraid. All you have to bother about is collaring villains.'

'Mmm. Rather you than me. I'll have to think about it.'

'If you would, old boy. Now what can I do for you?'

I told him about Goodrich, and the SCTs against his name, and that we now suspected he may have been laundering drugs money by investing it in diamonds. 'Yesterday,' I said, 'I interviewed his girlfriend and she told me that Goodrich was in cahoots with a character called K. Tom Davis, who was MD of the investment diamond company. She said that Goodrich told her, in a moment of alcohol-induced weakness or high passion, that Davis was involved in the Hartog-Praat bullion robbery.'

I heard Fearnside say, 'Jeeesus!' under his breath.

'So,' I went on, 'what can you tell me about the bullion robbery?'

'Right. Well, it was World War Two gold, recovered from a sunken destroyer – British – by treasure hunters, somewhere in the Baltic, I believe. Hartog-Praat is a Dutch security company, and it was their job to transport the bullion to the assay office in Sheffield. They went for the hush-hush approach, rather than maximum security, but somebody spilled the beans. It was a nasty job. If I remember rightly they doused a guard in petrol and threatened to ignite him. One guard died, but much later.'

'Was anybody caught?'

'Ye-es. Can't remember his name. He was a known bank robber, who handled the actual hijack. Definitely not the brains. He went down for a long time and a couple of minions were given a year or two for allowing their premises to be used, something like that. I'll have to dig the file out, put you on to the investigating officer.'

'Was any of the gold recovered?'

'No, not a bloody sniff of it. Tell you what, Charlie: gold would be a damn sight more attractive to these drugs dealers than diamonds. Gold can't tell lies.'

'Mmm. One of my DSs said exactly the same thing. I'll be grateful if you could send me anything relevant, soon as pos.'

'I'll put someone straight on to it, Charlie. Good luck, and it's been nice talking to you.'

'Likewise. Just one last thing, before you go.'

'Yes?'

'What's pink and hard, first thing in the morning?'

'Ha ha! Go on.'

'*The Financial Times* crossword.'

'Hee hee! That'll do, Charlie. That'll do.'

Another unwanted reputation reinforced. I replaced the phone and drew a doodle on my pad. It showed a ship, long and lean, with a gun on the front. I added some fish and bubbles, to indicate that it was on the sea-bed. Bits of the story came back to me. There was a big controversy after the wreck was discovered. It was an official war grave, sacred to the memory of the men whose bodies were still down there. But even sanctity has a price, these days, and when the value of the destroyer's cargo was estimated there were an awful lot of noughts after the pound sign. Had it been Communist gold, coming here to pay for the convoys? Or allied gold, to support the carnage on the Russian front? I didn't know, but either way, it was blood money, and no good could come of it.

I drew a line down the middle of the page. At the top of one column I wrote 'Drugs Dealers', at the head of the other, 'Gold'. The drugs dealers were awash with cash. Cash that they needed converting into something more solid, more negotiable across the world. Such as gold.

The bullion men were just the opposite. They needed their collateral converting into something more acceptable in straight society. Cash, for instance.

They needed each other like Yorkshire pudding needs onion gravy. I drew a circle round 'Drugs Dealers' and wrote 'The Jones Boys?' against it.

But what about the diamonds? The first payments were invested – wrong word – in diamonds. But the diamonds went bust and the payments kept on coming in. So what did the dealers get for that money after that? Gold? When we were role-playing, Jeff Caton said he preferred gold. I pinned the sheet on the wall above my desk, next to the photograph of Shirley Eaton.

Gilbert was clearing his desk, prior to his holiday. 'Put the kettle on as you pass,' he greeted me as I walked in.

I tested its weight and clicked the switch. He was rummaging in a filing cabinet so I flopped down into his chair and swung my feet on to the desk. 'I think I could get used to this,' I told him.

'Then go for it,' he said, lifting a whisky bottle from a drawer.

'No, the boredom would get me down.'

Gilbert stood the bottle on the cabinet and crouched, squinting at the level, and carefully drew a line on the label.

'You're wasting your time,' I told him. 'We just widdle in the bottle to bring it back up to the mark.'

'That I can believe,' he said, nodding enthusiastically.

We discussed priorities and a couple of low-level meetings he wanted me to attend. I didn't mention the raid on Michael Angelo's planned for Wednesday. I would have liked to have grilled him about Dominic Watts, the father, but resisted, in case he asked why I wanted to know.

Nigel was in with several of the other troops when I arrived back in the CID office. We spent an hour discussing ram raids and burglaries, and generally slagging-off some of the problem families that give us most heartache. Sometimes, a programme of selective assassination sounds highly attractive, until you realise where it would lead. Plenty of my colleagues would be prepared to risk it, I'm ashamed to admit. Then we all went home.

Tomorrow was the big day. Once a year, towards the end of his term of office, we have a Lord Mayor's parade, to raise money for his nominated charity. This time it was for the children's ward of Heckley General Hospital. A cavalcade of vehicles would start at the Town Hall at noon and slowly wend its way round the town to the sports field, where there would be various other events taking place. The classic car section of the Police Sports and Social Club would take part in the parade, and I was invited. It was their only event of the year. When I got home, I reversed the E-type out of the garage and gave it a wash and leathering. Then I sat on the wall and just gazed at it until the street lamps came on.

Last year, Annabelle came with me, and we had a good day. This time I'd be on my own, and I wasn't looking forward to it. I picked up the phone and dialled Sparky's number. His wife answered.

'Hiya, Shirl. It's Charlie,' I said.

'He's out,' she responded. 'No, he's drunk. That's it: he's had three pints of home-made lager and is in no fit state to drive, or anything else.'

'Relax, it's you I want to talk to.'

'Oh. In that case, hello, Charlie, how are you?'

'It's nice of you to ask, eventually. Look, it's the Lord Mayor's parade tomorrow, and I've promised to take the Jaguar along. If the kids aren't doing anything I was wondering if they'd like to come, too?'

'Oh, that's nice of you. But won't Annabelle be going?'

'Er, no, she's got something else on.'

'Right. Hang on, I'll see if they can be torn away from the television.'

They weren't doing anything, and they would love to come to the parade with their Uncle Charlie.

Hunger drove me out of bed early Saturday morning. I settled for toast and marmalade for breakfast but decided to treat myself that evening. I trimmed the fat from a couple of pork chops and seared them in the frying pan. I arranged them side-by-side in the slow cooker and covered them with a selection of vegetables and a can of condensed soup. They'd be done to perfection by tea time.

Nigel was in the office when I swung the long nose of the Jag into the super's place in the car park. We discussed the Dean brothers' case that was coming to court, and, after great deliberation and much soul-searching, I wrote 'No further action' on several documents Gilbert had left for me. The feeling of power made me feel light-headed. At eleven thirty I tore myself away and drove round to Sparky's.

Daniel hadn't changed much since I last saw him, just grown a little bigger and cheekier. He was the type of exasperating fourteen-year-old that you curse one moment and then say a little prayer of thanks for. 'Hi, Uncle Charlie,' he greeted me as they came down the garden path.

But Sophie had changed. No wonder Sparky's grumpier than ever, I thought. In less than a year she'd grown up. She was my god-daughter, and just past her seventeenth birthday. I reluctantly accepted that this was possibly the last time she'd want to be seen out with an old fogey like me. I held the door open and Daniel scrambled into the back. 'Thank you,' Sophie said, swinging her legs into the low car as if she'd been doing it for years. I waved to Shirley and slipped into the driving seat.

The parade was fun. Sophie practised her regal wave and Daniel pretended to be manager of Manchester United, back from another triumphant visit to Wembley. At first we were behind a steamroller, but we out-gunned him on the High Street without too much trouble. It was driven by the local scrap dealer, whose skin is the colour of an oily rag and who drives the biggest Mercedes in West Yorkshire.

The rest of the afternoon was a drag. While the kids enjoyed the fun fair and the police dog demonstration, I stayed with the car, and told several hundred people that it did a hundred and fifty miles per hour and nineteen to the gallon. They brought ice-creams back with them and

Sophie presented me with a fridge magnet she'd won. It was a little plastic Sherlock Holmes, complete with magnifying glass. Then I left them in charge while I took a stroll round.

They were deep in conversation with an older boy and girl when I arrived back. 'We've had our pictures taken for the paper,' Daniel boasted when he saw me.

'Ask him, he won't bite,' Sophie said to the young couple, adding, 'he's quite nice, really.'

'Ask him what?' I said, giving them a smile.

She was quite bonny, and he looked presentable, with the obligatory earring. 'It's a fabulous car,' the boy said, his expression supporting his words.

'Thank you. Do you want to buy it?'

'Uh, chance'd be a fine thing,' he replied.

'We were wondering if you did weddings,' the girl said.

'Weddings? No. My name is Priest, but I can't marry people.'

'No! We meant with the car. Like, a taxi service?'

'Oh, I see. Well no, not really.'

They looked disappointed. 'Never mind then,' the girl replied. 'I hope you didn't mind us asking. We wanted a white Rolls-Royce, but we've been let down. We just thought you might . . . you know.'

I tried, but I couldn't think of a decent reason for not doing it. 'When do you get married?' I asked.

'Next Saturday.'

'Leaving it a bit late aren't you? Er, for the taxi, I mean.'

They both blushed, which made three of us.

'My Uncle George has a Granada,' she said. 'We'll use that if we can't find anything else.'

'Which church?'

'St Bidulph's.'

'Oh.'

'Do you know it?'

'Yes, I do.' Annabelle lives in the old vicarage. 'So where's the reception?'

She was smiling now. 'At the Masonic Hall,' she said.

'In the town centre?'

'Mmm.'

'Right. Give me a number where I can contact you, and I'll give you a ring through the week. But I'm not making any promises.'

I took the kids for a drive on the M62 to the Birch services, where we had hamburgers and chips. Daniel said, 'Doctor, Doctor, I keep thinking I'm a pair of curtains.'

'No wonder you look drawn,' I replied.

'No! You should say, "Pull yourself together."'

Sophie said, 'I think Uncle Charlie's answer was best,' to which Daniel retorted, 'Well you would, wouldn't you,' and poor Sophie blushed like only a seventeen-year-old can. Anybody watching would have thought we were a family.

I was in trouble for feeding them when we arrived back. Shirley, their mother, teaches cookery and had prepared beef stroganoff for us, with jam roly-poly to follow. I wasn't hungry, but still managed large helpings of each. The pork chops made a pleasant change for Sunday breakfast, before I went to the office for a couple of hours. Paperwork, like rust, never sleeps.

The Dean brothers were due in court Monday morning. They are considerably brighter than the average tea leaf who passes through our hands. Computers and videos are standard fare for most of them, exchanging hands at about fifteen per cent of their market value. But a young crook can only carry one of each out through the window and up the garden path to his waiting Fiesta, and he looks suspicious with it. The Dean brothers know that it's the chip, deep within the computer, that gives it its value. And you can carry hundreds of them in your pockets and still have room for a UB40 and a packet of three. They hit the new British Gas offices six months ago at two in the morning. The security videos showed them moving quickly from computer to computer, spinning the screws out with rechargeable drivers and removing the chips and hard-disk drives which represented well over half the value of the machines.

What the Deans didn't know was that, as they entered the building through a fanlight at the back, they were sprayed with an invisible dye called FOIL – fluorescent organic indexing liquid – that was impossible to remove and would show bright orange under ultra-violet light.

Another thing that they didn't know was that their getaway driver, a neighbour with a reputation for his skills behind the wheel, had all the imagination of a stuffed warthog. He'd stolen a car and fitted it with false plates. For hours he'd wracked the sawdust inside his skull, trying to think of a suitable registration number. Something catchy, without being memorable. Sort of a Eurovision Numberplate Contest entry. Eventually, in desperation, he copied the number off an old motorbike he'd owned years ago. The video cameras captured his image and later that morning our Nigel captured his substance. The Deans lived next door and glowed like a pair of Jaffas under a u/v light. Because of its organic content the FOIL spray has a DNA fingerprint unique to each installation, and would prove that they had been in British Gas's offices. The technical term we guardians of the law use in a case like this is 'bang to rights'.

I did the morning meeting in record time and went over the case with Nigel before he went to court. They were our first FOIL arrests, and the system was on trial as much as the Deans. An expert from the company that makes the sprays was due to attend, to say how foolproof it was.

When Nigel had gone I made a coffee and studied the outstanding crimes printout. Prioritising them is our biggest heartache. Do we concentrate on Mrs Bloggs' stolen jewellery – sentimental value only, not insured and no chance of recovery – or on the ram raid at Microwaves-R-Us in the High Street? You make your decision and offer a silent apology to Mrs Bloggs.

After that I made a few calls to organise Wednesday's rhubarb run, when we would hit Michael Angelo Watts' fortress on the Sylvan Fields estate. Most of all we needed technical assistance from our scientific people at Wetherton. Professor Van Rees is head of the Home Office forensic laboratory that we use, and agreed to loan me a couple of technicians and some equipment. I was arranging some uniformed muscle from the Woodentops when Maggie caught my eye. She was on her phone, and I heard her saying, 'Put them in an interview room. I'll tell him.'

'Tell him what?' I asked when I'd finished.

'Tell him that Mrs Joan Eastwood just walked in, accompanied by a brief and asking to speak to you. That's all.'

I rocked my chair back on two legs and sipped my coffee. 'Now what on earth can she want?' I wondered aloud.

'Perhaps her husband's finished that boat,' Maggie suggested.

'The *Temeraire*? She wouldn't know, not living with him. I went to see her on Friday, leaned on her a little.'

'I know. I've read your notes. You think she did it, don't you?'

'It's possible. Let's give them five minutes, then see what it's all about.'

The brief was female, mid-thirties, in a suit that made her look like a Dallas undertaker and an expression to match. Appropriately sombre, but with one eye on the cash register. She introduced herself as Mrs Bannister, of the local big-wig law firm, and said that her client wished to make a prepared statement. I took the typed sheet she offered and inspected the aforementioned client.

'Hello, Mrs Eastwood,' I said, directly to her. She was wearing ski pants and an anorak with embroidery down the sleeves, and alongside her was what looked like an overnight bag. She'd come to stay. Her face was the same shade of pale as the walls and she was trembling. She just nodded a greeting.

A brief glance at the statement told me that Mrs Eastwood admitted hitting Goodrich on the head. The only intention had been to express her anger at him, not to inflict any injury, and there were mitigating circumstances. As she was no danger to the public, bail would be applied for when she appeared before a magistrate in the morning.

I passed the paper to Maggie and leaned on my fist, rubbing a forefinger against my cheek. Mrs Eastwood shuffled in her plastic chair.

'Would either of you like a coffee?' I asked.

Neither of them would.

After a long silence I said, 'In that case, with your permission, Mrs Bannister, I'd like to do a recorded interview with Mrs Eastwood.' I don't go in for all this 'my client' bullshit. Without waiting for a reply I spun my chair round to face the tape recorder and checked it for tapes.

'OK,' I said. 'Let's go.' I pressed the red button and the one with a single arrow on it and peeked through the little window to confirm that the wheels were turning. I read the date off the calendar on the wall and the time off my Timex – water-resistant to forty metres but I've no intention of proving it – and introduced everybody.

We started with an ice-breaker: 'Mrs Eastwood, would you mind telling us your address and date of birth?'

She stumbled through it, hesitating and mixing her words up. Her hands moved from the table to her lap, and back to the table again. Her fingers were long and bony, with no rings on them. She'd left her earrings at home, too.

'You were formerly married to Derek Eastwood, and shared the marital home at Sweetwater.'

She nodded.

'For the tape, please, Mrs Eastwood, if you will.'

'Yes.'

'Do you mind if I call you Joan?'

'No.'

'Thank you. Will you tell me, Joan, why you are here, today.'

'It's in the statement, Inspector,' Mrs Bannister interrupted.

'I'd like to hear it in Joan's words, if you don't mind.'

'But I do mind. The statement makes it perfectly clear why my client is here.'

'Fair enough. According to the statement, Joan, you have admitted hitting Hartley Goodrich on the head with a plant pot.'

She nodded.

'Mrs Eastwood nods,' I said.

'Sorry. Yes. I hit him.'

'That's all right. Would you please tell us, Joan, what led up to this?'

She gathered her thoughts for a few seconds, then launched into it. 'I was ... annoyed ... mad with him. It was just like you said. I let myself in ... picked up the milk bottle from the doorstep. He was watching television. We were supposed to be ... supposed to be ...'

'Supposed to be what?'

'Supposed to be going away together.'

'I see.'

'He should have picked me up, Sunday evening, when I finished work. I thought something must be wrong – he hadn't been too well. When I saw him, dozing in the chair, glass of whisky ... I just snapped. I ... I ...'

'You picked up the nearest thing that came to hand and hit him with it.'

Our eyes met for the first time. 'Yes,' she whispered.

'It was a heavy plant pot,' I told her. 'Surely you realise that hitting a person on the head with something like that was likely to cause a very serious injury.'

'I didn't mean to hit him with it.'

'Come on, Joan. It was on the table. You picked it up and brought it down on his head. How high did you raise it? This high?' I held my hands level with my face, palms inwards.

'It wasn't like that,' she protested.

'Then tell me what it was like.'

She was ringing a handkerchief between her fingers, twisting it around them. 'I ... I just picked it up. It was there on the table, where he'd left it.'

It had been the only piece of greenery in the house. All

else was dark colours, mainly shades of grey, and the only other non-geometric shapes in the place were the curves of the nymphs and bodybuilders that adorned his walls and low tables.

'What do you mean by "Where he'd left it," Joan?' I asked. 'Did you buy him the plant?'

She sniffed and nodded.

'Go on, please.'

She realised that she'd strangled the hanky lifeless and put it away. 'His house needed brightening up,' she began. 'I gave him the *Dieffenbachia* about a fortnight earlier, as a little present. Thought it might encourage him to buy a few more. When I saw it on the table, right where I'd left it, I realised he cared for that about as much as he cared for me.'

'So you saw his neglect of the plant as reflecting his attitude to you. The plant was a symbol.'

Mrs Bannister shuffled in her chair, but didn't speak. I was earning her fee for her.

'Yes,' Joan confirmed.

'Go on, please.'

'I picked it up. I only intended emptying it on his head. I turned it over and the plant pot fell out of the bowl. I hadn't realised it was in a separate pot. It landed on his head and he fell sideways. I dropped the bowl – the planter – and waited for him to sit up, but he didn't. I looked at him, and realised he was dead. I'd killed him. I was quite calm. There was no pulse. I was on my way out when I thought about fingerprints. I took the tea-towel and wiped everything I'd touched, just like you said.'

Mrs Bannister sat back in her plastic chair, a why-am-I-always-the-last-to-know expression on her face.

'Were you and Hartley having an affair?' I asked Joan.

She nodded, but I let it go. 'For how long?'

'About three years, I think.'

'Since before you went on the cruise?'

'Oh, yes.'

'Joan, what happened when you left York and Durham? Did you lose your job?'

She jerked upright, staring at me. Mrs Bannister chipped in with 'Is this relevant, Inspector?' because she realised she'd completely lost control.

'I think it might be in your client's interest to answer the question, Mrs Bannister. Were you sacked, Joan?'

She heaved a huge sigh, as if sloughing off all her worries. 'Yes, I was.'

'Could you tell us why?'

'I suppose it has to come out. I was caught copying the files of some of our wealthier clients. Hartley – Mr Goodrich – asked me to do it.'

'And then he would approach them with a view to offering alternative investments. More lucrative ones.'

'Yes, something like that. I couldn't see any harm in it, but it was dishonest.'

Not really, I thought. The bank would have sold them to him without a second's hesitation, if there'd been anything in it for them. Disloyal, maybe. 'And they sacked you,' I said.

She nodded and gave the tiniest hint of a smile at the memory. 'Escorted me from the premises. It was very embarrassing for Derek.' Notoriety can be fun, she'd discovered. I've known it for years.

'Go on.'

'That's when my marriage collapsed. I left Derek and found a flat. Soon after, I took a job at the hospital and moved to Leeds.'

'But you stayed friends with Goodrich?'

'Yes. He was very supportive.'

I should think so. He'd only destroyed her career and her marriage. I said, 'And when you received your share of the marital home, he invested it for you.'

'Yes.'

'In an investment diamond?'

'Yes.'

'So he lost you your money, too, or most of it.'

'Yes. Hartley said he was trying to recover it for me, but I'm not sure.'

'Mmm. You might be interested to learn that when we found Goodrich he was clutching a three-carat diamond. I've a suspicion that it was yours.' I turned to Maggie and suggested we check it. 'Unfortunately,' I continued, 'it will only be worth a fraction of what you paid for it.'

'Yes, I know.'

Mrs Bannister looked at her watch. 'Could we speed things up, Inspector? I've another appointment at twelve.'

She brings in a client to confess to a killing and worries about missing lunch. 'Joan, you said you and Goodrich were going away. For a holiday or for ever?'

'No, just a few days together. We ... I ... We'd considered moving in with each other. Well, I had. He went along with the idea at first, then changed his mind. Said he'd been on his own too long – it wouldn't work. We decided to go away as a sort of trial, I suppose.'

'So, come Sunday evening, you finished work and were waiting for him with your bags packed, but he didn't show up.'

'No. I mean, yes, that's right.'

'And first thing Monday morning you went round to see

him. He was calmly watching telly, and something inside you snapped.'

Mrs Bannister stirred in her seat, wanting to object to my putting words in her client's mouth, but couldn't see anything wrong with what I was suggesting.

'Yes,' Joan agreed.

Mrs Bannister said, 'We intended offering a plea of guilty to causing GBH, Section Twenty, but in the light of what we've just heard I'd suggest a Section Forty-seven assault might be more appropriate. May I have a copy of the tape and hand my client over to your custody, Inspector?'

I had some thinking to do. Section Forty-seven is actual bodily harm, but you can't commit it against a dead body. Technically speaking, a charge of *attempting* to commit ABH was possible, if Mrs Eastwood hadn't realised he was already dead. Attempting to commit a crime is still an offence. If someone puts his hand in your pocket, not realising it only contains fluff, he is still guilty of attempted theft.

Trouble was, she had a good defence. Mrs Bannister would claim that her client only wanted to embarrass Goodrich, cause him discomfort, and who could prove otherwise? If she'd known he was already dead we could have done her for an offence against the coroner's legislation, but she didn't, and although it might be a crime to conceal a dead body, there is no compulsion to report one. I felt the case go wriggling through my fingers and back into the river, like the eels I caught when I was a kid. But now, like then, I didn't mind.

'No,' I said.

'No?'

'No. I think we'll let her go home.'

'What do you mean, go home?'

'Exactly that. Mrs Eastwood, Mrs Bannister, Hartley Goodrich died of a heart attack, sometime on the Sunday evening. When you saw him, Joan, on Monday morning, he had already been dead for about ten hours. You struck a dead body with that plant pot. You didn't kill anybody. What I propose to do is pass the file to the Crown Prosecution Service for them to consider. I feel certain that they will deem it unlikely that it is in the public's interest to proceed further, and recommend that no charges be made.'

I'd considered dropping the whole thing myself, there and then, but decided that this way we would keep the coroner happy, if he asked any questions about the bump on the head.

Neither of them moved, apart from a slight sinking motion. Joan appeared not to comprehend that she was a free woman. Mrs Bannister recovered first. 'This is all highly irregular, Inspector,' she declared. I think she'd have preferred a murder-one rap.

'Mmm, it is, isn't it?' I agreed, amiably. 'But at no time have we said that this was anything other than a suspicious death. Mrs Eastwood has admitted to an assault, but she has aptly demonstrated that she was provoked, and that her intentions were not unduly malicious. As the victim was already dead . . .' I upturned my palms.

'In that case . . . You said my client is free to leave.'

'Yes. At no time has she been under arrest.' I turned to the tape recorder. 'Interview terminated at . . . eleven thirty-two.' I clicked it off and extracted the tapes.

Joan smiled for the first time in a week. 'I . . . I don't know what to say,' she mumbled.

'How about "Goodbye"?' I suggested with a grin.

Mrs Bannister grabbed her briefcase and jumped to her feet. She had an urgent appointment to attend.

'Before you go,' I said, 'do you mind if I have a quick word with Joan in private?'

She hesitated, and a look of panic flickered across Joan's face, as if she expected me to make a dramatic denouement and tell her that she was under arrest.

'Don't worry,' I assured her. 'It's nothing to do with Goodrich's death.' I handed a copy of the tape to Maggie, who led Mrs Bannister to the front desk to sign for it.

When they'd gone I said, 'It must be a great relief to know that you didn't kill Hartley.'

'Yes,' she agreed. 'I . . . don't know if I'm supposed to thank you, or not.'

'I doubt it,' I told her. 'I'm afraid I did lead you on a bit, but the truth came out, eventually.'

'Yes, and I wasn't very honest, was I?'

'You're not a very convincing liar,' I told her.

She blushed, saying, 'I'm sorry for all the trouble I caused you, Mr Priest. And ashamed of myself for being so devious. At one time . . . before . . .'

She let the rest of it hang in the air. She was going to say that at one time, before she met Goodrich, she wouldn't have known how to tell a lie.

'Joan,' I began, 'the conversation you had with Hartley about K. Tom Davis and the Hartog-Praat robbery. That's what I want to ask you about. Is there anything at all you can remember him ever saying about the gold?'

But there wasn't. He talked about it once, then warned her never to mention it again, and she hadn't. It looked as if the trail petered out with him. I walked Joan to the foyer, where we met up with Maggie and Mrs

Bannister again. The solicitor asked Joan if she was all right, and she nodded and smiled.

'There's just one final thing, Mrs Eastwood,' I said.

The three women gave me their attention.

'When we searched Goodrich's car,' I told her, 'we found a packed suitcase in the boot. It looked as if he was about to go away for a few days. Just thought you'd like to know.'

She smiled briefly, and her eyes filled with tears. It was drizzling outside, which must have felt good on her face. When they reached the car Mrs Bannister put an arm around her shoulders. I wouldn't have told her if I'd known it would upset her.

I collected a hot chocolate from the machine and walked upstairs with Maggie. 'Another one for the clear-up rate,' I boasted.

'Not even a piddling Section Forty-seven,' she replied.

'But a blow for justice, Maggie. Who do you think we should catch this afternoon?'

'Ah, I'd like a word with you about this afternoon. Do you think I could have an hour off to visit the optician?'

'God, yes,' I said. 'In fact, I ought to come with you. I either need some reading glasses or longer arms.'

I held the office door open for her and she gave me one of her exasperated looks. 'Oh, I can read all right,' she assured me. 'Reading's no problem. Reading's just fine. It's the bigger objects that I can't see. Do you know, about a week ago I examined this car, and guess what? There was a suitcase in the boot, and I completely overlooked it. Never saw a thing.'

Chapter Seven

Commander Fearnside caught me at home, halfway between boil-in-the-bag cod in butter sauce and *Look North*. Five minutes earlier the phone had rung but nobody had been there, although I thought I heard breathing.

'Did you try ringing a few minutes ago?' I asked him.

'No, Charlie. This is my first attempt. Why? Somebody playing silly buggers?'

'Probably. What can I do for you?'

'Right. Well, the file for the Hartog-Praat robbery is in the post, but I've had a chat with the SIO and thought I'd fill you in with the relevant stuff.'

'Great. Fire away.'

'First of all, just over a ton and a half of gold was stolen, worth about ten million pounds at today's prices. None has been recovered. Money like that causes rifts in the underworld community, and tongues wagged. Someone put the finger on a certain bank robber and general blagger called Cliff Childs. Prints in one of the getaway cars led us to a property in the East End owned by a pal of his, so we lifted him. He was ID'd by one of the guards through a tattoo on his neck. He's well into a twenty-year sentence, could be out in three or four, but he was only the sharp end. The brains were never caught.'

'So someone is still sitting on a pot of gold, holding it for him.'

'Ha! I hope they are, for their own sake. He'll be bloody annoyed if they've blown it in, what?'

'Mmm. Anything else?'

'That's only the beginning. All of Childs' associates, visitors, phone calls, et cetera, are monitored, as far as is possible. Most of them are predictable, but a couple of visitors were interesting. Early in his sentence a small-time crook called Jimmy McAnally called on him a couple of times, right out of the blue. Their paths had crossed in Strangeways, so they could have known each other. Then, blow me down if he didn't visit him again, about eighteen months ago. Another crook called Morgan had visited Childs at about the same time as McAnally's first two visits, but he died in a brawl shortly afterwards.'

'So what did you make of these visits?'

'Nothing, except that, just popping up like they did, they could have been messengers between Childs and whoever was holding the gold. Everything else coming out of his cell has been perfectly innocent.'

'Doesn't he have a wife?'

'She ran off to Majorca with his worst enemy, before the trial.'

'That sounds suspicious.'

'No, we've kept tabs on them, and they're running a little bar, struggling to get by. Let me tell you about McAnally.'

'Oh, sorry, Mr Fearnside. Fire away.'

'Jimmy McAnally worked the Billingsgate market, hence his nickname – Jimmy the Fish. He did three years for several offences of handling. Then he had a leg amputated after a car crash and married someone he met in hospital. She's a Yorkshire girl, with more than her fair share of that common sense you're supposed to be imbued with up there. She insisted that they move north, and now they live in . . . Bridlington, is it?'

'Could be.'

'Right. Well, it'd be interesting to know why he visited Childs, don't you think?'

'Mmm, yeah. And you don't mind if I go along and ask him?'

'Be my guest, Charlie. Nobody else is working on it.'

'Thanks. I'll keep you informed.'

'That's all we ask.'

'How did the talk go?'

'What talk?'

'Friday, to the City gents.'

'Oh, them. All right, thanks.'

In other words, not brilliant. I replaced the phone and wondered why talking to Fearnside always made me feel like Hercules couldn't make it, so could I do his labours for him? Cleaning out the Augean stables is just a euphemism for shovelling shit.

The phone rang again, but nobody spoke. I dialled 1471, and a pleasant, if stilted, lady's voice told me that she did not have the caller's number. It was all the excuse I needed, so I tried Annabelle, but she wasn't in.

Next day I took the prayer meeting and wasted the rest of the morning waiting for the CPS to come up with some answers. They eventually rang me back to say they couldn't see any purpose in charging Mrs Eastwood, but would I still submit the paperwork? They could cocoa. I was wondering what to do about lunch when Nigel breezed into the office, smiling with a mischievous smugness, like a little boy who'd broken his best friend's Tonka toy. When he saw me he put his hands to his head and yelled, 'Aaargh!'

There's a ritual to go through with Nigel. 'So?' I said, inviting him to explain.

'Do you want the good news or the bad news?'

'The good, please, if it's not too much trouble.'

'Four years each for the Deans, with eighteen months for the driver.'

'Great,' I replied. 'That should keep them out of our hair for a while. And the bad?'

'They're suing us.'

'Suing us? What for?'

'Would you believe it? Subjecting them to unnecessary danger in the form of liquids that may be of a carcinogenic nature, and exposing them to ultra-violet radiation, which is a proven carcinogen.'

'Are they serious?'

'Mmm. Deadly. Their brief is demanding to see any safety and health guidelines that come with the products.'

'Silly pillocks.'

I took him across the road for a sandwich and a glass of shandy, and asked him to do some final polishing of arrangements for the rhubarb run.

'And what about the warrant?' he asked. 'Does that need collecting?'

'Warrant?' I echoed. 'We won't be using a warrant, Nigel. Warrants is for cissies.'

Now he looked worried.

I left him in the pub and drove to my CADs meeting at the Civic Hall. The Community Action against Drugs committee is a new venture, meeting every month or so at the request of various concerned groups, mainly tenants' associations on the estates. To offset unilateral action by some more militant factions, we'd decided to hold a 'Shop a Pusher' campaign. The *Gazette* would be asked to publish a pro-forma, saying something like 'The following person has tried to sell me drugs . . .' We were meeting to finalise the wording. I suggested that we add a footnote saying that the police would only take action after a person had been named six times from separate sources. The committee talked me down to four, but I didn't mind. It was only there for reassurance; we'd ignore it if it suited us to.

Back at the office I typed up the CAD committee decisions and did a report of the previous night's conversation with Fearnside. As an afterthought I added a note about the two silent phone calls I'd received. I looked at the mess in my office and wondered about putting everything in order, just in case I was told to stay away, after the rhubarb run, but I decided to risk it.

At home I had a frozen Christmas dinner for one, which was ghastly, and the only phone call was from Mike Freer to wish us luck. I slept like a vulture on a dead tree.

The dawn chorus on the Sylvan Fields estate is just as likely to be the police helicopter as a vocal blackbird. It's a busy time there. Some towns have a park 'n' ride scheme; on the Sylvan Fields it's park 'n' torch. Clattering overhead, a helicopter would arouse less interest than a three-legged dog peeing against a lamppost.

As soon as I heard it, I clicked the tit and ordered all units to stand by.

'Sewer Rats in position,' came back to me, followed by, 'JCB approaching target, ready when you are,' and, 'Zulu Ninety-nine in position.'

'Look at that,' I said, nudging Sparky and nodding. The clouds had dissolved, and through the windscreen we could see Venus in the pale sky, bright as a daisy in a lawn.

'It's Venus,' he confirmed.

'It's beautiful,' I said.

'Some of us see it every morning. C'mon, let's go.'

'It might be an omen,' I told him. 'Did you know that the Sioux called General Custer the Son of the Morning Star, because he always attacked at dawn?'

'I do now. They'll be having their breakfasts if we hang about any longer.'

I raised the radio to my lips. 'Rhubarb to all units: Tallyho! Tallyho!'

Sparky leaned across and shouted, 'Scrag the bastards!' into the instrument.

Instantly the air was filled with the warbling of sirens, drowning out the chopper. We screeched around the corner and saw the JCB that we'd borrowed from a nearby building site turn to point at the front door of Michael Angelo Watts' fortress. Cars came from all directions and angled in beside it.

Police were leaping out on to the pavement, slamming doors and slamming them again just for effect. Curtains were flung back all down the street as bleary-eyed neighbours in their night attire, or lack of it, wondered what the excitement was. Sparky and I strode down the short path, the front of the building illuminated by the chopper's searchlight.

'What happened to him?' Sparky said as we reached the front door.

'Who?' I asked, reaching through the bars.

'General Custer.'

I glowered at him and beat the door with my fist. 'Police! Open up!' I yelled.

Sparky reached through and thumped harder and yelled louder. We'd have heard feet running up and down the stairs, people shouting and toilet-flushing noises if it hadn't been for the helicopter.

He squinted up at it, saying, 'He's fading my jacket with that fucking light.' He only swears when he's nervous.

We hammered for nearly five minutes before the door opened as far as a security chain would allow it and a wide-eyed boy aged about twelve peered through the gap. He was wearing a giant-sized T-shirt with a catchy logo, and probably nothing else. 'Hello, son,' I said. 'We're the police. Is your father in?'

He shook his head.

'Is Michael Angelo Watts in?'

'No.'

'Then will you please fetch whoever is in charge to the door.'

He closed it and we heard the latch being applied again. I waved at the JCB driver and he revved the engine and raised the shovel in a menacing gesture. Two minutes later a bare-chested adult with short dreadlocks was addressing us through the gap. 'What the fuck you want?' he demanded.

'Are you Michael Angelo Watts?' I asked.

'Yeah. Whad if I am?'

'We're looking for a man called Moses Sitole. We believe he's a friend of yours. Can you tell me if he's here?'

'I don't know no Moses Sitole.'

'So he's not here.'

'Never fuckin' heard o' him.'

'Let me show you a picture.' I removed a carefully cropped photocopy of a Bob Marley album cover from my inside pocket and passed it through the gap to him.

'You a fuckin' joke, man,' he assured me.

'So you don't know this man?'

'I never see him before.' His teeth were magnificent.

'OK,' I said. 'Looks like we've been given some bad information. Sorry to have troubled you, Mr Watts. Try to have a nice day.'

As I walked off I heard him call, 'Hey, you.'

I turned, but it was Sparky he was talking to. They glared at each other for a second before Watts said, 'Who the fuck he think he is?'

'We call him Crazy Horse,' Sparky declared, winking at me as he came away.

I gave Zulu Ninety-nine a thank-you salute and he lifted effortlessly into the sky. Next time, if there is a next time, that's the job I want. Sparky went to thank the JCB driver and I walked to the back of the next block, where the Sewer Rats were crouched around a manhole.

Van Rees's two assistants were wearing white coats and looked like a pair of earnest sixth-formers.

'Any joy?' I asked.

They nodded enthusiastically and gestured towards a row of plastic sample bottles, each containing about half a pint of cloudy water. 'It looks very promising,' one of them told me.

It had bloody better be, I thought.

We drove back in silence, Sparky in his morose York-shireman mode. 'Do you?' I asked, as we approached the nick.

'Do I what?'

'Call me Crazy Horse?'

'No.'

'Oh.' I was disappointed – he was a hero of mine. 'What do you call me?'

'Don't ask,' was all he'd say.

I rang Van Rees to tell him that the samples were on the way, and Mike Freer to update him.

'You know what they say,' he said.

'What?'

'If you're not part of the solution, you must be part of the sediment.'

'Yeah, very apt. And people who live in glass houses shouldn't throw orgies.'

I wrote, 'If anybody rings for me, I'm at the CADs meeting,' on a sheet of A4 and Blu-Tacked it to my window. With luck, I'd be able to hold them off until the results came in.

The clap hit the propeller at about two p.m. A pale-faced DC popped his head round the door and told me that the assistant chief constable wanted me, as soon as possible. 'He sounded annoyed,' he added, unnecessarily. I needed a change of scenery. Sparky volunteered to field all my calls and I went for a drive.

I left the car in the Sculpture Park and took a pleasant stroll towards K. Tom Davis's mansion, about half a mile away by the lanes, but probably much nearer across the fields. Word would soon be around that Goodrich's death was from natural causes, so I needed to do as much interviewing as possible while everybody was on the defensive. We didn't have much to go on, just a garbled boast into Joan Eastwood's shell-like in a moment of alcohol-induced passion, but murderers have been hanged by less. And Mrs Davis had claimed that her husband went all over the Continent with Justin, although Justin said he never saw him. If he didn't go with Justin, where did he go?

It was a long shot, but I like to keep the pressure on. Maybe the bullion robbers had got clean away with it, but I'd like them never to be free of that dread of the early-morning knock on the door. The same goes for war criminals. May they go to the grave expecting every policeman they see to be the one who puts his hand on their shoulder.

Neither K. Tom nor Mrs Davis was in, which wasn't my number one preferred case, but I made the best of it. I wandered round, looking in through all the windows, being careful not to trigger the alarm. The conservatory was a beaut. Leisurely afternoons spent inside, catching up on my reading, with an occasional dip in the pool, sounded idyllic. Especially if Annabelle could have been there, too.

No. *Only* if she could be there. And if she was there, everything else was secondary. Who needed a swimming pool? Or a conservatory? I didn't. In fact, I wouldn't have had a swimming pool and a conservatory given. So stuff 'em!

Phew! That was a narrow squeak. Sometimes, middle class values sneak up on you.

I tried the sliding door, not sure what I would do if it opened. But it didn't. The garage was detached, and designed for two cars, with separate doors that had little diamond-shaped windows in them. I assumed the diamond shapes to be coincidences. Mrs Davis's VW Golf convertible was inside, but the Range Rover was nowhere to be seen. They were probably out in it.

There was a side door to the garage. Breaking into the garage wasn't as serious as breaking into the house, I decided. At this point, according to popular fiction, I should have removed my credit card from my wallet and slid it behind the catch. That only worked on the first day that credit cards were invented. On the second day, every lock in the world was modified to make it credit card proof. Besides, I have difficulty extracting money from a cash dispenser with mine.

I have a different technique. I stood, gracefully poised on one leg for a moment, and thumped the door good and hard with the sole of my other foot, close to the handle.

Wood splintered and the door flew open. If doors opened outwards, it would be impossible to do that. Maybe I should tell someone.

I broke off a few pieces of the shattered frame and carefully closed the door behind me, grateful that no alarm had sounded. It was gloomy in there, but I could see well enough. A sit-upon lawnmower stood in the space for the other car, and there was a workbench, with lots of tools, along the back wall.

The Golf was locked, so I turned my attentions to the other stuff. In a corner was a big gas-fired barbecue with a butane cylinder beside it that wouldn't have looked out of place on an oil rig. Maybe he had the contract for feeding Brent Spar. Under the workbench was a rusty iron gas-ring, standing on three legs, with a couple of ladles and some tongs like blacksmiths hold hot horseshoes with. This man took his barbecues deadly seriously. Hanging on a hook were a pair of thick gloves and some dark goggles.

A motorbike, if you could call it that, leaned against the far wall, under a sheet. I uncovered it, revealing a spindly frame and a huge engine, with handlebars that were wider and more threatening than a Texas longhorn. Its smell took me back to when I was a kid, when dope was what you painted model aeroplanes with.

Tyres scrunched on gravel. I threw the sheet back over the bike and tiptoed over to one of the little windows. A car, only half visible, was parked in front of the house. Someone slammed a door. The Davises had a visitor.

I stood back from the shaft of light, peeking out, but my view was limited. Surprise, surprise, nobody answered the door to him. After a few minutes he wandered round the side of the house and I saw their visitor for the first time. That was another surprise.

Spying on people isn't fair. After a good scout around he relieved himself into a drain, with much shaking-off of droplets, then cross-pollenated his nostrils with an elegantly curled middle finger. He was dressed so cool you could have chilled a six-pack of Mongolian lager on him, but the manner was agitated, restless, which wasn't really surprising. In a burst of inspiration he removed a portable phone from a pocket and stabbed at the keys. He spoke a few words and looked puzzled, then stared at the instrument and tried again. I'm not the only one who has difficulty with them, I was pleased to see. After another couple of futile attempts he gave that a shake, too, and put it away.

He opened the passenger door of his car and slid in. Shit, he was waiting. Ah, well, I was wanting to be incommunicado for a few hours – Davis's garage was as good a place as any. He cranked the seat back a couple of notches and settled down. I perched on the lawnmower, facing the wrong way, and watched.

It was a short wait. Ten minutes later the Range Rover swung round the end of the house and parked nose-up in front of the garage door, six feet from me. Davis jumped out, apologising for being late. His wife followed him, removing several carrier bags from the back of the vehicle. There must have been big queues at the Sainsbury's checkouts.

I watched them move out of sight, towards the front door, and gave them five seconds to unlock it and step inside. When I calculated they'd be there I pulled the garage side door open and left. Keeping as much blank wall as possible between me and them I sneaked down the garden and out through a gate. I crossed the paddock, about a hundred yards long, and climbed a fence. I was in the Sculpture Park. Apart from not having a ticket, I was safe.

The first one I saw was about fifteen feet high, made of bronze, twisting and writhing towards the sky. Six-inch nails stuck out from it at intervals, like footholds put there for the man who changed the light bulb on top. Except there wasn't a lightbulb on top, just a round thing a bit like a bicycle wheel. I didn't rate it.

The next one, sitting in the middle of the field like something out of *The Prisoner*, could have been a Moore, but he has many imitators. I strolled towards it in a long arc, to lose the buildings of the local college and the distant motorway from my field of view, and stopped to admire. It was uphill from me, with a line of trees behind, and looked perfectly natural, but like nothing you'd ever seen before. I smiled my approval. When I reached it I saw the little plaque on a post. It said, 'Henry Moore, *Hill Arches*, bronze,' with some dates.

I was supposed to be working. I passed another couple of pieces on my way back to the car and memorised their names. When I brought Annabelle I'd impress her with my knowledge.

Nigel and Sparky were in when I rang the nick, and the news was bleak. Assistant Chief Constable Partridge wanted me in his office at ten in the morning, or else. Death was the only excuse.

The best way to deal with trouble is to charge headlong at it. But only after all else has failed. I went home to bury my head in the sand.

On the way I called at the supermarket to stock up with comfort food. I still had a sheaf of bullbars posters in the glovebox, so before I went in I wandered round the car park and left five of them behind the windscreen wipers of offending vehicles. I pinned one on the store's notice board and when I came out I found homes for another two.

There was an envelope with familiar handwriting waiting on the doormat for me, along with a glossy brochure from the council telling me how lucky I was to live under their protection, a catalogue from a thermal underwear company and the new edition of the *Gazette*. On the front page of the paper was a photograph from the Lord Mayor's parade, with the promise of more inside.

I binned the unsolicited stuff and tore open the envelope. It contained a picture postcard from Annabelle, put there because she'd taken up all the space with writing. I put the kettle on and perched on a stool, reading.

She'd decided to visit her sister, Rachel, for a few days, then was moving on to Winchester, where Peter's mother now lived. I wasn't flattered. Annabelle and Rachel go together like marshmallow and mustard, and it looked as if I'd always be standing in Peter's shadow. She'd left on the spur of the moment, she said, and would be very gratful if I could have a look at the house, if it was convenient, to make sure it was all right. She'd be home a week on Saturday, at the latest. Love, Annabelle.

The only ray of sunshine was the picture on the other side of the card. It showed traffic on the Guildford by-pass, taken about forty years earlier. I could imagine her rejecting the views of the South Downs and the floral clock and choosing that one especially for me. I pinned it to the fridge door with Sophie's magnet, but I didn't feel any happier.

Life goes on, I thought, searching in my wallet for the scrap of paper with a telephone number on it. I dialled the number, and a few moments later C. Priest Taxi Services had confirmed its first booking for a wedding.

I wasn't too sure about my next call. After picking up the receiver I hesitated until the warbling noises came. I flicked the cradle again and dialled Kim Limbert's home number.

'It's Charlie Priest,' I said.

'Hello, Charlie. This is a pleasant surprise. What can I do for you?'

'I was just wondering if you'd reconsidered your decision. You were rather hasty, you know.'

She laughed. 'Aw, Charlie, that was five years ago. You're not still carrying a torch for me, are you?'

'I said I'd give you some more time to think about it.'

'Five years!'

'And six days. I'm a patient man.'

'Ah ah! Shall I tell you something, Charlie. Once or twice, when I've been really low. *Really* low. I've wished you'd meant it.'

I said, 'Gosh, I never realised you got that low. Didn't you consider suicide?'

'Oh, yes. This was long after I'd rejected suicide. So how are you?'

'I'm having a little local difficulty, Kim. I'd like you to

make a written statement, saying that I once proposed marriage to you.'

'It doesn't count if you were drunk at the time. What have you done now?'

'Sometimes it's the real you that comes out when you're drunk. I'm on a fizzer. Mr Partridge wants me standing before his desk tomorrow morning. I think it's to ask me about my racist attitude, and about harassment of one of our citizens called Michael Angelo Watts.'

'Oh, Charlie! I am sorry. Watts, did you say?'

'You know him?'

'Heard of him, and of his father, Dominic. Is it big trouble for you?'

'Listen, Kim, if you can't help, it's OK, I'll understand. This morning we called at Michael's house, on the edge of the Sylvan Fields. A little boy answered the door, wearing a T-shirt with "Make my day, kill a pig" written on the front.'

'With a picture of a pig wearing a policeman's helmet. I've seen them.'

'That's right. Well, apparently, father Dominic owns several sweatshops and outlets selling all this funky gear, and I was wondering if one of your many nephews might be able to obtain one for me, to be used in evidence at my hearing. What do you think?'

'Is it Dominic who's making the complaint?'

'I'm assuming so.'

'Is it official, or "Leave it with me"?'

'I don't know, yet.'

'Mmm. For the record, I have two nephews.'

'Noted. Look, if you'd rather not involve them, it's OK. I'm not relying on this for my defence.'

'They won't mind. I'll leave it at the desk.'

'Great. And good luck with your panel. We'll be rooting for you.' Kim was up for Inspector, and I expected her to go further.

'Thanks. Let me know what happens. And if you need me, shout.'

I replaced the phone and sat there for a few minutes, biting my knuckles. It had been a long time ago, and I was drunk. But I'd meant it. Every word of it.

I was drinking my last cuppa of the evening, Radio Four's *Book at Bedtime* droning in the background, when I noticed the still-folded copy of the *Gazette*. I opened it at the middle pages, where all the photos from the parade were, and saw Sophie and Daniel smiling at me, leaning on the Jag like a couple from *Bugsy Malone*. The registration number was plainly visible, and the caption said it was the proud possession of Detective Inspector Charles Priest, head of the Heckley CID.

Seven thirty next morning saw me ringing Van Rees from the office. He promised to have a written report ready by lunchtime. 'There is something in solution over and above what one would expect,' was as positive as he would be. Cautious buggers, these scientists.

As the second-hand on the wall-clock slipped silently over the minute hand at eight o'clock I lifted the phone again and thumped in the City HQ code.

'Assistant Chief Constable Partridge, please,' I told the telephonist.

'Mr Partridge's office,' came the reply.

'DI Priest, from Heckley. Could I speak to him please?'

After a short silence he was barking in my ear. 'That you, Priest?' he demanded. Usually it's Charlie.

'Yes, sir.'

'What the bloody hell have you been playing at? I want you in my office at ten sharp. Didn't you get my order?'

'Yes, sir. But I was hoping that we could delay things until some results come in from Wetherton. Then I'll be able to answer all charges and prove that my actions were justified.' I sounded as convincing as a government minister in the Iraqi supergun enquiry.

'This had better be good, Priest. You know how delicate we have to be with these things. Bloody Sylvan Fields is a tinderbox – actions like yours could ignite the place. How long do you need?'

Emotional bullshit. Sylvan Fields was ninety per cent white, and the only revolutions the white residents understood were made by car engines. 'Could we make it two o'clock, please?' I suggested.

'Two o'clock I'm seeing the complainant. Supposed to be placating him. I've already persuaded him to keep it unofficial, leave it with me.'

'I've no objection to you seeing us together, sir. Kill two birds with one stone.'

'Two it is, then. I'll tell him, so he can please himself whether he comes then or later. But I'm warning you, Priest, this had better be good.'

'Thank you, sir. It will be.'

Traffic were next on my list. 'DI Priest here. Could you please send your fastest car over to the Wetherton lab and pick up a report for me at lunchtime today. It's very important. It should be ready about noon and I need it here at, er, thirteen hundred hours, prompt.' They use the big clock in Traffic.

'Right, sir. We'll do that for you.'

'Thank you. As I said, it's very important, so tell the

168

driver that if he crashes, on no account must he burst into flames.'

I was politely but firmly informed that all Traffic drivers were highly trained and did not crash. Finding a sense of humour in Traffic is as likely as discovering life on Mars, but I like to launch a probe in their direction, now and again.

All that was left was the waiting. I turned my pad over to a clean page and tried working out my pension, but I couldn't concentrate. It was quieter in Gilbert's office, so I trudged up the stairs and sat in his chair with my feet on the desk, pretending to be Mr Partridge. 'Well done, Priest,' I said to myself, gruffly. 'Damn good show. Why don't you start taking a bit more time off? Relax a little?'

There was some mail in the tray: Gilbert was invited to attend a bash at the Town Hall, dress formal; our year-after-next's provisional budget forecasts were overdue; and we hadn't replied to a survey on the effects of closed circuit TV on rowdyism in the town centre. A nice letter from the Police Authority congratulated us for having the joint best clear-up rate in the region. Perhaps that's because we don't spend all our time going to piss-ups and answering bloody useless questionnaires, I thought. My last Fin 23 form was still there, unsigned, which explained why I hadn't received any expenses for six weeks, so I did a passable copy of Gilbert's scrawl and slid it into the out-tray.

The Traffic car was thirty-five minutes late. I was pacing up and down the foyer like a pregnant tiger when the driver strode in carrying a manila envelope.

'Is that for DI Priest?' I asked, reaching for it.

'Er, yes, sir.'

'That's me. Now could you get me to the City HQ before two, please.'

These Traffic boys can drive, I'll say that for them. He sliced a good ten minutes off my best our-nick-to-their-nick time and deposited me near the entrance with ninety seconds to spare.

'Don't wait, I may be some time,' I told the driver as I slammed the door, before he could protest that he had no intention of waiting. It occurred to me that I might not have the clout to hitch rides in police cars when I came out.

The desk was unmanned, as is usual. I leaned on the bell push.

'DI Priest,' I told the irate-looking WPC who came to see what the fuss was about. 'Is there a package for me?'

'A package? What sort of package?'

'Any sort would do. What sorts do you have?'

'I'm not sure. I've just come on.'

'Could you look? Please? It is rather urgent.'

She rummaged under the counter and straightened up holding a plastic carrier with something about reggae written on the side.

'That'll do,' I said, snatching it from her. 'If anybody wants me I'll be in Mr Partridge's office.' I sprinted up three floors and only slowed down when the thickness of the carpet told me I was there.

'Come in!' someone growled when I knocked. The clock above his desk told me I was exactly on time, to the second. I wondered about using Jean Brodie's line, 'I was so afraid I might be late, or early,' but I settled for, 'Good afternoon, gentlemen.'

Chapter Eight

Dominic Watts was seated at this side of the ACC's desk, the placatory cup of coffee perched on his knee, as if he was afraid to sully the polished magnificence of the desk. He was a small man, neatly dressed in a shiny suit. Shiny all over, not just at the backside and elbows, like mine. His briefcase was on the floor beside him, with a leather trilby hat balanced on it. His expression indicated that it was unlikely we'd end up swapping funny stories and fishing in our wallets for family snapshots.

'Sit down, Priest,' the ACC said. I pulled the chair back from the desk to make room for my legs and sat down, placing the envelope and the carefully folded carrier bag on the desk.

'I don't believe you two have met,' he went on. 'DI Priest, this is Mr Watts. Mr Watts, this is DI Priest.'

Watts barely nodded at me. I said, 'Hello.'

'Mr Priest,' Partridge continued, 'Mr Watts approached me yesterday, as I am standing in for the chief constable, with some serious allegations about a . . .'

'They are not allegations,' Watts interrupted. 'They are definite charges, with many witnesses who will confirm . . .' He had a clipped, precise way of speaking, every word carefully enunciated, the result of having a better primary education than you get here.

171

Partridge held up a hand. 'Mr Watts, please. At this moment in time I am just trying to establish the ground rules. I'll give you every opportunity to air your grievances in a while, if you'll bear with me.'

So, we were having ground rules, were we? I'd tell him a few rules of my own, if he'd bear with me, at this or any other moment in time.

'As I was saying. Serious allegations about a raid Heckley CID made on the home of Mr Watts's son, Michael Angelo, who happens to live next door to Mr Watts.'

In a house with bars on the doors and six inches of reinforced concrete over the manhole covers, I thought.

Partridge went on. 'Now, Mr Watts has kindly agreed that this meeting, and any subsequent action, will be off the record. I assume you have no objection to that, eh, Priest?'

Subsequent action meant disciplinary action. I did object, actually, but it was a finer point of the rules of the game, and above all I wanted to get on with it. 'No, sir,' I said.

'Right. Good. So what I propose is that you, Priest, explain what you were playing at yesterday morning, and then Mr Watts will have an opportunity to state his case. That way, hopefully, we'll be able to iron out this problem to everyone's satisfaction. Is that understood?'

Fat chance, I thought, as I nodded.

'Yes, Assistant Chief Constable,' Watts replied. 'It is perfectly understood.' His precise constructions reminded me of Enoch Powell, and I almost smiled.

'Very well.' Partridge turned to me. 'So what was the purpose of this raid, Priest?'

'Thank you. First of all, sir, can I say that we were not playing. We were acting on information that Michael

Angelo Watts' home is used as a safe house for the distribution of class A and class B narcotics. In other words, he is a . . .'

'What is your evidence for this?' Watts demanded, rising from his chair. 'These are scurrilous allegations, completely without foundation. I demand to know where . . . ?' A fleck of saliva landed on the polished mahogany and the leather hat rolled off the briefcase.

'Please! Please!' The ACC jumped to his feet. 'Mr Watts, you will be given every opportunity to respond, in due course. If you will only let Mr Priest finish.'

'I demand to know what evidence he acted upon!' Watts insisted.

'Right. Right. Mr Priest, could you answer that specific point before you continue?'

'No,' I said. 'Evidence about the movements of drugs is obtained at great danger to the officers and others concerned, and I cannot risk lives or prejudice enquiries by giving that information.'

'Just as I thought!' Watts insisted. 'There is no information. This attack on my son and his young family, which took place early in the morning when they were all in bed, was nothing more than blatant racial harassment by a police force where racism is . . .'

'Mr Watts!' Partridge shouted, shutting him up. 'These outbursts will get us nowhere. Let Mr Priest continue.'

'Ask him if he had a warrant,' Watts demanded.

'Well, Priest?'

'We didn't need a warrant. We knew we couldn't obtain access to the house until it would have been too late, so we didn't try.'

Partridge shook his head. 'If you didn't have a warrant, why did you go there?' he asked.

Watts jumped in first. 'To inflict more suffering on my son and to terrorise his family – that is why they went, so early in the morning,' he claimed.

I said, 'We regret that any children were involved, but the total responsibility for any stress imposed on them must lie with Michael Angelo Watts and his lifestyle.'

'What do you mean, his lifestyle?' Watts demanded.

'The lifestyle of a drugs dealer,' I replied.

'Where is your evidence?' he shrieked, saliva spotting the desk like the first flurry of a snowstorm. I eased away from him.

'Yes, Priest,' Partridge said. 'These are very serious allegations you're making. I hope you've some evidence to back them up.'

I pulled the envelope from under the carrier. 'It's all here, sir. If I may . . . ?'

Watts wiped his mouth and retrieved his hat. The ACC lounged back in his big chair, rotating a silver propelling pencil in his fingers. It looked as if the stage was all mine.

I said, 'It is well established that pushers and dealers flush drugs down the toilet when they think they are in danger of being discovered. So we lift the cover of the manhole outside and try to catch whatever comes through the drains. The next step in the game is that they cover the manhole with concrete and reinforce the fall-pipe so we can't break into it. Our progress is further impeded by iron grilles over the windows and steel barred gates outside the doors. The house at Sylvan Fields belonging to Michael Angelo Watts has all these modifications.'

'Because of the crime rate in the area!' Watts told us. 'Why do you not address that problem, instead of harassing honest citizens? Tell me that.'

I ignored him. 'I decided to make a mock raid on the

house, acting on information that heroin from the Continent was being distributed from there.' Watts waved his arms, but stayed silent. 'We posted a team from the Wetherton laboratory at the next drain down the circuit, with other people at all the stench pipes coming from the block of houses where the Wattses live, and the next block of houses down the line. When we knocked on his door there was a flurry of action inside, accompanied by much flushing of the toilets both there and next door, where you live, Mr Watts.'

'This is ridiculous,' he said. 'Fanciful nonsense. It is obvious to me, Mr Partridge, that by listening to this you are as prejudiced as he is. This is a waste of my time.' He jammed the hat firmly on his head and rose to his feet.

'Sit down, Mr Watts!' Partridge insisted. 'This meeting was called at your request. Please have the courtesy to hear us out.' He inclined his head towards me, the signal to continue.

I pulled the report from the envelope, and studied it for a few seconds. 'In a nutshell,' I told them, 'somewhere between one hundred and one hundred and fifty litres of water came from the two houses. None came from the other four drains that fed into that manhole. Samples were taken and checked for specific gravity, and then the water was boiled off and the residue analysed. The laboratory have given us low and high estimates which indicate that between six and twenty kilograms of substance were in solution in the water that came from the Wattses' households. That substance, gentlemen, was fifty per cent pure heroin. Working on the lowest figures, it would have a street value of approximately a quarter of a million pounds.'

'Lies, lies, lies!' Watts shouted at me. 'All lies. If any

drugs were found it is because they were planted, by you.' He reinforced his words by stabbing a finger at me. 'Twice before my son has been falsely incriminated. Now he is not allowed to sleep in the safety of his own home without being persecuted by you. This is not over yet, Mr Partridge. I will take this up with my MP.' He jammed the hat on his head again and grabbed the briefcase. His parting shot was, 'This whole sad story has been motivated by jealousy and racism, purely and simply, but I will stamp it out. Believe me, I will.'

Before he reached the door I said, 'I understand you have a shop in Lockwood Road, Mr Watts.'

He turned and took a pace back towards me. 'Yes, I have. Are you now about to tell me that I am charged with peddling drugs from there, too?'

I pulled the T-shirt from the carrier and held it up for Partridge to see. 'Make my day, kill a pig,' I read from it. 'A young friend of mine bought this, earlier today. A black friend, from your shop. Printed on your machines, no doubt. He's as disgusted with it as I am.' I hurled the T-shirt at him. 'Take it back where it came from, Mr Watts, and never dare accuse me or my men of racial prejudice again.' It draped itself across his shoulder, then fell slowly to the floor.

He yanked the door open. 'You will be hearing from the Council for Civil Liberties about this!' he shrieked at me.

'And you will be hearing from the Crown Prosecution Service!' I shouted after him.

Partridge had his head in his hands. As silence fell in his office he removed them and peered at me.

'He's gone,' I confirmed.

He let out a long sigh. 'You'd, er, better leave me a copy of that report,' he said.

'Yes, sir.'

'And, er, before you embark on anything like this again, er, have a word with someone, eh?'

'We took at least six kilograms of heroin out of circulation, sir. Probably a lot more. At a conservative estimate it cost them a hundred thousand pounds, so they'll be hurting. It's called pro-active policing, sir.' The ACC is big on pro-active policing. He wrote a paper on it. He's written papers on most things.

'Quite,' he said.

I sat there, feeling awkward, wondering if that was it, and I was dismissed from his presence. He didn't exactly smile, but the frown slowly slipped from his face, like the shadow of a cloud passing from shrubbery.

'I, er, might have a little job for you,' he said, and nodded slowly and repeatedly, as if congratulating himself on finding just the sucker he'd been looking for.

'Oh,' I said.

'Ye-es.' He opened a drawer and pulled a big envelope from it. 'In fact, you're just the man. Next Friday – week tomorrow – I'm supposed to be delivering a lecture at Bramshill to a bunch of . . . a party of overseas officers. Unfortunately I can't make it. I rang them and they said, "That's OK. Just send someone else." It'll be a nice day out for you. You can have my first class rail warrant, too. How about it, eh, Charlie?'

Suddenly it was Charlie again. I thought about offering to wash his car every week for two years, but he didn't look in the mood for bartering. I said, 'Fine, sir. What's the lecture about?'

'Ethics. Here you are.' He passed the envelope over.

'Ethics?'

'Yes. What do you know about them?'

'They beat Yorkshire by ten wickets, didn't they?'

I was still a policeman when I left his office, which was a surprise. I popped my head round a few doors, looking for Sergeant Kim Limbert, only to be confronted by shiny faces that I'd never seen before. She wasn't in, so I missed out on a coffee and sympathy. I walked out of the building with my car keys in my hand, then realised I needed a lift. A friendly panda took me back to Heckley, and as we drove past the municipal sewage works I looked into the sky and watched the huge flock of seagulls that scavenge a living there. They were looping the loop and practising their barrel rolls.

I needed to unwind. Nigel had a date and Sparky shook his head when I suggested going for a drink.

'Sorry, Chas,' he said. 'Going out with Shirley.'

'Oh. Anywhere special?'

'No. Just . . . out.' He was uncomfortable, almost blushing. This was a rare event, like a visit from Halley's comet, or Mrs Thatcher contemplating that she might have made a mistake.

'Whaddya mean, out?' I demanded.

'Out. Just . . . out. That's all.'

'Why all the secrecy?'

'It's not secrecy. We're just going . . .'

'Out.'

'Yes. Out.'

'Why don't you tell me to mind my own business?'

'Because I'm too polite.'

'Since when?'

'There's a first time for everything.'

'But you're thinking it.'

'Yes!'

'Right. I will.'

I went home, showered, and walked down to the pub about half a mile away; the nearest thing I have to a local. I only go there as a last resort.

Nothing had changed since my last visit. The landlord resented my interrupting his conversation with the three cronies who occupied their permanent positions at the little bar, and checked the tenner I handed over by holding it up to the light. I did the same with the fiver he gave me in my change. The regulars were local business-men of the upstart variety. Their Pringle jumpers had crossed golf clubs on the breast, and they fell silent while I was being served. I ordered a home-made chicken pie and chips and found a table away from the door.

The food was reasonable. No, fair's fair, it was good. I enjoyed it, and a second pint relaxed me. Long time ago I started hitting the booze hard, but not any more. It's an occupational hazard, an antidote to the long hours and the stress of the job. I saw where it was leading me and looked for a different strategy. I decided it was all a matter of attitude.

A third was tempting, but I decided to stick to my two-pint limit. As I placed my empty glass on the bar one of the cronies said, 'You're the policeman, aren't you?' making it sound like an accusation. He had a Zapata moustache that made him look much older than he prob-ably was, and would have been horrified to learn that in some circles it was a badge of homosexuality.

'That's how I earn my living,' I confessed.

He elbowed his way round his colleagues. 'I've just been done for speeding,' he declared, which was more-or-less what I'd expected. 'Said I was doing fifty-five on the by-pass, and I wasn't doing an inch over forty-eight.

Bloody diabolical, I call it. When somebody had a go at the wife's Clio you didn't do a thing about it.'

'It's a forty limit on the by-pass,' I said. 'And three people have been killed on it so far this year.'

'One of them was in a stolen car.'

Presumably that didn't count. I smiled at him. 'Just regard it as payment for all the times that you weren't caught,' I suggested, turning to leave.

'It's all right for you, though, isn't it?' one of the others said.

'What is?'

He nodded at the glasses on the bar. 'This job.'

'You mean drinking and driving?'

'That's right. It's all right for you.'

'No,' I told him. 'It's the same for me as it is for anyone. Possibly even worse. That's why I walked here tonight.' This time I made it out of the door before they could reply.

As soon as I arrived home I rang Sparky's number. 'Hello, Sophie,' I said when she answered. 'It's Uncle Charlie. Can I have a word with your dad, please?'

'Hello, Uncle Charlie. They're not in. Did you see our picture in the *Gazette*?'

'Yes, it's good, isn't it? Are you sending for a copy?'

'Mum said she would, and one for you, too.'

'That's kind of her. Where have they gone?'

'Um, I can't tell you.'

'Oh, why not?'

'Because Dad said that if you rang to ask where they'd gone, he'd kill us both if we told you.'

'Honestly?'

'He meant it.'

'Right. Put Daniel on.'

He was right there. 'Hi, Uncle Charlie,' he said. 'Did you watch the match?'

'Never mind that. If you don't tell me where your dad is I'm coming straight round and I'll dig your kidneys out with a chair leg. Understood?'

'He made us promise, Uncle Charlie.'

'Right! And I'll wear my flared jeans with budgie bells on the bottom and play a Bob Dylan tape while I'm doing it!'

'Whaaa! Anything but that! I'll tell you.'

'Go on . . .'

'They've gone line dancing.'

'Line dancing!'

'I never said a word!'

'Right, Daniel. Let's just call it our little secret. See you sometime.'

Line dancing! I'd struck pay dirt. This could run for weeks and weeks.

I had one shoe off when the phone rang. I clip-slopped over to it, smiling like a toyshop, willing Annabelle to be on the other end.

'Priest,' I growled, in my pretend officious tone.

It was Heckley control room. 'Hi, Mr Priest,' the duty sergeant said. 'Sorry to disturb you, but a woman's been asking for you. Said she's called Lisa Davis. Do you know her?'

'Hardly. Interviewed her husband sometime last week. Did she say what it was about?'

'No. Wanted to speak to you and you alone. She sounded ferret and skunk to me. I'll give you the number . . .'

I wrote it on the pad. 'Cheers. I'll give her a ring.'

'Please yourself, Charlie, but I said I'd pass it on. One of your many fans, I expect.'

'Work, Arthur,' I told him. 'You know how it is: CID never sleeps.'

I flipped the cradle and dialled the number he'd given me. She must have been sitting right by the phone.

'Hello,' a husky little voice greeted me.

'It's Charlie Priest, Lisa. You wanted me to ring you.'

After a hesitation she drawled, 'Hello, Charlie. I didn't think you would.'

'Why ever not?'

'I'm not sure. I just didn't. Nobody seems to want to talk to me, tonight. I don't know why.'

'I'll talk to you, Lisa. What can I do for you?'

'Thank you. I could tell you were kind. I bet you're a Virgo, aren't you? That man at Heckley police station wasn't very polite.'

'Wasn't he, by jove! I'll have a word with him, first thing in the morning.'

She gave a little laugh. 'You don't mind me ringing the station, do you? I hope I haven't got anybody into trouble.'

'Of course not, Lisa. So what's it all about?'

'Oh, you know, I'm feeling a bit fed up. And lonely.'

'Has Justin gone?'

'Yes. Is Annabelle there with you?'

The message coming through was that Lisa Davis could be bad news. I remembered the warning Annabelle had given me. 'No, she's not here at the moment,' I replied. No need to say she was two hundred miles away.

'So you're on your own, like me,' she observed.

'That's right.' I didn't feel like playing counsellor to a spoilt bitch, which was what I suspected her to be. I needed some TLC myself, but not from her.

'Do you get lonely, Charlie?'

'Yeah, sometimes.' I reached down and unlaced the other shoe. 'Everybody gets lonely sometimes, Lisa. It's all part of life. When do you go out to Australia?'

'Oh, I don't know. I might not go.'

'I think you should. Justin will be disappointed if you don't go.'

'Him!' she sniffed.

There was an awkward silence. She broke it, saying, 'I'm frightened, Charlie.'

'Frightened? What of?'

'This house. It's spooky up here, when you're alone.'

'There's nothing to be frightened of. Why don't you have a nice warm bath, a cup of cocoa, and go to bed, eh? Then you'll feel a lot better.' She had a point. I think I'd have been scared, living up there on my own, with the wind howling round the eaves like Heathcliffe on Carlsberg Special.

'Why don't you come up and go to bed with me?' she replied. 'That would make me feel better.'

No doubt about it, bits of me wanted to. I said, 'Er, no, Lisa. I don't think that's a good idea.'

She sounded disappointed. Offended, probably. 'Don't you like me?' she sniffed.

'Yes,' I replied. 'You're a very attractive woman, but I think we'd both regret it, afterwards.'

'I wouldn't,' she declared, sounding as if she spoke with the confidence of experience.

'Well, I would. How much have you had to drink?'

'Just a little bit.'

She was as tight as a screw top. A thousand gallons is a little bit, when you're talking about leaking tankers. 'What a pity,' I said. 'It's an offence for a policeman to take advantage of an intoxicated woman. Didn't you know that?'

'Is it?'

'Mmm.' I decided to change the subject. 'How's the parrot?' I asked.

'He's lovely, but he's not very cuddly.'

I had an idea. 'Why don't you stay with Justin's parents?' I suggested. 'They have a big enough house.'

'Are you joking?' she exclaimed.

'No. What's so funny?'

'Ruth wouldn't have me anywhere near. That's what.'

'Oh, why?'

'It's a long story.'

Good, I thought. We were moving on to safer territory. 'I'm all ears,' I said. 'Tell me about it.'

'She hates me.'

'Why? For marrying her precious son and taking him away from her?'

'Mmm. Partly.'

'And what's the other part?'

'Oh, me and K. Tom, you know.'

'No, I'm sorry, but you've lost me.' I made myself comfortable, sitting on the floor with my back against a radiator.

'Well, let's say I knew K. Tom a long time before I knew Justin. That's all.'

'In the biblical sense?' I risked asking.

She laughed. 'What do you think?' she replied. 'He didn't insult me like you did.'

'I'm sorry about that. It's nothing personal. I just don't like too many complications.'

'It needn't be complicated, Charlie,' she assured me.

The last thing I needed was convincing that it wouldn't

be complicated. 'So how did you meet Justin?' I asked.

'Through K. Tom. I worked as a temp for him and he was good to me. Helped me start up on my own. When Ruth became suspicious he introduced me to his step-son.'

The ultimate revenge. It sounded damn complicated to me.

'Does Justin know about you and K. Tom?' I asked.

'No! Of course not,' she exclaimed.

'So why have they fallen out?'

'Ah! Wouldn't you like to know?'

'Yes. Are you going to tell me?'

'Why should I?'

'It's just conversation, Lisa. Like you said, we're both on our own, and I like talking to you.'

'Do you really?'

'Of course.'

'That's nice.'

'Wait a minute,' I told her. 'I've got cramp.' I stretched my legs and adjusted my position. 'I'm sitting on the floor and it's a bit hard.'

'Ooh!' she cooed. 'Tell me more!'

'Lisa Davis, you're a wicked lady,' I reprimanded her. 'Ah, that's better. Now, you were telling me why Justin and his dad fell out.'

'Oh, you know, it was because K. Tom asked Justin to do him a favour, and Justin refused.'

'That doesn't sound like Justin. He must have had a good reason. What sort of a favour was it?'

'He wanted him to bring something into the country. Or take something out of it. I'm not sure.'

'You mean . . . smuggling?'

'I suppose you could call it that.'

'Well, I'm not surprised Justin wouldn't do it. There's big penalties for smuggling drugs these days. It's just not worth the risk. So what happened?'

'It wasn't drugs!' she protested, jumping to her father-in-law, and lover's, defence. 'What made you think it was drugs? K. Tom wouldn't have anything to do with drugs.'

'What was it, then?'

'I . . . I can't say.'

'Money!' I announced. 'Bet it was money.'

'Money? Why would anybody want to smuggle money?'

'Good question,' I replied. 'It does sound silly, but people do it, I'm told. Suppose you get a better exchange rate, that way. Hardly sounds worth bothering.' I paused for a few seconds, then, as if realisation had at last dawned, I proclaimed, 'Oh, it'd be the gold. I'd forgotten about the gold.'

'W-What gold?' she stuttered.

'Never mind. No more questions. How are you feeling, now?'

'I don't know.'

'What did you have for your dinner?'

'Ah! Do you really want me to tell you?'

'I wouldn't have asked if I didn't.'

'I had yoghurt, banana and a small jacket potato.'

'It sounds horrible.'

'No, it wasn't. It was quite nice.' She'd resorted to her little girlie voice. 'Charlie . . .'

'Mmm.'

'Will you come and see me, sometime?'

I'd be seeing her, sometime, no doubt about it. I just wasn't sure about the circumstances. 'No, I don't think so, Lisa,' I said.

'I thought you said you liked me.'

'I do, Lisa. I think you're terrific.'

'Tomorrow?'

'I can't make it, tomorrow.'

'Saturday?'

'No. I'll be seeing Annabelle over the weekend.'

'Then it will have to be tomorrow.'

'I'm busy, tomorrow.'

'I thought you wanted to know all about K. Tom. And the . . . you know . . . the stuff.'

'You mean the gold?'

'I might do.'

'I don't believe you know anything about it,' I teased.

'You'd be surprised what I know,' she claimed. 'But I'm not saying anything on the phone. Why don't you come and see me in the morning, about ten o'clock?'

'That's a very tempting offer.'

'So you'll come?'

'I might.'

'Good. And if you're a very good boy, Aunty Lisa might tell you all about . . . you know . . . *it.*'

'Right,' I replied, my voice coming from somewhere down in my bowels. 'I'll do that. Ten it is.'

I let Gareth Adey run the morning meeting. Soon as it ended I strode into the CID office and said, 'You, you and you. Inner sanctum.' I was in a good mood. I'd changed my normal route to work in order to drive past the local pub again. Two posh limos were standing forlornly in the car park, their windows opaque with morning dew for the first time in their lives. After my visit the silly prats at the bar had shared a taxi home.

Nigel, Sparky and Maggie followed me into my corner. 'First of all,' I told them, 'I'm giving a lecture a week today at Bramshill. It's on ethics.' I turned to Nigel. 'Could you have a little think about it?' I asked him. 'Write down a few ideas for me, if you don't mind.'

He nodded.

Sparky gasped. 'Ethics! You!'

'What's so funny?' I demanded.

'It's like asking Genghis Khan to talk on road safety.'

'Right,' I said, pointedly ignoring him. 'The enquiry into Goodrich's death is over. Where are we with the Jones boys?'

'You mean the suspect bank accounts?' Maggie said.

'Yep.'

'It's all in the reports, just like you insist.'

'I know, but let's hear it in the spoken word.'

Nigel said, 'Maud and Brian reconciled three of the Jones' lists of money in Goodrich's book with real accounts in local banks.'

'And where did it go from there?'

'About half went to IGI, for diamonds. The other half went on a variety of things: one cheque of eighteen grand to Heckley Motors, presumably for a car; some went into legitimate investments.'

'Goodrich was a big wheel in second-hand endowment policies,' Maggie told us.

I pulled the flip chart from the corner and handed a pen to Sparky. 'You can be teacher, this morning, Dave,' I told him. 'Good night, last night?'

He grimaced at me and stood up. 'No, bloody awful,' he admitted, turning over the pages until he reached a blank one.

'Sorry, Maggie,' I said. 'You were telling us about second-hand ... endowment policies, did you say? What are they?'

'Maud explained it to me. If someone takes out an endowment policy, then finds out that they are dying, say of AIDS, they want the money now, not after the event. The insurance company will pay them a surrender value, based on the number of payments they've made, but another option is to sell the policy to a third party for a lot more money. This third party then takes over the payments, and draws the full amount when the original holder pops it.'

'And that's legit?' I gasped.

She shrugged. 'Everybody benefits, Charlie. It's a brutal world out there.'

'The insurance companies benefit, Maggie. Why can't they pay the full amount early, minus payments? They'd have to, eventually, if some poor sod didn't need the money.'

Nigel said, 'We're not the morality police, Boss. If it's legal, it's legal.'

'Ok. So what next?'

'Michael Angelo Watts knew Goodrich,' Sparky told us, writing the information on his chart.

'And,' I said, pausing for effect, 'he also knows K. Tom Davis.' They looked at me, inviting an explanation. 'I had a ride round there, Wednesday afternoon,' I went on. 'Did a little spying. Saw him pay them a visit.'

'That's interesting,' Nigel said.

'And he's a drugs dealer,' Maggie added.

'Allegedly,' I said, smiling. 'Go on.'

'IGI go bust,' from Nigel.

'Right.'

'Michael Angelo Watts very annoyed,' Sparky suggested.

'I'd bet he was,' I said. 'The surprising thing is that we

found Goodrich dead in his chair and not standing on the riverbed with his feet in a concrete block. So how did he sweet-talk Watts into leaving him be?'

'Blame IGI – K. Tom Davis – for the failure?' Nigel wondered.

'Can't see Watts falling for that,' Sparky said.

'Nor me,' I confirmed.

'How about an alternative method of payment?' Maggie proposed.

'Such as?'

'Well, what's this about the gold?'

'Right,' I said. 'I'll tell you what we know. Mr Smart Arse Caton said right from the beginning that the drugs dealers would prefer payment in gold, because they're awash with cash, but, on the other hand, anybody holding gold would welcome the opportunity to convert some of it into cash.'

'Jack Spratt and his wife,' Sparky said.

'Precisely. It's a marriage made in heaven. And now there are rumours that K. Tom was involved in the Hartog-Praat bullion robbery. Only rumours, sadly, but the fact is that someone, somewhere out there, is sitting on a ton and a half of a very desirable metal.'

'So what's next?' Sparky asked.

'Next,' I replied, 'is that I am going to interview K. Tom's daughter-in-law, Lisa Davis, later this morning. She reckons to know something, but I'm not sure. Then, when I have the time, I want to talk to a man called Jimmy the Fish, in Bridlington. Hopefully, they'll put some flesh on the rumours. Have you all got plenty to be going on with?'

They always say they have. I turned to Dave. 'I'm seeing Lisa Davis at ten, so I'd better be off. I want you to give me a ring on my mobile at ten thirty, no later. In fact, better make it twenty past. Say there's been a murder, and I'm urgently needed. OK?'

'Will do, Chas,' he replied.

We were on our way to the door when Nigel said, 'Have we time for a quicky?' He meant a joke, not sex. Nigel tries, bless him, but his timing lets him down. We all stopped.

He turned to DC Maddison. 'Maggie, how many menopausal women does it take to change a light bulb?'

'I don't know, Nigel. Please tell me.'

'Three.'

'How do you work that out?'

'No, you're supposed to say? "Why three?"'

'Oh, sorry. Why three?'

'BECAUSE I SAY SO!' he yelled.

I smiled – it wasn't bad, for him – but I was alone.

'Very funny,' Maggie stated. 'Tell me, how many menopausal men would it take to change the same light bulb?'

'I don't know,' he obligingly replied.

'Ten.'

'Why ten?'

'It's just a fact of life, Nigel. Just a fact of life.'

Sparky decided to join in. 'I don't understand all these silly jokes about light bulbs,' he told us. 'About a year ago I was in Sainsbury's and I saw a man with one arm changing a light bulb with no trouble at all.'

'You mean . . . single-handed?' I said.

'Exactly. No trouble at all.'

'How did he manage that?' Nigel wondered.

The merest twitch of a mouth corner betrayed Sparky's triumph. He said, 'He just showed them his receipt, same as anybody else would.'

Chapter Nine

One of the hill farmers chose that very morning to transport twenty tons of hay from the outskirts of Heckley to his barn up on the moors, so I was stuck in the half-mile procession that followed his tractor and trailer most of the way, bits of dry grass swirling in his wake like confetti. It's a sign of a hard winter when they stock up with hay. I was ten minutes late when I parked outside Broadside and Lisa would be worried I wasn't coming, if she remembered I was supposed to be. The big gate was half open, but I left the car outside. The gate swung shut on well-oiled hinges and the galvanised catch held it there, like a man-trap gripping an ankle.

A lilac Toyota MR2 stood outside one of the garages, with 'Lisa Davis Agency' and a phone number emblazoned on the side. It pays to advertise.

The front door of the bungalow was ajar. I knocked and pressed the bell, simultaneously. After about forty-five seconds I repeated the exercise.

'Mrs Davis!' I shouted through the gap.

No reply. I eased the door open a little and called again. 'Lisa! Are you there?'

There was a movement in the shadows at the far end of the hallway. I pushed the door wide to admit more light, and saw the parrot on the floor, waddling towards me.

'Lisa!' I yelled.

The macaw was nearly on me. When I'd told Sparky about it he said they cost about two thousand quid, and this one looked bent on freedom.

'Good boy,' I said, followed by, 'LISA!!!'

It kept coming, picking up each foot with the deliberation of a deep-sea diver, the long tail swishing from side to side on the carpet. I stepped inside and tried shooing it back, but it wasn't having any.

I closed the door behind me, and a few seconds later the bird had me pinned against it. That's when I did the bravest deed of my career. I pulled the sleeve of my jacket over my fist and offered my arm to it, like that hapless fool at the dog-handling centre who spends his working days rolling about under a slavering Alsatian. The macaw gently gripped the material in a beak that looked as if it came from Black and Decker's R and D department and decorously placed one foot on my arm. Its claws went straight through to the skin as it juggled for balance, then it stepped aboard with the other foot and the pressure eased a fraction. I stood up, the bird wobbling alarmingly, but it may have been me. I had a sudden panic attack as I realised why so many pirates wore eye-patches.

Parrots like to climb, and that means upwards. Unfortunately that's in lesson two, and I was still struggling with the first. I should have raised my arm, but I didn't. The bird pulled its way up my sleeve like a rock climber – beak, claw, claw, beak, claw, claw – until it reached the back of my neck. I stood there, bent over like Quasimodo meets Long John Silver, and wailed, 'Lisa! Help! Please!'

But no help came. You're in this on your own, Priest, I thought, and slouched towards the door into the lounge, where the bird's stand was. The door was open, the room much as I'd seen it before, except for some magazines strewn on the floor. Fashion and gossip. It was easy for me to read them because my eyes were pointing downwards. I sidled against the perch and made jerking movements to encourage the bird in that direction. It banged its beak against the bell once or twice and stepped off my neck, on to the perch. I straightened my back gratefully and said, 'Phew! Good boy.' I was speaking to myself.

The poor bird's food tray was empty, so I gave it an apple from a bowl on a low table. The macaw held it down with a foot and its beak carved a great wedge out of it as easily as a spoon passes through a bowl of custard. I'd had a narrow squeak.

But where was Lisa?

I was in the hall, calling her name, when my foot kicked something. I looked down and saw a mobile phone lying there. The room opposite was the kitchen, where she'd entertained Annabelle. Next was a dining room, then two bedrooms straight out of a film set and a third done out as an office. This was where Justin kept his trophies and souvenirs. I'd have liked to have studied them but this wasn't the time. The last door, I presumed, was the bathroom. I knocked, and pushed the door with the tip of my knuckle. It swung back, revealing a white and gold suite but not much else. I wasn't in the mood for gathering ideas about interior decoration.

So where was she? I shouted her name again, for no sensible reason.

Surely there's another bathroom, I thought, probably *en suite* with a bedroom. I went back to the biggest room and stepped on to the thick shaggy carpet. The curtains were closed, so I put the light on.

In an alcove was another door, slightly ajar. 'Are you there, Lisa?' I called, softly, but there was no answer. I placed the knuckle of my first finger against the door and slowly pushed it open.

This was Lisa's bathroom. A large Victorian bath stood in the middle of the room, and she was in it.

Her throat had been cut.

Her head lolled sideways, face as white as the porcelain, and one knee was drawn up. She looked like a discarded Barbie doll, with another mouth where there shouldn't have been one, trapped in a bowl of strawberry jelly.

I reached a finger down towards the surface of the water, smoother than a newly opened tin of paint, and saw its reflection coming up to meet it. A drip fell from the tap, plinking into the surface and sending a single ripple arcing outwards, so a wave of distortion passed through the image, a momentary glitch on the TV screen. The water was cold.

A warbling noise startled me. After a moment's confusion I realised it was my mobile phone. I took it from my pocket and said 'Priest,' into it.

'Hello, Hinspector Priest,' Sparky greeted me in his music hall Yorkshireman voice. 'This is 'Eckley po-leece station. Could you cum back quickly becoss we've got a murder for you to investigate.'

I stared down at her. No matter what I thought of her morals she'd been a good-looker. She'd run her own business and successfully managed Justin's affairs. But she'd loved life just a little too much for her own good. Her hair was dry except for where it dangled into the water and capillary action had carried its dark stain upwards a little way.

'I know, Dave,' I mumbled into the mouthpiece. 'I'm already there. Believe me, I'm already there.'

I was sitting on the wall when Les Isles arrived, fifteen minutes later. There were no hay-wagons to slow his progress.

'What's this all about, Charlie?' he asked, slamming his car door.

I told him about my conversation with Lisa the night before, about the suspicions that her father-in-law was mixed up in the Hartog-Praat robbery, and about her intimation that she knew all about it. He gave me a sideways look, as if to hint that there were other reasons, too, for my visit.

'And her throat's cut?' he said.

'That's right.'

'Tell me what you know.'

'Front door open – wide open, that is. I've had a look round the outside and there's no other sign of entry. Either the door was unlocked or he had a key. No sign of a struggle. He must have known exactly where she was. It's an *en suite* bathroom, not where you'd find it if you didn't know the layout of the house. The water was flat cold. No rigor mortis, but skin macerated. She rang me about ten last night. I reckon she died not long afterwards. The killer left in a hurry. Are you having a look?'

'I believe you, Charlie. No, I'll wait till the anoraks have done their stuff.'

'One more thing. There's a mobile phone lying on the hall carpet. With a bit of luck he'll have dropped it on his way out.'

Les's eyebrows shot up. 'In the hallway?' he asked.

'Mmm.'

'Just inside the doorway?'

'About three yards inside.'

'C'mon, then. Let's see it.'

It was a Sony. We knelt on the carpet and examined it. Look but don't touch, as my mother used to say. There really should be a standard for what all the buttons do.

'Looks to me as if it's still on,' Les observed, pointing at the display. 'Any idea what's what?'

I shook my head. 'No, but one of them should tell you the number of the owner.'

'But which one?'

'No idea. On mine you press the F button and another, but don't ask me which. Have it checked for prints, then consult an expert.'

'I suppose so.'

Someone outside shouted, and we let the SOCOs in. We showed them the phone and they cordoned-off that side of the hall with their coloured tape. Superintendent Isles donned a disposable overall and went with them to examine the body, while I waited outside, where the air was fresher.

He was visibly ashen when he emerged, ten minutes later. 'It's at times like this I wish I still smoked,' he admitted.

'I doubt if it would help,' I said.

'Probably not. How long had you known her, Charlie?' he asked, concerned.

'Only met her once, plus a long phone call. She was lonely. She hinted that she'd rung other people, but nobody wanted to talk to her. A look at her list of calls might be a good idea.' I didn't mention that I'd suggested she have a hot bath and go to bed.

'Mmm. She was certainly a looker. Can I leave the calls with you?'

'No problem.'

'Where's that bloody pathologist?' he snapped.

We stood in the doorway, arranging the mechanics of another murder investigation to go with the two unsolved ones that Les was already overseeing for other divisions. I was hoping he'd leave this one to me, as with the Goodrich case. A red grouse landed on the wall, saw us, and flew off again, cluck-cluck-clucking impatiently as he went. Spots of rain were blowing about in the wind.

My phone was ringing again. I plunged my hand inside my jacket and withdrew it, clutching the dreaded instrument. 'Priest,' I said.

The warbling continued. It wasn't mine. 'It's yours,' I told the super.

'No, it's not,' he said, looking at it. We both turned and stared through the open doorway, to the phone on the floor, chirruping its song of greeting.

Someone was determined to get a reply. 'Answer it,' I suggested.

'God, what if it's someone for her?'

'Then they got a wrong number.'

We stepped inside and resumed our kneeling positions around the raucous piece of electronic wizardry. Isles removed a pen from a pocket and pointed at a button. 'That one, you reckon?' he asked.

'I'd say so.'

He eased the aerial out with a fingernail, pressed the button with a little green telephone on it and said, 'Hello.'

I couldn't hear the other end of the conversation, so I stretched upright. Isles listened, careful not to touch the phone with his ear. An earprint is as distinctive as a fingerprint, and we use all the help we can get.

'Yes, sir,' I heard him say, 'we were hoping you'd ring. Your mobile phone has been handed in to the City Police headquarters.' More listening, then, 'Earlier this morning. Would you like to collect it, sometime?'

I couldn't help smiling. This was too good to be true. Isles said, 'Shall we say in about an hour. That would make it twelve noonish. If you could give me your name, sir . . .' He held a hand up to me, for writing material. I pulled the cap off his pen for him and held my notebook at an open page.

'And your first name, sir . . . Thank you. And your address is . . .'

I couldn't read his scrawl upside down. He lowered the pen and said, 'Thank you, sir. So we'll see you in about an hour. Goodbye.'

I turned the book around and held it towards the light.

'Know him?' Isles asked, standing up and flexing each leg to restore the circulation.

I nodded. 'Yeah,' I said, when I'd deciphered his hieroglyphics. 'I know him all right. We go back a long way.'

I'd only met Dominic Watts the day before, but it felt like a lifetime ago.

Personally, I'd have hung on to the phone and let Watts go. Made some feeble excuse about doubting his ownership of it, but we'd let him know, soon as pos. We could have picked him up any time. Mr Isles arrested him and made him strip bollock naked. Even confiscated his shreddies and leather hat for forensic examination. I could have gone down to the cells at City HQ and gloated at him, sitting there in his nifty paper one-piece suit, but I didn't.

What I did was spend several hours explaining to Isles, a fresh-faced DCI unknown to me and a couple of DSs the relationships between Watts, Goodrich and the Davis family. They met, we suspected, through the diamond investments, which were legitimate but unwise. How Goodrich and K. Tom talked their way out of that, when they crashed, was only conjecture, but maybe the Hartog-Praat gold came into it.

'Did Watts know Lisa Davis?' Isles asked.

'Can't be sure,' I told him, 'but there's no reason why he should have. Maybe his address book will tell us different.'

'He's denying everything,' Les told us. 'Claims he never heard of her. He lost the phone somewhere in town and is threatening us with a wrongful arrest suit. He's an indignant so-and-so,'

'Tell me about it,' I said.

We were interrupted several times as bits of information filtered through. First of all it was the fingerprint section. The mobile phone was covered in marks, as one might expect, but they didn't match the ten-print form made by Dominic Watts after his arrest. A small piece of lateral thinking and a call to Criminal Records did produce a comparison, though, indicating that the phone had been last used by Michael Angelo Watts, son of Dominic.

'Shit!' growled Isles. 'It looks as if Sonny Jim borrowed his daddy's phone. We got the wrong person.'

'Let's drag the son in, then,' the DCI, who was called Makinson, suggested. 'Then see what Forensic can come up with to put one of them at the scene. One of them did it.'

'Maybe Forensic won't find anything,' I argued. 'Picture what happened. Someone walks straight in, cuts her throat, walks out again. If they got blood on their clothes they had over twelve hours to destroy them or lose them somewhere . . .'

'We're looking,' Isles interrupted.

'Right,' I continued. 'Then there's the possibility of the transfer of fibres the other way. Watts's suit looked like silk to me. Something shiny. Not the sort of material that sheds like a moulting labrador. And the son doesn't exactly wear Harris tweed. We could be on a loser.'

'We found several tyre tracks,' Les told us, glumly, popping a Polo mint into his mouth. 'None match Dominic's car and it's looking doubtful for Sonny's. Anybody want one?'

I took one from the tube and passed it on. Makinson shook his head. 'Thanks,' I said. 'And what was the motive supposed to be? Remember motives?'

'If we can put one of them at the scene of the crime at the right time,' Makinson argued, 'we don't need a motive.'

'*We* don't need a motive,' I told him. 'But *they* need a motive, unless you're saying one of them is a psychopath. We're relying too much on forensic evidence. When I retire I'm setting myself up in business as an expert on forensic evidence. For the defence. I reckon I could drive a motorbike and sidecar through most of it, and that includes fingerprints and DNA.' There. I'd ridden my hobby horse in front of Les's shiny new DCI. He looked at me as if I'd peed in the font.

The next interruption saved us from a falling-out. A female DC came in with a list of Lisa's telephone calls for the day before. Les studied it, checking the date against the calendar and writing against the entries until the relevant bits emerged. 'OK, pin back your ears,' he said.

'She made ... ten calls in the morning and four in the afternoon. All the names are here but they don't mean much to me at this stage. Presumably they're to do with the agency she ran. Did she work from home, Charlie, do you know?'

'Sorry, Les, I don't,' I admitted.

'What sort of agency was it?'

'Office temps, I believe, but she also handled the publicity, and whatever, for her husband.'

'OK. We'll check 'em out. Let's jump to the relevant time. According to this she rang K. T. Davis at nine thirty-seven, the call lasting seventeen minutes. At nine fifty-six she rang Heckley police station. That'll be when she asked for your number, Charlie.'

'Yep.'

'That call lasted three minutes. Did you ring her straight back?'

'Yes. It was about ten o'clock. Not much later.'

'And how long did you speak for?'

I shrugged my shoulders. 'Ten minutes, at a guess. It felt like longer, but I don't suppose it was.'

'That's all right,' Les said. 'That takes us to ten past ten. According to this, Lisa rang K. T. Davis again at nine minutes past ten. This time they were only speaking for two minutes. What does all that tell us?'

I'd been making notes, adding the times, as all the others were. I said, 'She rang K. Tom and they spoke for seventeen minutes. Immediately after that she rang Heckley nick and asked for me. I spoke to her for, say, eight minutes. As soon as I put the phone down she rang K. Tom again. This time their conversation was short and sweet.'

'So what do you make of it?'

'Plenty, but it's all conjecture. She'd told me that nobody wanted to talk to her. She was playing me off against K. Tom. It's painful to admit it, but it was really him she wanted to see, not me. Maybe she rang him to say I was coming round to see her, this morning.'

'Mmm,' Les nodded. 'He refused to go round and fettle her, so she rang you. Then she told him that if he couldn't do the job, she'd found a nice policeman who would.'

'Well, I, er, wouldn't have put it quite like that,' I protested.

Les reached out and put his hand on my arm. 'Don't worry about it, Charlie. You're a single man, and I'm satisfied that your reasons were completely noble. Wouldn't like to have to convince a jury, though. Seriously,' he went on, 'you think there's a lot more in this, don't you?'

Les is older than me, but has slightly less service. He joined after an unhappy spell in the army, and I showed him round for his first few days. He's ambitious, and very thorough, but sometimes lacks imagination. Or maybe I have too much.

'Yes,' I told him. 'I believe the Hartog-Praat gold figures in this somewhere. Perhaps Lisa told her father-in-law that I knew something about it. Maybe she threatened him. Told him I was coming round in the morning, when she would fill in the gaps in my knowledge. Hell hath no fury, and all that.'

Isles said, 'So Davis hot-footed straight over and silenced her.'

'Mmm.'

DCI Makinson could contain himself no longer. 'All this is getting too complicated,' he complained. 'We have a suspect in the cells and another in the frame. What's the point in dragging up all this far-fetched stuff about Hartog-Praat just because Inspector Priest's girlfriend had too much to drink. I say we concentrate on what we've got. In my experience if there are two theories then the simple one is invariably the right one. It's called Occam's razor.'

A DS sitting opposite raised his eyebrows at me with a wicked grin. Makinson had clearly heard of my service record: inspector at twenty seven, then zilch. I drummed my fingers on the chair legs and bit my tongue.

Superintendent Isles pursed his lips and nodded. 'Maybe,' he said.

The DS broke the awkward silence. 'What did we learn from the Watts' mobile?' he asked.

'Not much,' Isles replied. 'Only half a dozen numbers stored on it. We're looking at them. Haven't received a record of calls made, yet.'

I said, 'Did you find an answerphone at Lisa's house?'

The DS nodded.

'Was the last message still on it? Mine stores the last one until it's recorded over.'

'Yeah. So does hers.'

I looked at him, inviting him to reveal its contents. After a few seconds he said: 'It was from her mother, inviting Lisa to join them for Sunday lunch. That's all.'

'Jesus,' I mumbled.

The other DS said, 'You reckon K. Tom Davis was in debt to the Wattses, because of the diamond failures?'

'Mmm,' I agreed.

'Any idea how much?'

'Not accurately, but we could easily be talking about a million pounds.'

'That's a lot of money,' he observed. 'Maybe killing Lisa was a warning. Like, a last reminder.'

'A final demand, calling the debt in. Could be.'

Superintendent Isles was deep in thought. 'Charlie,' he said, 'you told us that the son's house, which adjoins Dominic's, is fortified.'

'Yep, that's right.'

'But you reckon there's a door knocked through between the two.'

'Can't be sure, but I'd gamble your salary on it.'

'Fair enough. OK, here's how we handle it. We go for the simple explanation. You, Charlie, hang fire for a couple of days and see what we turn up. We can search Dominic Watts' house because he's under arrest with a murder charge hanging over him. Michael Angelo Watts is implicated, so we take out a warrant to search his house. But we don't go in waving the warrant. We enter via the internal door from Dominic's and *then* we wave the warrant. Hopefully we'll be able to shepherd everyone downstairs before they know they've been busted.'

'Sounds good to me,' I declared, rising to my feet. 'Let's go.'

'Not so fast,' Les replied. 'I've told you to hang fire. We'll see to the Wattses, one way or the other, then you can take it from there. OK?'

I sat down again. 'Yeah. Fair enough,' I said. 'But do I get to talk to Dominic?'

'I can't see why not. And we will have to interview your witness, K. Tom Davis, about the telephone calls.'

'OK. You talk to them about the murder, I'll concentrate on their financial dealings. Another thing. Can I send someone from the Fraud Squad with you on the raid? They know what to look for. Then we'll compare notes, what, Monday morning?'

'No problem. Monday it is,' Les replied, gathering his

papers together to indicate that the meeting was over.

Makinson said, 'You have a weekend off, Mr Priest. I'm sure you've earned it. Monday morning you'll find that it's all neatly sewn up. Then you'll be free to run about after your money-launderers.'

Isles turned to him and smiled like a May morning.

'Inspector Priest,' he confided, 'has a tendency to see bogeymen where the rest of us see nothing. He believes that behind every little crook there is a conspiracy of big crooks feeding off him.' His face hardened as he added, 'The only trouble is, he's caught more big-time villains than you and me put together have ever dreamed about. When Charlie speaks, I listen.'

Thanks, Les. I don't like slapping down senior officers. These young ones can't take it; go running for the rule book. It causes unpleasantness.

On the way home I called in at a jeweller's and asked to see the top man. He confirmed that it was normal practice to melt gold with a butane flame. It didn't oxidise or corrupt in any way.

The wedding wasn't until three o'clock, Saturday afternoon, so I had plenty of time for other things. I swapped the cars round after breakfast and waited for the postman, but there wasn't a letter or card from Annabelle.

The chief constable had no reason to be visiting the City HQ on a Saturday morning, so at precisely eight forty-five I swung the long nose of the E-type into his parking spot.

Les Isles was in, looking out of his window. 'Saw you come, he said. 'The car looks fabulous. Your dad would have been proud of it. Did he ever see it finished?'

'No. He died two years before it was completed. Thanks for yesterday, Les. I'm grateful.'

He screwed his face up, like when you don't want to laugh out loud, or even cry, so you give the muscles something else to do.

'What's so funny?' I asked.

'Nothing.'

It was a laugh he was suppressing. 'Something's amusing you.'

He leaned back on the radiator and waved a mug at me, his composure regained. 'Want a coffee?'

'No thanks. I'll pop down and see Dominic Watts, if you don't mind. You still have him, I presume.'

'For another five hours. I was thinking about your dad.'

'Go on.'

'Oh, I just owed him one.'

'I'll accept it on his behalf. Call it paid back in full. What did he do?'

He smiled at the memory. 'It was during that time we were all sergeants. You'd gone to Leeds, I was here with him. I dropped a bollock. An almighty, gold-plated bollock. One of those that either finishes you or makes you a figure of ridicule for the rest of your career. Did he ever tell you about it?'

I shook my head. 'No.'

'Well, I'm not going to. I don't know what he did, who he had a word with, but he covered up for me. Nothing happened. Years later, when he was ill, I went to see him in hospital. I thanked him for what he'd done. He said we had to stick together. Times were changing. He said that he worried about you, because you were reckless. He asked me to look out for you.'

Now it was my turn to gaze out of the window, over the roofs and chimney pots and tower blocks and steeples, without seeing any of them. Les was suggesting having a pint together sometime when his phone rang. He said, 'Yes, sir,' into it, and rolled his eyes at me. I gave him a wave and sneaked out.

Dominic Watts's expression made me feel about as welcome as a shit fly on a prawn sandwich. 'I presume you have come to rejoice at my predicament,' he said, every consonant present, the cadence rising and falling like a waltz rhythm.

'No,' I told him. 'I derive no pleasure from seeing a man of your age in a cell.'

'Then why are you here? I have nothing to say to you or anyone else. First you accuse my son of dealing in drugs, now you are attempting to pin a murder charge on me. These are false accusations.'

'I want to ask you some questions, I said. 'As you know, you are entitled to have a solicitor present. Do you require a solicitor?'

'I have nothing to say, either in the presence of a solicitor or without one.'

'How well did you know Hartley Goodrich?' I asked.

'I have no comment to make.'

'Did he act as your financial adviser; arrange some investments for you?'

'You have examined his papers – his books – I presume.'

'Yes.'

'Then you know the answer to your own question, Inspector Priest.'

'We know he placed some money for you with a variety of financial institutions. Do you know anybody called Jones?'

'No, I do not.'

'Then how do you explain these?' I removed some

photocopied pages from my inside pocket and passed them across to him. When his house was searched, Maud had found entries in a notebook that corresponded with the amounts of money paid into one of the Jones accounts.

His eyes flicked downwards for an instant, before he said, 'I cannot explain them, Inspector, for I do not recognise them.'

'They were found in your house.'

He didn't reply.

'And similar lists were found in Michael's house.' He stiffened at the mention of his son's name. 'Along with a quantity of cannabis and a few hundred ecstasy tablets. What's gone wrong? Can't he afford heroin any more? Starting at the bottom again, is he?'

'They were planted by your officers.'

'That won't do, Dominic,' I told him.

'And I am not a murderer. No doubt if you try hard enough you will pin one of these crimes on us.'

'Did you know Lisa Davis?'

'No!'

'So you didn't cut her throat?'

'Does it matter how many times I deny it?'

'Your son keeps a Filofax. Handy things, Filofaxes, though I never felt the need for one myself. Lisa Davis's phone number was found in it. He knew her, and his fingerprints were found on the phone.'

He shook his head in frustration. 'I have been over this many times with Chief Inspector Makinson. I did not murder that unfortunate young woman. My son did not murder her. What will it take for me to convince you?'

I'd strayed over into the wrong investigation. 'Know what I like about you?' I asked.

'No, Inspector,' he proclaimed. 'I am surprised to find that I have any redeeming features, in your eyes.'

'It's your use of the language,' I said. 'Day after day we interview people who were born in this country who cannot string a subject, verb and object together – they communicate in grunts – but your English is impeccable. Under different circumstances it might be a pleasure to talk to you.'

'Thank you. I was taught by nuns – the Little Sisters of Saint Theresa. Thou shall not kill was another of their precepts that I took to heart.'

I smiled. 'Nice one. I walked into that. I believe you, Dominic, but Mr Makinson doesn't.'

'I find your confidence in me most moving. Presumably you believe my son did it.'

'No,' I admitted. 'I don't believe he did it, either.'

'You don't?' he repeated, wide-eyed. 'You amaze me.'

'No,' I confirmed.

'Then why are we being harassed?'

'It's not my case. I'm interested in your financial dealings. It's Makinson wants to do you for murder. Tell me all about K. Tom Davis, and the diamonds, and I might have a word with him.'

'Inspector!' he exclaimed. 'Are you suggesting we do a deal? That is not the way I thought justice worked in this country. Whatever happened to innocent until proved guilty?'

It went out of the window, along with full employment and respect for old people. 'Not a deal,' I replied. 'Just cooperation. You were laundering money through Goodrich. First of all into diamonds, then into gold. We'll find the proof, slowly. You'd be making it easier on yourself if you realised that and helped us.'

He leaned his chin on his fists and nibbled his thumb-nails. After a while he asked, 'Has Michael been arrested?'

'No,' I said. 'We can't find him.'

'He's a good boy. He would never kill anyone, I swear it.'

Not by drawing a Stanley knife across their throat, I thought. But he'd feed them drugs until they crawled away and choked on their own vomit in a dark corner. 'If you say so,' I replied.

We were talking in his cell. Ten by eight, eau-de-nil walls and a grille on the door. He was sitting on the bunk and I was on a plastic chair I'd taken in with me. Someone had brought him his own clothes – a pair of slacks and a polo shirt. Very Anglo. He leaned forward, conspiratorially.

'Is it safe to talk in here, Mr Priest?' he whispered.

'There's no one in the cells next door,' I told, him. The Friday night drunks had all gone home and the other remandees were across the corridor. 'Business is bad. And the custody sergeant is at his desk. You can talk.'

He moved forwards, squatting on his heels close to me. 'This . . . cooperation you mentioned, Mr Priest.'

'What of it?'

'I think a spirit of cooperation might be to our mutual advantage.'

'In what way?'

'Nothing very heavy. Just, let us say, helping each other. Believe it or not, I trust Britsh justice – it is the police I have no respect for. Eventually the courts will set me free and prove that Michael is not a murderer. Then life will go on, for all of us. We are not evil people. We are businessmen, and business is difficult in the present economic climate, as I am sure you are aware, Mr Priest.'

'I read the papers,' I said. And clean up the debris, I thought.

'I am sure you do. Someone in your position could be very useful to us. We could call it a ... consultancy. I imagine you have not many years left before you retire. On half-wage, if I am not mistaken. That would make running an expensive car very difficult, would it not, and I believe you have a certain penchant for the good things in life. Why don't you go away and think about what I have said, Mr Priest?'

Two-thirds salary, actually, but yes, the Jag would have to go. I stood up and hooked my arm through the chair and lifted it. 'Sorry, Watts,' I said, 'but that's not the kind of cooperation I had in mind.' I tom-ti-tom-tommed on the cell door and heard the latch click on the outer gate. A few seconds later the grille slid back and the jailer peered in at me.

'All done?' he asked.

I nodded, then turned to Watts as the door swung open. 'The nuns let you down,' I told him. 'They forgot to drill into you the golden rule of English grammar.'

'And what is that?' he snarled.

I gave him my most disarming smile. 'Never start a sentence with a proposition,' I said, and walked out. My visit had been a waste of time, but at least I got the one-liner in. Sometimes, that makes it all worthwhile.

Chapter Ten

Then came the icing on the cake. As I strolled out of the main entrance I recognised the back of DCI Makinson, briefcase in hand, ogling the scarlet torpedo parked in the chief constable's place.

'Good morning, Mr Makinson,' I said as I walked round him and unlocked the door. I drove away without giving him another glance. I was having a magnificent day, and it was still early. Enjoy it while you can, I thought. It won't last.

At the supermarket I stocked up with bananas and cornflakes and purchased an aerosol of car polish. I looked for some white ribbon, but couldn't see any, and they didn't have any Occam's razors, either, so I settled for Gillette. The wedding was scheduled for three. I had an early lunch, then waxed and buffed the Jag until my fingers ached and my eyes were burning from the glare. I was determined the bride wouldn't regret that the Rolls-Royce people had let her down.

I put my best suit on and went to collect her with plenty of time to spare. For a few minutes it looked as if the car would steal the show, but when she appeared from her old home for the last time she looked beautiful. It struck me that she wasn't much older than Sophie.

Her father folded himself into the back seat, ruining the

creases in his trousers, and we went to the church the long way, via a few laps of Heckley town centre. I did a final flourish down Annabelle's cul-de-sac when we reached the church, but her car wasn't there. I hadn't expected it to be.

I sat in the Jag for the service, and afterwards posed, hand on door, for the photographer.

'Are you sure you won't stay for the reception?' the bride asked, as I drove her and her new husband to the Masonic Hall. 'It'll be no problem to fit you in.'

'We'd like you to stay,' the groom added.

'No,' I insisted. 'It's kind of you, but I've a few things to do.'

'Then what about the disco, tonight?' he asked.

'Yes!' the bride enthused. 'Then you can dance with Aunty Gwen. I think she's taken a shine to you.'

I couldn't think of a reason to refuse. Annabelle was incommunicado and the bride's father was a great story-teller. He was a rep with Armitage Shanks, which made you smile before he started. It was either the disco, the local, or stay in. One of the bridesmaids was attractive. 'What time does it start?' I asked.

After I'd eaten, carefully checking the list of ingredients on the side of the packet for garlic, I showered and floppped on the bed for a nap. I felt relaxed for the first time for ages, and fell asleep. When I awoke it was nearly dark and I was under the duvet.

It was half past nine when I arrived back at the Masonic Hall, still in the Jag because I'd forgotten to swap the cars round again. I had to park it in the alley round the back.

'We thought you'd changed your mind,' the bride's father told me. 'You missed some great speeches at the reception. What'll you have?'

He bought me a pint and propelled me towards the buffet. It looked as if a bomb had hit it, but I found some chicken drumsticks and little sausage rolls. I leaned on the wall, plate balanced in one hand, watching the dancers.

They were probably the bride's old schoolfriends, boys and girls. I was always tall for my age. These days, I'd be considered average. Junk food must be good for you. The girls wore baggy T-shirts that reminded me of those sheets they drape over new models in car showrooms, hiding, but hinting at, the bodywork concealed underneath. One wore fishnet tights, and her legs were so long they resembled twin, if upside-down, Eiffel towers.

My free hand was in the pocket of my leather jacket, and I fingered the keys of the finest bird-pulling car God ever invented. I did a little calculation and smiled, wistfully. Biologically speaking, and possibly legally, too, I was old enough to be her granddad. I let go of the key and reached out for my glass.

Aunty Gwen hit me as I finished my last drumstick. She was too much of everything. Too much Estée Lauder, too much make-up, too much . . . Aunty Gwen.

The group was playing seventies stuff, so I allowed myself to be dragged on to the dance floor and pretended to enjoy it. Twenty minutes later the sweat was running down Aunty Gwen's face like a flash-flood in the Kalahari and she begged to sit down again.

That'll learn her, I thought, and went back to my wall, collecting an orange juice on the way.

I stayed a polite hour, wished the happy couple all the best and turned to leave. The bride's father followed me. At the door he said, 'Er, Charlie. Thanks for stepping in like you did. It was good of you. Made her day. A hundred and twenty, was it?' He pulled a roll of notes out of his top pocket and offered them to me.

'Don't be silly,' I said. 'Call it a wedding present.'

'Nonsense. You can't be expected to do it for nothing.'

I took the roll from him, peeled the first twenty-pound note of it and popped the rest back in his pocket. 'That's fine,' I said, waving the twenty.

'Are you sure?'

'I'm sure. It was a good excuse to polish the car and it's been a bit of a change for me.'

'Smashing. I'll say the rest's a present from you, eh?'

'Good idea.'

'Oh, and, er, sorry about our Gwen.' He laughed.

It was drizzling outside. I turned up my collar and walked between the parked cars out into the main road and up the side street, lined with the overspill. The trees still had leaves on them, blotting out the feeble street lights. As I turned the next corner the sound of the group inside came through an open window as they started playing the hokey-cokey. Thank God I'd left. Trouble was, I was wideawake. Blame it on the afternoon nap, the music, those legs. Eggs, chips and a pot of tea on the motorway sounded inviting, so I decided to take the Jag for a burn-up.

Several other late-comers had parked behind me, and the E-type is so low you don't see it until you're there. As it came into view it seemed to be leaning. The camber must be bad, I thought. And it wasn't shining like it should be.

It was like a fist in the stomach. I stood and looked at it, gasping for breath. My lungs were empty, but I couldn't inhale. I dropped the keys and sat on the low wall, forcing my head down, trying to drag the cold night air into my chest.

It had been done over. They'd slashed three of the tyres,

poured a gallon of brake fluid on it, smashed the driver's window and razored the leather seats.

I forced my breathing: in, out, in, out; until I'd calmed down. 'It's only metal and rubber,' I said over and over to myself.

The glove box is lockable, so they hadn't been in there. I retrieved my portable and rang Heckley nick. I needed Jimmy Hoyle and his breakdown truck, fast, but didn't carry his number around with me. They passed the message on and told him it was urgent.

'How about the SOCO giving it a going-over,' the sergeant asked.

'Not here,' I told him. 'I want it away before anybody else sees it. No point in ruining everybody's day. It'll have to be at Jimmy's, in the morning.'

Jimmy Hoyle and I played in the same football team, a long time ago. We were in a cup final against Halifax Town juniors, who we regarded as professionals. Jimmy scored what should have been the winning goal in the last period of extra time, but I let in a penalty in the closing seconds. We were thrashed, four-nil, in the replay.

'Chuffin' 'ell!' he exclaimed when he saw the Jag. He'd done most of the restoration, so it hurt him as much as me. 'Aw, Charlie, you must be gutted.'

'It's only metal and rubber,' I asssured him, without conviction. 'Just get it away, quick as pos.'

We winched it aboard his truck and fifteen minutes later left the Masonic Hall behind us, the strains of the Gay Gordons filtering through the ventilators. I realised what I was missing and didn't feel too bad.

Jimmy said he could manage to unload it, so he took me straight home. All the neighbours peered through their curtains as I jumped down from the cab and waved him off, his yellow flashing light washing the fronts of the houses with waves of jaundice.

Sleep was impossible. I watched a movie on TV, followed by a couple of CDs. Then I turned the lights off and stared into the fire until the birds started singing. It wasn't the car. That could be repaired. Earlier in the day, twelve thousand miles away, Justin Davis would have been getting off a plane, or maybe the highway patrol pulled his car over. A stranger's hand would have fallen on to his arm in a show of sympathy. 'Could you come with us, sir,' they'd have said. 'I'm afraid we have some bad news for you.'

How in the name of evil do you tell a man that his wife was found in the bath, dead, with her throat slashed?

Superintendent Isles released Dominic Watts and circulated an APW for his son, Michael Angelo Watts, backed by a warrant for his arrest. We'd do him for drugs, if not murder. I spent the rest of Sunday on household chores and gave my little patch of grass what I hoped was its last cut of the year. I had a key to Annabelle's, so I took my mower there and gave her a short-back-and-sides, too. I removed the mail from behind her door and came home. It had only been an excuse to see if she was back. I don't fool myself, most of the time.

On Monday morning Mr Isles admitted that no forensic evidence to link either of the Wattses with Lisa had come to light. Her telephone number was in Michael's Filofax, that's all, and he could have dropped the telephone anywhere. Information was coming through that he was hiding in Chapeltown, Leeds. Makinson had interviewed K. Tom and Ruth Davis. K. Tom claimed Lisa rang him about her agency and problems she was having with her

VAT payments. He did her tax returns for her, he said. She'd rung back later to confirm a figure. Ruth had gone to bed early with a migraine, and Makinson reported that their relationship appeared strained. How jolly astute of him.

'Did he ask what the VAT figure was?' I wondered.

'What, and cast doubts on the man's integrity?' Les answered sourly. 'He couldn't do that. Today we're interviewing Lisa's agency girls,' he continued. 'That should be interesting. Might even do them myself. DCI Makinson can talk to Michael's friends.'

'Ha! Good idea,' I agreed. 'If I can get away I might have a ride over to Brid. See if I can find this Jimmy the Fish character that went to see Cliff Childs.'

'It was Childs who lifted the Hartog-Praat bullion?'

'That's right.'

'OK. Give it some priority, then, Charlie.'

'Will do.'

'Have you seen the papers?'

'Not yet. Is she in them?'

'You're in for a treat,' he sighed.

Most of the troops were out. Several of them collect a morning paper on their way to work, for the football results, the pin-ups and a lightning résumé of the news, in that order. Their choices are depressing. I wandered round their desks, collecting a small forest's worth of bumfodder, and took them into my office.

One or two had done the crosswords, presumably while waiting at the traffic lights. I refolded them all and spread them out, front pages uppermost.

The *UK News* set the tone, as usual. The headline was only two words, but it covered well over half of the page. It said, 'BLOOD BATH'.

Underneath, it told the reader that the beautiful wife of daredevil motorcycle ace Justin Davis had been found naked in the bath with her throat cut. Presumably many of their readers didn't realise it was customary to remove one's clothes before taking a bath.

What was it that Phineas T. Barnum said? Nobody ever lost money by over-estimating the bad taste of newspaper proprietors? I turned to page two, as instructed, where it revealed that her body was found by an off-duty CID inspector who was making a 'social' call. The inverted commas were their shorthand for nudge-nudge, wink-wink. I scanned the others, but *Yuk! News* said it all. I gathered them together and dumped the lot in the WPB.

Commander Fearnside had given me Jimmy 'the Fish' McAnally's last known address and details of where his shop was, so I awarded myself a day at the seaside. It was a bright but blustery morning and the sun was in my eyes as I joined the procession of HGVs on the M62, heading towards Hull. I slipped into the fast lane and hit the local radio button for the news and traffic information.

I learned that the police were looking for a man in connection with Lisa's death, and that her husband was coming home from Australia. All traffic was flowing normally, they said, but the champion jockey had taken a heavy fall at Newmarket and been rushed unconscious to hospital. His condition was stable.

At the end of the motorway I took the North Cave Road, through Beverley. I caught up with a line of traffic and dropped in behind them. After a few miles the young woman in the car following me pulled out and made a death-or-glory bid to overtake us all. A lorry heading the other way loomed out of a dip in the road and blazed his headlights at her. She hit the brakes, blue smoke puffed from under a wheel and she squeezed back into line. Hanging in her rear window was a sign that said 'Baby on board', and I could see the top of the child's head over the seat. The poster might have been more effective pinned to her steering wheel.

I parked on the south promenade, about half a mile from the town centre. It was pay and display down one side, so I left the car on the other, with everybody else's. Bridlington was much as I remembered it, but huge signs and a compound filled with earth-moving plant indicated that changes were coming in the off-season. Bringing the place into the twentieth century would be a good idea, before the rest of us hit the twenty-first. Unless, of course, that meant more fast food outlets, amusement arcades and soopa-loopa rides. On second thoughts, leave it as it is.

The place was busy. The boarding houses and hotels extend the season by offering ridiculously cheap rates, and senior citizens take advantage of them. They wandered along the prom in couples and little groups, raincoats buttoned against the breeze, waiting for the next mealtime or cup of tea to come around. I looked for a suitable pub and memorised its name. The gulls hovering over the harbour or perching on the masts of the fishing boats were enormous. These were proper seagulls.

Jimmy the Fish's lock-up was in the harbour wall, along from the museum, the candyfloss stall and the fishing tackle shop. I knew it was his, because it said 'Jimmy the Fish' in big letters over the open front. It's in the training.

He specialised in little packets of shellfish and dressed crabs, with white fish available from a cold cabinet at the back of the shop. The man himself was small and wiry, with a weatherbeaten face and tiny, twinkling eyes. A woman was behind him, her back to me, busy at some task that involved running water and a big knife.

I eat mussels occasionally, so I opted for a change. 'Winkles, please,' I said, after making an inspection of his wares.

He said, 'Well blow me darn wiv a fevver duster, me old cock sparrer. One tennis racket of all that twinkles coming up. Get them darn yer hat an' coat, mister. They'll put rabbits on yer shirt an' vest, no tin-lidding.'

No he didn't. He said, 'Certainly, sir. Help yourself to vinegar.'

I gave him a pound coin and the winkles a quick squirt of acetic acid. None of them cringed in agony, so they must have been dead. Vinegar apart, it was a bit like eating the contents of a puncture outfit. I threw the paper bag into his bin and wiped my hands and mouth on serviettes from the dispenser he had thoughtfully provided. Mrs McAnally was hacking at something with a hatchet. McAnally served a tall elderly gent with 'his usual', and when we were as alone as we'd ever be I flashed my ID at him and said, in a low voice, 'I want a word.'

'Jesus Christ, I knew it!' he hissed and dropped the tray of crab sticks he was fitting into his display.

I leaned across his counter. 'The Marquis,' I told him, 'in twenty minutes.'

His eyes had lost their sparkle. 'Right,' he croaked, with all the resignation of a man whose past had caught up with him.

I was halfway down my orange juice and soda before the taste of vinegar went away. The Marquis is the type of pub I prefer to avoid: all pool tables, slot machines and loud music. The only consolation was that they were playing Hendrix's 'Hey Joe'. There was a small snug, just inside the front door, so I settled in a corner and waited.

I didn't recognise him in his cap, without the white coat. He poked his head furtively round the corner, then limped over and sat opposite me. I'd forgotten about his leg.

'Jimmy McAnally, I presume?' I said.

'Yeah, that's right.' His hands were shaking.

'DI Charlie Priest, East Pennine CID. Want a drink?'

'No fanks. I've told the wife I'm putting a bet on. Best not go back smelling o' beer, know what I mean?'

'Fair enough.' I decided to go for the jugular, pretend we knew he'd liaised between Childs and K. Tom Davis. If I'd asked him and he denied it, I was wasting my time. If we were wrong, then we'd lost nothing. I said, 'I've been doing some work on the Hartog-Praat bullion robbery, in conjunction with the National Criminal Intelligence Service. They have a file on you thicker than prison gravy.' Might as well remind him of what he was missing. 'They tell me that you carried messages between Cliff Childs and a man in Yorkshire called K. Tom Davis. I want you, Jimmy, to tell me all about those messages.'

I could almost see the cogs going round. He'd come prepared to deny everything, but I'd jumped in first with half the story. 'I d-don't know no T-Tom Davis,' he blustered.

'You mean you don't know the name of the man you carried the messages to? One about eighteen months ago, two more not long after Childs was sentenced? I've got the dates, if that would help.'

'No, yeah. I mean, I don't know.'

'You've got me confused, there, Jimmy. Are you saying you didn't know Davis's name?'

'Yeah, that's right.'

'So how did you contact him?'

'I had a telephone number. I'd to ring him, local call, and we met at a pub. That's all.'

'Can you remember the number?'

'Nah. It was a long time ago.'

'So what did he look like?'

He looked around for inspiration. 'Big feller. Prosperous, if you know what I mean. Bit similar to the landlord here.'

'That sounds like Davis,' I admitted. He was carrying a rolled-up copy of one of the tabloids, racing page outermost.

'Read the headlines, Jimmy?' I asked, nodding towards it.

'Headlines?' he repeated unfolding the paper. There was a photo of Lisa there, in a bikini and a professional pose. 'Yeah. What about it?'

'That's Davis's daughter-in-law,' I said. 'She was found with her throat cut. Some of us are wondering if it was a warning to him. We reckon he's looking after the Hartog-Praat gold for Cliff Childs. Maybe he's been dipping his fingers in. What do you think?'

The paper was shaking as he read it, amplifying his nervousness. 'Mother o' Mary,' he whispered, turning to page two for the rest of the story. 'I don't fink noffing, Mr Priest,' he replied, clumsily refolding the pages.

'Well, I do, Jimmy. I think plenty. First of all, I think you'd better tell me the contents of the messages you carried between Childs and Davis. So let's have it.'

He stared at the Formica table top for a while, then said, 'I'd like that drink now, if you don't mind.'

He was playing for time, trying to calculate how much would satisfy me, how much he could keep concealed.

'Uh uh,' I said, shaking my head. 'Later. You'll enjoy it a lot more.' I drained my glass and pushed it to one side, waiting.

'Yeah, you're right,' he conceded. 'I was inside, got a message from Childs to come up to Yorkshire as soon as I was free and ring this number. Somewhere near Wakefield, he said it was. Told me there might be a bob or two in it for me, one day. So I did.'

'And what was the message?'

'Noffing much. Davis had to 'ide the stuff some-where—'

'The stuff?' I interrupted.

'Yeah, that's right.'

'Did he say what it was?'

'No. Just the stuff.'

'But you had a good idea what he meant?'

'I knew what 'e was inside for, Mr Priest.'

'OK. Davis hides the stuff. Then what?'

'He'd to give me half of the 'iding place. Childs was scared that Davis might snuff it while he was inside, but he didn't want anybody else to know where it was. I took 'im half of it, someone else took 'im the other half.'

'Who was the someone else, Jimmy?'

'Lord 'elp me, Mr Priest, I don't know.'

So that was it. McAnally only knew half of the story, so there was no harm in stringing me along. And the other guardian of the holy grail – Morgan – was already safely dead. McAnally had nothing to lose. I picked up my glass, realised it was still empty and pushed it away again. 'I'm not interested in you, Jimmy,' I told him. 'I knew the dead girl, Lisa Davis. This is personal. I want to find that gold before anyone else finds themself breathing through their larynx. You'd better tell me the rest of it.'

'I'm sorry about the girl, Mr Priest, I really am, but blimey, I've told you everyfing I know, so 'elp me.'

'Well, for starters, you could tell me your half of the hiding place.'

He waved his hands in the air, agitated. 'It didn't make sense, Mr Priest, honest it didn't.'

'Jimmy,' I said. 'All this "Mr Priest" is making me feel old. Call me Charlie. Don't read too much into it – I'm still the cop and you're still the cheap ex-crook, but call me Charlie. OK?'

'Right. Fanks, Charlie.'

'So what was it?'

'Like I said, it didn't make sense.'

'Go on,' I urged.

'It was just . . . St Sebastian, that was it. The martyrdom of St Sebastian. Crazy, innit?'

'The martyrdom of St Sebastian?'

'Yeah.'

'You're right, it doesn't make much sense. Maybe if we knew the other half . . .'

'Yeah, well, that'd be different. We're only singing off 'alf the hymn sheet, ain't we?' He leaned forward on to the table and smiled for the first time. A load was off his shoulders, and he hadn't disclosed anything worthwhile. He'd confirmed what we'd guessed, and given us a cryptic clue that was about as much use as a Teflon flypaper.

I hit him with, 'Tell me all about Johnny Morgan.'

He slumped backwards in shock, as if a sniper across the street had taken him out. 'J-J-J . . .' he stuttered, then shut up.

'Johnny Morgan,' I reminded him. 'The two of you shared a cell. I've heard that you can become quite close, banged up like that. Happen with you and Johnny, did it?'

'Johnny's dead,' he whispered. 'You brought a ghost up, that's all.'

'He was the courier for the other half of the message.'

'Was he? I didn't know. Anyway, he's dead.'

'He's dead and you lost a leg in a car accident. Any chance the two are linked?' I asked.

He shook his head. 'Nah, no way. He was knifed by a Paki in a pub brawl. I got 'it by a young bird in a Lada. She was Brahms and Liszt. Just the luck of the draw.'

'You're probably right,' I conceded. 'But I don't believe you're being straight with me, Jimmy. Look at it from my point of view. Two old pals, you and Johnny, have the key to a ton and a half of gold. All you have to do is go and dig it up. Then you could live in luxury, anywhere in the world, for the rest of your naturals. Are you seriously asking me to believe that you didn't compare notes? Pull the other one, Jimmy.'

'Johnny's story died wiv 'im, Mr Priest. I swear it.'

'And I'm the Princess of Wales.'

We sat watching each other across the table. The landlord came and took my empty glass, giving us a look that said, 'If you aren't drinking, piss off.'

'Can I go?' McAnally asked. 'I've work to do.'

'How old are you?' I said.

'Fifty-three.'

'Fifty-three and still dreaming of the big time, Jimmy.' I waved a hand round. 'This is it, Jimmy. This is reality. You're as far as you'll ever get, and so am I. I'll retire soon, make do with my pension. You'll sell your fish for a few more years, then retire to your little bungalow with Mrs McAnally. Surely that's better than living on the Costa del Crime or somewhere, drinking yourself to death, never sure when the knock's coming on the door.

It's time to abandon the pipedreams, Jimmy, and accept your lot in life. I'd say it wasn't a bad lot. Plenty I know would be glad of it, and I'm talking about policemen.'

'Yeah, you're right. I got a good 'un when I married the missus. We weren't evil, Charlie. It was a way of life if you were born where I was. I did a bit of fieving, some receiving, that's all. I've paid me debt. Never had noffing to do wiv Hartog-Praat, I swear it.'

'So what was Morgan's half of the message?'

'I told you. It died wiv 'im.'

I hadn't wanted it to go this far. I fingered a beer mat, wiped the wet circle my glass had left. When the table was as clean and dry as it would ever be I said, 'N-CIS have you down as the driver, Jimmy. That makes you an equal partner.'

'Oh no,' he groaned, his face whiter than the cod fillets his wife had been preparing.

'A twenty would make it unlikely·you'd ever come out again. As long as Childs knows where the gold is and keeps *shtoom* it'll be full terms for everyone. Like I said, your file is mighty thick. I'll tell you something, though.' I leaned forward. 'N-CIS are always on the lookout for bigger premises, just because of all the paperwork. You know all about the price of property in London, I imagine. A big file like yours, they'd just love to lose it. A little bit of cooperation, Jimmy, and I could ask them to stamp NFA on the front cover. Next time they had a clear-out, it'd be thrown in the skip. I can't guarantee someone wouldn't find it on a rubbish dump near the Epping Forest, but it couldn't hurt you anymore.'

'NFA? What's that?' he asked.

'No . . . further . . . action.'

A little bit of the old twinkle came back. 'And that would be . . . that?'

'No promises, but I can't see why not.' Especially as we didn't have anything on him. The fat file I'd told him about was half a line in Cliff Childs' *curriculum vitae*.

Through the open door I could see the landlord polishing glasses. 'Fancy that beer now?' I asked.

'Yeah, please. Pint o' bitter.'

I fetched two while he did some thinking. Sometimes it pays to give them no time, keep the questions coming, pile on the pressure, but Jimmy was a professional. His instinct would be to clam up completely. I wanted him to realise that he had nothing to lose by talking to me.

I placed the glasses on beermats on the table. 'Thought you lot drank light and dark, or some other muck,' I said, sitting down.

'Nah. 'Aven't you heard? We got Tetley's now.'

'Civilisation has reached you,' I declared, taking a long appreciative draught. 'Cheers.'

'Cheers.'

'So what was the purpose of the third visit, eighteen months ago?' I asked him.

'He got in touch wiv me,' he began.

'Childs?'

'No. This bloke you say is called Davis. I really didn't know 'is monicker.'

'But he knew where to contact you.'

'Yeah. That was part of the deal.'

'And what did he want?'

'I'd to fix up a visit to see Cliff Childs. Tell him that this bloke in Yorkshire could offload some of the stuff at a good price. Cliff had to phone him, and when he did, any numbers mentioned would be pounds per ounce. That's all.'

'And you assumed they were talking about gold, not drugs?'

'Yeah, it was gold all right.'

'So you and Morgan didn't find it?'

He chuckled and lifted his glass. I watched the level fall as his head tilted back, the froth sliding down the inside. 'Nah,' he said, licking his lips. 'Didn't stand a friggin' chance.'

'So what was Morgan's half of the message?'

'Uh!' he exclaimed, a faraway smile on his face as he realised he was about to relinquish a dream. 'Five yards in, at five yard intervals. That's what it was.'

'Five yards in, at five yard intervals?'

He nodded.

'And the other half was the martyrdom of St Sebastian?'

'Yeah.'

'So where did you look?'

'Where didn't we? We rang directory enquiries until they recognised our voices. "Not friggin' you again," they'd say. St Sebastian didn't have many churches named after him, fortunately, and no pubs, but we could have been talking about anywhere between London and Yorkshire. It was hopeless. Then this happened.' He raised his gammy leg. 'Bit later, Johnny was killed. I decided I'd just 'ave to be patient, see what they offered me for being their running boy.'

'Or what your cut was for being the driver,' I suggested.

'I wasn't on the job, Mr Priest,' he insisted.

'If you say so. Do you reckon there are a few people out there, waiting to get their hands on the stuff?'

'I wouldn't know.'

'Are you happy that Johnny's death and your accident weren't related?'

'Yeah. This bird what 'it me was coming up a slip road the wrong way. You couldn't plan anyfing like that.'

'Mmm. Probably not,' I agreed, lifting my glass and draining the last of my pint.

'So what 'appens now?' he asked. He sounded scared. I'd revived too many ghosts.

'I'll go home,' I replied. 'Type up my report. I'll have a word with N-CIS suggesting your file be quietly disposed of, as you have been very cooperative, and hopefully, we'll all live happily ever after. You've got it made here, Jimmy,' I told him. 'You've got it made. Why don't you accept it?'

'Yeah, you're right, Mr Priest. Trouble is, the grass is always greener at the other side of the wall, innit?'

'That's because of all the shit that's there.' I took a CID card from my wallet and signed it, saying, 'If you think of anything else, let me know. Thanks for your help, Jimmy, and look after yourself.'

The original plan was to eat in Brid but I wanted to get back, so I skipped lunch. It might be the seaside, but experience had taught me that their fish and chips are not as good as ours. The fish has still been frozen in a factory ship, somewhere off Cape Farewell, and they cater for a passing trade. I listened to Classic FM on the journey back to Heckley, and thought about Jimmy and his cryptic clues. They were meaningless to me, but he could have been bullshitting. I had a suspicion that he would quietly sell his little business and sneak away to fresh pastures, without his name over the door. That's what I'd have done, in his shoes.

Maud was coming down the stairs as I went up them. 'Hi, Maud,' I greeted her. 'Looking for me?'

'Hello, Charlie. Yes, I've left you a note with Sparking plug.'

'You mean old Grumpysod? Coming back for a coffee?'

'No, if you don't mind. I want to be off early. We've identified all the Jones boys accounts, so I've left you a breakdown. Oh, and while I was at your desk I took a message from a PC Young. He's our new DVLC Liaison Officer. Could you ring him, please?'

'Oh, right. Wonder what he wants.'

Sparky was sitting at the word processor, typing a report. 'Hello, Dave,' I said. 'Where's this message from Maud?'

'I left it on your desk,' he replied. 'Can I have a word, Charlie?'

'Sure.' This was Sparky at his most formal. I hung my jacket behind the door and pulled a chair out, alongside him.

'I, er, heard about the car, the Jag,' he said.

'Yeah,' I replied. 'I nearly cried when I saw it, but I soon put it in perspective. That reminds me – I need to collect a claims form. Don't suppose you've heard if the SOCO has had a look at it, have you?'

'It was Sophie's fault, wasn't it?' he said.

'No, of course not.'

'It was,' he insisted. 'She must have told the photographer at the Lord Mayor's parade who the car belonged to. That's how someone knew it was yours. I'll have a word with her, Charlie.'

'No, you won't,' I told him. 'They're growing up fast enough as it is. It's not Sophie's fault that some maniac has a grudge against me.'

'Well, I'm sorry.'

I thumped his knee with my fist. 'Let's have a look at these figures from Maud,' I said.

The gist of it was that the seven Joneses, whoever they were, had deposited between two and three thousand pounds each with Goodrich, nearly every week, for just over two years. That amounted to the tidy sum of £1·78 million.

Four hundred thousand had gone into diamonds, and therefore down the drain; and another eighty-eight thousand was safely deposited in legitimate investments. That left nearly £1·3 million unaccounted for, possibly converted into something else, like, she suggested, gold. Her footnote commented that seven bank managers were heading for a bleak Christmas.

Not long ago a mugger stabbed a pensioner in Heckley for fifty pence. There was no shortage of candidates who'd kill for a share in a million and a bit.

PC Young's number was written on the bottom of the report. I dialled it.

'Hello, Mr Priest,' he said, after I'd introduced myself. 'I'm the DVLC Liaison Officer. I understand you own an E-type Jaguar, licence number . . .'

Any enquiries about car numbers and owners have to be directed through each force's liaison officer, who then talks directly with the licensing centre in Swansea. 'That's right,' I said. 'Want to buy it?'

'Sorry, but no. Maybe if it had been a Ford Escort . . . According to Swansea you have a block on your number.'

'Yes, and I've instructed all my staff to do the same.'

'That makes sense. What I rang for is to tell you that the West Pennine Liaison Officer took a call from one of their PCs this morning, asking for the name and address of the owner of your Jag. I just thought you'd like to know about it.'

'You bet I'd like to know about it!' I declared. 'Did he give it to him?'

'No, of course not.'

'Good. Thanks. It might be legitimate: maybe he's seen me speeding somewhere – not that I do, you understand.'

'Wouldn't dream of suggesting it, sir.'

'I should think not. Look, on Saturday night someone trashed the Jag for me. Slashed the tyres and seats, poured hydraulic fluid over everything else. I'm afraid I'm going to have to follow this up. Can you find out the name and number of the PC for me, please?'

There are informal ways of dealing with situations like this. We go on courses, get drunk together, stray over into each other's territory, and slowly build up a network of inter-force contacts. In my case, with my service, it's more like a labyrinth. I rang a DI in West Pennine that I once shared a park bench with when we were locked out of the academy and asked him to do some nosing around.

I wanted to write my report on the meeting with Jimmy the Fish, but the telephone wouldn't stop ringing. We grumble at Superintendent Wood, but miss him when he's not there to field all the calls that come down the channels. The chief constable's secretary rang from Force HQ for our projected figures for crimes of violence and burglaries, needed for a meeting he was attending tomorrow.

'Ah!' I improvised. 'Haven't they arrived, yet?'

'No, I'm afraid not,' she replied in her snootiest voice. She rarely addresses anyone as low in the pecking order as me.

'Right. Well, I can't remember the actual numbers, and the computer's playing up, but crimes of violence are expected to rise by, er, three per cent, and burglaries by, er, four per cent. If you have the last figures there, could you work them out, please?'

She said she would, but wasn't pleased about it. Tough Tipp-Ex, I thought. Reports, I'm keen on. I give every member of the team plenty of time to do their reports, and sometimes we catch a criminal through them. Statistics are for politicians. All they catch are votes. We were really hoping for a decrease in crime, but it wasn't in our interest to admit it. I slammed the phone down, grabbed my coat and fled before it could ring again.

Jimmy Hoyle helped me fill in the claims form I collected on the way home. We surveyed the Jaguar in his garage, walking round it with glum faces, as if it were the last, dying specimen of an endangered species, which, in a way, it was. It looked as if it had been engaged in a monumental struggle against an ancient enemy, fought to the death. And lost.

'It's all superficial,' Jimmy assured me. 'It'll put right.'

'Of course it will,' I replied with forced enthusiasm. It was hard to believe, looking at the wreck they'd left me with.

'Don't mention the wedding,' Jimmy advised as I read out a question about the purpose of my journey.

'Why not?'

'Because you're not insured for it. It's called hire and reward. Just put pleasure.'

'Right. So what do you reckon, about?'

'Oh, thick end of four grand.'

'Blimey.'

Jimmy wanted to go for a pint, but I declined. Once he gets in a pub he believes it's bad manners to leave before closing time. Driving home I thought about our conversation and one I'd held earlier in the day with Inspector Adey.

I'd seen him in the washroom at the station, wearing his full uniform, and asked him what the celebration was. He was handing out cautions to juveniles, and the uniform was to impress them with the gravity of the situation. He'd just done the first three. One had consumed a Mars bar and a can of Coke while pushing an empty trolley around the supermarket. He fell into the poverty trap: unemployed, but too young to claim benefit. Said he was hungry. Another had paddled in the koi carp pool in the shopping mall and the last one stole all the garden gnomes on the Barratt estate and lined them up across the road.

They'd have criminal records until they were eighteen. And here was me, plotting to sting an insurance company for four thousand pounds, knowing there'd be no comebacks. It was a so-called victimless crime, but it was still fraud. To he that hath, it shall be given; or to put it another way, life's a bitch.

I typed my report of the day trip to Bridlington on my own word processor, in the spare bedroom-cum-office. I checked it, made some alterations and ran off a copy for our files and another for Fearnside. It would be easier to transmit it electronically, or send a disk, but it's forbidden. That's how you spread viruses. I talked to his office and a few minutes later he rang me from home.

I'll say one thing for him: he's a good listener. 'Tell me the messages again,' he asked, when I'd finished.

'McAnally's was, "The martyrdom of St Sebastian", and Morgan's was, "Five yards in, at five yard intervals."'

'Mmm. Sounds bloody nonsense to me. Do you reckon he was having you on?'

'It had crossed my mind. Oh, by the way, I suggested

that we might lose his file, if he cooperated. Is that OK?'

'He hasn't got a file.'

'I know, but I said he had a whole drawer to himself, that you thought he was the driver. Actually, he didn't bust a gut denying it.'

'Didn't he, eh? Suppose we could lose him, providing this is good information. What do you reckon, Charlie?'

'I really don't know, but in the absence of anything better . . .' I let it hang in the air.

'Right. You're not going to suggest that I domicile myself in the British Museum and swot up on the lives of the bloody saints, are you?'

'No,' I replied. 'That's for Hollywood. It'll be something more obvious than that. They had the right idea, looking for a pub or a church.'

'The simple explanation – Occam's razor, eh?'

'Took the words right out of my mouth, Mr Fearnside.'

'Splendid. Well, you keep on with it, Charlie, and let me know how it goes. I'll put some of our brainboxes on to these messages. One or two of them time their soft-boiled eggs by doing *The Times* crossword. Maybe they can put their efforts towards something useful for a change, eh?'

Chapter Eleven

All Tuesday we were bogged down with a missing thirteen-year-old girl. Monday morning she'd told her parents she was going to a chum's after school, but when she wasn't home by eleven p.m. they rang the other girl's parents. Samantha wasn't there, hadn't been there, and she hadn't been to school either. Nothing knackers the overtime budget like a vulnerable MFH. The nightshift, with some help from CID, looked into her background, friends, state of mind and everything else that might shed some light on her whereabouts. She had some strange acquaintances, and when I came on it was fairly certain that she'd run away. We'd have to go through the motions though, and the helicopter and the task force started an interim search of the local countryside.

We found her early in the evening, after somebody heard our appeal on *Look North* and put the finger on her boyfriend. They were drunk, in bed, at his council flat in one of the Sylvan Fields tower blocks. He was unemployed, thirty-eight, had four children elsewhere and normally slept with an eight-foot-long boa constrictor. He swore blind she'd told him she was seventeen and she said she loved him. We couldn't afford any more overtime for the next two months.

I was in the shower when the phone rang, washing that

man right outa my hair. It could have been anyone, and some folks don't like talking to answerphones, so I dashed downstairs leaving soggy footprints on the Axminster. 'Priest,' I said into it.

'Hi, Pissquick. How y'doing?' came Mike Freer's melodious tones.

'You got me out the shower!' I protested.

'It comes with the training. Always strike when the opposition least expects it. That's what we've just done. Since when did Drug Squad knock on anyone's door at eight o'clock in the evening?'

'Is there a point in this, Mike? I've stood here dripping so often I have flag iris growing in my hallway.'

'And frog spawn?'

'Buckets of it.'

'OK. Well, put some in a jar and take it down to City HQ. I'm sure Michael Angelo Watts would appreciate something to amuse him as he sits in his cosy ten-by-eight.'

'You've lifted him!' I exclaimed.

''Bout an hour ago, in Chapeltown.'

'Fantabulosa! What's he saying?'

'Would you believe: "Bring me my solicitor"?'

'I believe it. Great. I wonder how soon Les Isles will let me have a crack at him?'

'After everybody else, I imagine. Just thought you'd like to know. S'long.'

'Thanks, 'bye.'

The water was running cold when I went back upstairs. I thought about walking to the local again, and ruining all their evenings, but decided they weren't worth it. I settled for watching a science programme on Channel 4 and a reasonably early night.

* * *

The PC who'd tried to find my name and address from the DVLC said that a civilian had made an unofficial complaint to him about an E-type Jaguar being driven recklessly. He hadn't taken the civilian's name, but decided to look into it 'just out of interest'. What he meant was that one of his shady friends had slipped him fifty quid for the information. The liaison officer asked him all about it, prompted by my DI colleague. A discreet eye would be kept on his future behaviour. I thanked my opposite number for his assistance and put the phone down.

Simon Mingeles was Michael Angelo Watts' brief. He was in court on Wednesday morning, defending the AIDS virus against a crimes against humanity rap, so I had to wait until he was available to hold his client's hand. It was almost three thirty when I spoke the time into the tape recorder, in one of City's interview rooms.

Michael wore baggy pantaloons, some sort of ethnic top and an expression of bored arrogance. Mingeles had that glow that a two-hour lunch gives one.

'Inspector Priest,' Mingeles began, 'my client has already spoken at length to DCI Makinson and Superintendent Isles. I really do not know what we can learn from more of these pointless conversations. Until my client is charged I am advising him not to answer any more questions. He will, of course, vigorously deny any charges made against him.'

'Mr Watts is still under caution,' I reminded them. 'As it says, it may harm his defence if he does not mention, when asked, something which he intends to rely on in court. I've looked at the transcripts of the previous interviews and I'd hardly describe them as speaking at length, Mr Mingeles. Being downright evasive is more like it.'

'Very well, go ahead' he said, with a dismissive wave. Some would blame his assumed superiority and oily confidence on the claret he'd consumed with his lunch, but I knew he was always like this.

I turned to Watts. 'Where were you at ten thirty, last Thursday night?' I asked.

'Mr Priest,' Mingeles interrupted. 'My client has already explained his whereabouts to your superior officers. Is it really necessary to go through all this again?'

'We have senior officers, Mr Mingeles, not superiors. And while we're on the subject of titles, by *your client*, I assume you mean Mr Watts. Don't you think it more polite to address him by his name?' This was becoming another hobby-horse.

Mingeles blinked, but came straight back. 'I am touched by your concern for our relationship, Mr Priest, but that is something between us and nothing to do with you or your investigation. Could we stick to the business that brings us here?'

'So where were you?' I asked Watts again.

His big hooded eyes glared at me and gave a perfunctory flick towards his mouthpiece. Why not? He was paying him enough.

'My client was at a private drinking club, as stated earlier, on more than one occasion,' Mingeles said.

'An illegal club?' I wondered.

'Awaiting a licence, yes.'

Like I'm waiting for a call from Steven Spielberg. 'And where is this club?'

'In Heckley.'

'The address?'

Mingeles sighed. 'Mr Priest. This information is on record, with me. It can be furnished to you if and when my client is charged. Until that time he prefers not to disclose the whereabouts of the club or the names of the witnesses who can vouch for his presence there.'

I said, 'That's bullshit, Mingeles, and you know it.' The big PC standing at the door to make sure we didn't attack each other shuffled his feet.

'That is the position,' the lawyer stated, with admirable restraint.

'OK.' I wanted Watts to speak, say anything, just to get his jaw working. Who knows? Once he started, he might not be able to stop. I rocked my chair back on two legs and asked him, 'Do you remember me, Michael?'

The big eyes flicked from me to Mingeles, who extended his fingers in a gesture that told him to go ahead and answer. 'Yeah, I met you. You fuckin' Crazy Horse,' he said.

Mingeles looked puzzled, wondering if I was having sex with the spirit of the Sioux chief. I smiled at the memory of the rhubarb run.

'How much did that little venture cost you?' I asked.

'Don't answer that,' Mingeles insisted, placing a hand on his client's arm.

'So what is the street price of heroin?'

'No comment,' Mingeles snapped.

'OK,' I said. 'Let's try you with another one. How much is an ounce of gold, on the black market, these days?'

Mingeles jumped in again with 'My client has no comment to make.'

I turned to the tape and said, 'Accused opened his mouth to speak but solicitor intervened.'

'This is disgraceful!' Mingeles blurted out. 'You are putting implications on this that are entirely fictitious. I demand that you withdraw the comment or it be stricken from the tape.'

I said, 'No, Mr Mingeles. You jumped in because you assumed that your client might know the answer. I was merely underlining this.'

He turned to Michael and advised him not to reply again until they'd conferred.

'What's your date of birth?' I asked.

Mingeles nodded with a sigh of resignation.

'Third September, nineteen sixty-six.'

'And your shoe size?'

'We are not here to play games,' Mingeles complained.

'We found a footprint. What's your shoe size?'

Nod of approval, followed by 'Eight and a half.'

We hadn't found a print, but I could play silly buggers just as good as them. I said, 'So tell me how your fingerprints came to be on your father's telephone?'

The tame brief chipped in again with the usual complaint that this had already been explored, mulled over, analysed and generally put to bed with Makinson and Isles. 'I'd like to hear it for myself,' I said.

Watts received the go-ahead. 'I borrow it, and lose it somewhere. That's all.'

'Do you often borrow your father's portable telephone?'

He looked sideways, and when the nod came said, 'Yeah, all the time.'

'Doesn't your father mind about the bill?'

This time the glances were more urgent. 'No...' he began, cutting it off as a friendly hand fell on his arm.

'Is your mobile the same type as your father's?'

Mingeles nodded at him, he nodded at me.

'For the tape, please.'

'Yes,' Mingeles chipped in. 'My client has confirmed that his mobile phone is the same type as his father's.'

'Exactly the same?' I insisted.

'Yeah,' Watts said.

'A Sony?'

'Yeah.'

'Good. Thanks. So where did you lose it?'

'I don't know.'

'Can you remember where you went between the last time you used it, which was at three forty-seven on the Thursday in question, and noticing it was missing?'

'My client told Mr Makinson that he believes he lost it somewhere in Heckley town centre,' Mingeles informed me.

'I'd like to hear it from him.'

Mingeles nodded. 'That's right,' Watts confirmed. 'I lost it somewhere in town centre.'

'I don't believe you.'

There was a long silence, until Mingeles said, 'Fortunately, Mr Priest, what you believe is not important. Unless you have evidence to the contrary, my client's word will be accepted by any court in the land. Now, if there are no further questions, I suggest we terminate this interview.'

'Where did you lose the phone?' I asked again.

'My client has already answered that satisfactorily.'

'I want to hear it from him.'

'I fuckin' tol' you. In town centre.'

'How well did you know Lisa Davis?'

He'd rehearsed that one. 'Never heard of her,' he replied.

'So why was her number in your Filofax?'

Mingeles said, 'Ms Davis's agency is in the *Yellow Pages*. My client extracted the number for future use, in the event of his father needing any clerical assistance.'

'And, of course,' I declared, 'she just happens to employ several very attractive young ladies. Some might say gullible young ladies, don't you think?'

'We wouldn't know about that,' Mingeles informed the tape.

I leaned on the little table that separated us. 'Listen, Michael,' I said, 'you're going down for dealing. That's as sure as Haile Selassie was an ugly runt. Makinson wants to pin a murder rap on you. Believe it or believe it not, I happen to think that you didn't cut Lisa Davis's throat. But you have a good idea who did. Right at this moment I am the only friend you have that you haven't paid for. I'll ask again: where did you lose the phone?'

Watts didn't understand the Selassie jibe. He only joined the Rastas for the haircut. It's a bit like joining the Young Conservatives for the table tennis. 'You a fuckin' joke, man,' he told me for the second time. 'You know fuck all.' Mingeles silenced him by grasping his arm.

I leaned forward, closer to him. 'I'll tell you what I do know,' I said. 'I could get you off a murder rap. But why should I? Tell me where you left the phone, and get yourself off.'

Mingeles looked puzzled, sat back and listened.

'Where were you,' I asked, 'when you made those last calls on your dad's phone and got three wrong numbers? You thought it was your own phone at first, didn't you? You gave it a shake, then realised it was your father's. What did you do? Pick up the wrong one as you left home?'

He glowered at me, leaving the question unanswered.

I went on. 'So, you visited someone and left the phone on their hall table or the mantelpiece or wherever one puts a mobile phone. You had a discussion, maybe a little argument, and left in a hurry, forgetting to pick up the phone. That's what happened, isn't it, Michael?'

Sweat was dribbling from under his dreadlocks and his nostrils were flared, like he was halfway down the hundred metres track, or coming out for the third round.

Mingeles shuffled in his seat. 'You appear to know a lot about my client,' he stated. 'Sadly, for you, it is entirely supposition.' He lifted his briefcase and clicked the locks.

I turned to him. 'Listen Mingeles,' I said, 'this is all good stuff. I know how many times your client shakes his prick after a piss and which finger he picks his nose with.' I hooked a middle finger towards him and he shrank away. 'He is protecting someone because that person is the key to continued wealth for him. If you want to be of real service to your client, I suggest you advise him that the gravy train is off the rails.' I looked at my watch. 'Interview terminated at ... three fifty-four.' I pressed the button and ejected the tapes.

Mugging is a high risk business. High risk for the offender as well as the victim. It's an entry level offence, the first step on a pathway that usually leads to further, more violent, crimes. The mugger needs no tools, no training and no conscience. A fast pair of legs and an urgent desire for a few quid and you're in business. Old ladies out shopping are the first targets, for our young thief has never heard of osteoporosis. But they don't have much money, unless you catch them straight out of the Post Office on giro day. Male targets are often more prosperous, but might fight back, so he starts to carry a knife.

If he's carrying a blade, he might as well use it to threaten the victim. And so it goes on. Rapists, especially the ones who attack their victims out of doors, usually started their careers as muggers.

We were having a plague of them, with two on Thursday morning. Thursday was pension day – laddo was on the learning curve. Maybe we could find a place for him on a residential course. The Davis enquiry was going nowhere, and I wanted this latest pimple in the figures squeezing out before it became a rash, so I put everyone I could spare out on the streets, including myself. For once the two victims gave good descriptions which, surprisingly, tallied. Wearing a Forfar Athletic Football Club jersey anywhere outside Forfar could be considered eccentric. In Yorkshire it was downright weird. We scoured the town and a patrol car spotted him coming out of a betting shop after the last race at Hamilton.

'You've got to admit,' Sparky said later through a mouthful of biscuit, 'it makes the job worthwhile when you target a criminal like that and catch him so quickly.'

I took a well-earned sip of coffee and put my feet up on the desk. 'He's hardly John Dillinger,' I remarked.

'It's one less scrote on the streets. That's what counts.'

'I'll drink to that. Hopefully, when Mr Wood comes back we'll be able to spend a bit more time on the Goodrich affair. Anybody know where Nigel is? I suppose we ought to call him off.'

'He had a theory about someone up the Manchester Road.'

We were chattering away, pleased with ourselves, when my phone rang. It always does.

I swung my legs off the desk but Sparky beat me to it.

'Who?' he asked. His face screwed up in puzzlement and he said, 'Dances with Wolves? No, there's no one here called Dances with Wolves. Pardon ... It's a bad

line, could you speak up, please. Dances with *Anybody*?
Oh, you must mean Mr Priest. I'll put him on.' He
reached out with the phone, saying, 'It's for you.'

Before I put my ear to it I could hear Nigel protesting.
'I never said a thing! He's making it up, boss.'

'So that's what you call me, behind my back, is it?' I
growled.

'No, boss. Honest! I never said a word. He's winding
us up.'

'So what do you call Dave?'

'I don't call him anything! What's going on?'

'Botulism Feet? Aw, Nigel, that's not nice. That's *personal*.'

'I never said a word! You're as bad as he is! Put him
back on!'

'And what else, did you say?'

'Nothing!'

'The what?'

'NOTHING!' he shrieked.

'The Line Dance Kid? Sorry, Nigel. I don't know what
you mean.'

I glanced at Sparky who glowered back at me, slowly
turning colour. '*Bastard*!' he hissed.

'Put him back on!' Nigel insisted. He sounded hurt and
confused, like a dog in a cactus garden.

'He doesn't want to talk to you. What did you ring
for?'

'Oh, flipping heck. Put him on, please.'

'Sorry, Nigel. He's shaking his head. We got someone
for the muggings, so you can come back, now.'

'So I heard. Is he annoyed?'

'Well, he's not pleased, stuck in a cell like that.'

'I meant Dave.'

'Oh, he'll get over it. Thanks for those notes on ethics that you left me, Nigel. They look useful.'

'That's why I rang. I wasn't sure if you'd found them. Good luck with the talk, if I don't see you. Listen, boss. You are having me on, aren't you?'

'Having you on, Nigel? *Moi*?'

'Ha! You nearly had me going, there. Good one. Any instructions for tomorrow?'

'No, I don't think so. I'll leave the shop in your capable hands. You could always . . . Oh, never mind.'

'What?'

'I was going to say that it might not be a bad idea to put a little pressure on K. Tom Davis. Maybe go see him, ask a few innocuous questions; perhaps even suggest that Michael Angelo Watts might be released, for insufficient evidence; something like that.'

'Great. I'll try to do it myself.'

'OK, but take someone with you. Give me a ring tomorrow night.'

The first-class rail warrant didn't materialise, so I drove down to the staff college at Bramshill. The session on ethics was the last one on Friday, presumably put there to reinforce, or perhaps negate, everything they'd heard on the previous days. I rose with the sun and made it in time for lunch. It was the best meal I'd had since Annabelle went away, although the company was stuffy. They like to do things with decorum at the staff college.

The Assistant Chief Constable had supplied me with his paper on the subject, but I decided to personalise it, using a few ideas of my own and the notes Nigel had given me. There were about thirty-five people present when I rose to my feet, after being effusively introduced by someone I'd only met three minutes earlier. Some of the delegates were no doubt from overseas, but there was a fair smattering of what I took to be our top brass. Let's see if I could make them squirm . . .

'There was this high-ranking police officer . . .' I began. 'In fact, he was a chief constable. Being a chief constable he owned a very nice car – an extremely desirable vintage Rolls-Royce. There was nothing he liked more than swanning around in his Rolls, driving through town on a sunny Saturday afternoon, showing it off. One day, out of the blue, a young lady who lived a few doors away asked him if he would be kind enough to take her to the church for her wedding, the following weekend. She would, of course, be willing to pay him the going rate for his services. Sadly, while everybody was in the church, a lorry reversed into the Rolls-Royce and drove away, leaving over five thousand pounds worth of damage behind . . . Fortunately, the Chief Constable was insured . . .'

When I finished the story one or two of them were shuffling around uncomfortably. I like to think they were wrestling with their consciences, but it may have been boredom. I talked about how the miners' strike had overturned our guidelines, and about more recent problems with animal-rights activists and road protesters. How do we balance the rights of protesters with the rights of those who earn a living exporting veal calves and horses? It must have all been highly bemusing to anyone from Nigeria or Saudi Arabia. With five minutes to go I asked for questions and sat down. Timed to perfection.

It was the accents, not the questions, that caused me problems. I muddled through, and the chairman helped out a couple of times with responses that caused me to wonder which of us had misheard. At fifteen seconds to four a swarthy character with a complexion like the dark side of the moon rose to his feet. General Noriega's ugly brother. His voice was eerily light, as I imagine a torturer's to be, and I craned forward, hand cupped over an ear, to catch his words. He seemed to be asking why we didn't just shoot protesters, and cure the problem once and for all?

'That's an interesting point of view,' I declared. 'But unfortunately we haven't enough time to explore it fully. Perhaps it will make a good topic for you to discuss over a drink in the bar, this evening. Thank you for listening, gentlemen – and ladies – and I hope you enjoy the rest of the course.'

They applauded, but nobody stood on a chair and waved. Several of them did ask for copies of the paper, which didn't exist, so I promised to send it. The course director invited me to stay for dinner, but I declined and left as quickly as politeness allowed. I ate at the motorway services. It would have been cheaper at the Savoy, but I was on HQ's expenses.

There were no messages on the answerphone when I arrived home, just after ten, and no mail waiting on the doormat. I made a pot of tea and sank into my favourite chair, exhausted. It had been a long, stressful day, and I felt in need of something to unwind me. Nigel's phone call came as a relief.

'Hi, boss. How did it go?' he asked.

'Oh, so-so,' I told him. 'Nobody threw money at me, but they applauded at the end. That's all you can ask for.'

'I bet it was the highlight of their week,' he replied.

'Well, naturally. I was top of the bill, after all. What about you? Anything interesting happen today?'

'There's a couple of things you ought to know about. I went to see Davis, but he wasn't in. Apparently a pal had collected him and they'd gone for a game of golf. I had a fairly long talk with his wife and told her that Michael Angelo Watts might be freed soon, so no doubt he'll get the message. Apparently they didn't see much of Lisa, because Justin and K. Tom didn't see eye to eye, which we already knew.'

'Did she expand on the reason?'

'I encouraged her to. She said it was just the normal stepfather thing. General resentment. She expressed her grief over Lisa but it was hard to tell how sincere she was. She certainly wasn't overwrought about her.'

'I'll bet. So she didn't say anything about her husband and Lisa having an affair?'

'No. I asked how close they were and she said they had a business arrangement, that's all.'

'Mmm. Maybe we ought to be less circumspect with Mrs Davis senior, the next time. Did you have a chance to ask about her alibi?'

'Didn't have to ask. She said she went to bed with a migraine. K. Tom stayed in, watching TV. Lisa rang him twice; she said she heard him on the phone.'

'Fair enough. What about the rest of it? Is everybody behaving?'

'No problems. As I left K. Tom's I wondered about leaving one of your bullbars stickers behind his wipers, but I decided it was inappropriate. There's one other thing. I thought that K. Tom might try to skip the country, so I put out an APW on him. Is that OK?'

'Yes. Good idea, except they don't work, since we all became Europeans. Did you do it through the FIU?'

'No. As you say, they're not very efficient, these days.

Jeff and I spent an hour ringing all the ferry companies' security departments. They all promised to feed his details into their computerised booking systems. With luck, if he books a ticket they'll let us know.'

'Smashing. Anything else?'

'No, that's it. What are you doing tomorrow?'

Good question. Annabelle was due home, but I wasn't sure if I was still an item in her life. 'Oh, I'll call in to the office for a couple of hours,' I told him. 'Make sure everything is nice and tidy for Mr Wood, on Monday.'

'I can manage, if you fancy the weekend off,' Nigel volunteered.

'I had most of last weekend off,' I reminded him.

'Well, have another.'

It was tempting. 'You sure you don't mind?' I asked.

'Of course not.'

'Right. Thanks. I'll have a day out walking.' They'd be calling me one of the ESSO boys, soon: Every Saturday and Sunday Off. Before I went to bed I recovered my hiking gear from the spare bedroom and studied the Ordnance Survey map for the north-west lakes.

Hard physical exercise, fresh air and a change of scenery are a good cure for most kinds of blues. And I needed some time to think. I was up with the sun again, but there were still plenty of cars on the verge at Seathwaite when I arrived. There's always room for another, providing you don't mind parking halfway up a drystone wall.

Great Gable is a proper mountain. There's no need for ropes or anything at this time of year, but towards the top you can touch the rocks in front of your face and pretend you are on K2. First there's the long drag up to Styhead Tarn to put behind you, with a fearful drop into a raging beck just a twist of the ankle to your right. Then the ground levels out and it's decision time: Scafell or the Gables? I turned right, up Aaron Slack towards Windy Gap, which separates Green Gable from her big sister.

The rain spoiled it. I donned my waterproofs and from then on it was just a challenge to get to the summit. I ate my soggy banana sandwiches talking to a couple from Bolton, huddled behind the pile of stones, and accepted a square of mint cake from them. It rained all the way back to the car. I trudged on, carefully watching my footfalls, anorak hood knotted tightly under my nose. I was warm and cosy in there, and the going was all downhill. It was quality thinking time, but I didn't answer any questions. Something Nigel had said was troubling me.

The Chinese restaurant in Skipton did a decent won ton soup, followed by duck in plum sauce. I arrived home about nine. I was outside, unlocking the door, when I heard the answerphone making its beeping noises. Annabelle, I thought. I made a cup of tea and collected the mail. My AA subscription was due, the dentist wanted to see me and someone was offering to make me rich if I made them rich first. Why doesn't anybody send *letters* any more? I stuffed a custard cream sideways into my mouth, soggyfied it with a swig of tea and pressed the play button.

The electronic lady told me I had one message. There was a long pause, longer than usual, before a man's voice said, 'We got your car, Priest. Next we'll get your woman. Then we'll get you.'

I swallowed the mush in my mouth and let the tape rewind. The lady told me that the time announcement was off. I played it again then flicked the lid open and removed the cassette.

Annabelle didn't answer the phone. I grabbed my leather jacket and drove straight round to her house. Her little car was parked on the drive for the first time in a fortnight, but she wasn't in. The house was in darkness, all the curtains still wide open.

Next stop was Heckley nick. The duty inspector listened to the tape and arranged for a car to keep observations. I sealed the cassette in an envelope and obtained a new one from the pool while he rang the hospitals. Then I went looking for her.

A patrol car was there when I arrived back at her house, where the vicars of St Bidulph's had once lived. I sat in with them for ten minutes, gave them her description and told them about the Jag being vandalised. They made concerned noises and assured me she'd be all right.

Villains don't usually carry out their threats. They didn't threaten Lisa and they didn't threaten to do the car. They just got on with it. No warning, *fait accompli*, this is what we are capable of. Giving a warning is dangerous and pointless. I knew the theory, but it didn't convince me.

I took the long way home, meandering round the streets of town, not really knowing why. When I arrived I left the car out in the road, under the street lamp, because I hoped I'd be using it again before too long. My outside light casts a black wedge of shadow down the side of the house. As I opened the gate I saw a pair of long legs, clad in jeans, jutting out of the darkness where the doorstep was.

Annabelle was sitting there, hands stuffed in her pockets, head back against the wall to avoid the drizzle.

'You look frozen,' I said, sitting on the step beside her.

She nodded, and agreed that she was.

'How did you get here?'

'I walked.'

'It's five miles,' I said.

'The map is wrong – it's ten,' she replied. She still had a sense of humour.

'Why?'

She shrugged her shoulders. 'I came out for a walk, to do some thinking. And my legs brought me here. That's all.'

'You have very sensible legs,' I told her, putting my hand on her left knee. 'You should listen to them more often. How long were you going to wait?'

'As long as it took.'

I'm not usually lost for words. After a few seconds I said, 'Thank you,' and helped her to her feet. We went inside and I put the kettle on. Standing in the kitchen I asked her, 'Did you hear about Lisa?'

'Yes. It was horrible.'

'It was me who found her,' I admitted.

'I thought it was.'

I folded my arms because I didn't know where to put them and turned to face her. 'You read about it in the papers?' I asked.

'Yes.'

'I can explain. I . . .'

She interrupted me by placing her fingers across my lips and shaking her head. 'You don't have to,' she said.

We carried our coffees through into the front room and pushed the settee closer to the fire. 'Do you want something dry to put on?' I asked.

'No, I will be all right, thank you.'

'Music?' I suggested, leaning towards the CD player.

'No. I want to talk.'

'Oh. Right.' I took a sip of my coffee. 'I did Great Gable today,' I boasted. 'I wanted to do some thinking, too.'

'I wish I'd been with you.'

'So do I.'

'Did you come to any conclusions?'

'No. It's all out of my hands. Did you?'

'Yes.' She sipped her coffee, looking into the pretend flames of the gas fire. We sat in silence for several long minutes, until she began, 'When we were in Africa – Kenya . . .' She stopped and tried another tack. 'I want to try to explain why I've been so stupid, so difficult with you.'

'I'm the one who was stupid,' I confessed. 'Insensitive. In this job you . . .'

'No. It was me. When we were in Kenya . . . I left Peter. He had an affair, was unfaithful, so I came home, back to England.'

'I'm sorry . . .' Once or twice before there'd been hints that the perfect romance between the hard-working bishop and his young, glamorous wife had not been as blissful as the world had been led to believe, but I'd never dreamed it was this.

She continued. 'There's still the Happy Valley syndrome out there. Lots of bored women with nothing to do but gossip and drink gin. And have affairs with each other's husbands. Did you ever see *White Mischief*?'

'Mmm.'

'Not much has changed since then. Well, not in some circles. An eager young clergyman was fair game to them. All the more fun if he had a naive wife they could be charming to, afterwards. At first I thought that was the worst part, the humiliation, the laughing behind my back.

260

But it wasn't. I soon forgot that. A chance remark gave him away, and suddenly lots of things fell into place. I caught the next flight home, left everything behind, arrived on Rachel's doorstep carrying a duty free bag containing my allowance of booze. The worst part, Charles, was the sense of betrayal. That never went away.'

'I know. And Peter followed you?'

'Yes. He'd been ill with malaria, so he used it as an excuse to come back. We patched things up, in a way, kept up appearances like we were taught to do, and the rest, as they say, is history.' She looked at me for the first time and gave me a little smile.

'I'd ... no idea ...' I began.

'So, when this handsome detective appeared on the scene and swept me off my feet ...' This time the smile wrinkled her nose. Some women use tears, Annabelle wrinkles her nose and brave men fall at her feet.

'You mean I've a rival?' I said.

'I owe you an apology, Charles. Can we try again?'

'You owe me no apology. Don't be too hard on him, Annabelle. The temptation was just too much. None of us can be certain how we'd behave under those circumstances, no matter how strong our resolve. Most men might have gone the same way, who knows?'

She tried to smile again, saying, 'But you wouldn't have been able to stand in your pulpit and quote the seventh commandment while keeping a straight face. I doubted you, Charles, because of something Peter had done. For that, I'm very sorry.'

I took her cup from her and walked into the kitchen with them. When I returned I stood behind her and placed my hands on her shoulders, rotating my thumbs against her neck muscles.

'Mmm, that's good,' she said, rolling her head.

Over the fireplace I had an original painting of a World War II Halifax bomber that the squad presented to me when I made inspector and moved on. Every six months or so I rotate my pictures, and it was the Halifax's turn to have pride of place. Not great art, but I love it. A gang of us had been walking, and we found the remains of wreckage on Brown Tor. We did some research, found out all about it. Vaguely, I could see the outline of my reflection embracing the four engines, with an RAF roundel where my eye should have been. When I spoke, I talked to the reflection.

'When my wife – Vanessa – left me,' I began, 'I went a bit crazy. Nothing clinical, just hit the booze, you know. Did some silly things, took risks. One day, about a month after she'd gone, a letter came for her, in a Heckley General Hospital envelope. I wasn't sure where she was, so I carried it about with me for several days, thinking I'd ask the force doctor to read it, decide if it was important. One day, I found it there and thought, what the hell, and opened it.'

A Halifax bomber had a crew of seven, average age about twenty. The chances of surviving ten raids were less than fifty per cent. The one we found had flown into Brown Tor on a training flight in bad weather – they didn't even make the starting line. I'd never told anyone else about the letter, and I wasn't sure if I could make the words come out. 'It was from the ante-natal clinic,' I went on, 'fixing her an appointment. She was pregnant.' My hands had stopped massaging Annabelle's neck, but I left them on her shoulders. 'I was fairly certain that she was living with a tutor from the art college. I went straight round there, gave her the letter, told her she had to come home with me. I wasn't having my baby brought up by him. He was sitting on the arm of her chair, all protective. It was like talking to a bloody tableau. She read the letter, then passed it back to me. "You've had a wasted journey," she said. "There isn't a baby any more."'

There, I'd done it. Annabelle placed her fingers over mine and twisted to look up at me. 'Oh, Charles,' she whispered, very softly, 'I'm so sorry.'

I gave her neck a final rub and disentangled my hands. I walked round and flopped in an easy chair, facing her. 'Now, I think it was for the best,' I told her, with a dismissive wave, but the gruffness in my voice betrayed me.

After a silence I said, 'Annabelle. I know you loved Peter, in spite of what happened between you. I don't want to replace him or compete with him. Your time in Africa was an important part of your life, probably the most important part, and I like to hear you talk about it. But Vanessa means nothing to me, now. She was just part of the growing-up process. As far as I'm concerned, all that was just . . . something that happened to someone else, in the past.' I stood up, not knowing how much more to say, how much to tell her about my feelings. I decided to leave it at that. 'Come on, love,' I said, 'you've had a long day. I'll take you home.'

Annabelle didn't move, just sat there, looking at me. Her hair was nearly dry and some colour had returned to her cheeks. Little lines in the corners of her eyes gave her age away but only underlined her beauty, like the date on a bottle of wine confirms its quality. Hers had been a good year. 'Charles,' she began, 'I want to stay here tonight, with you. If you'd like me to.'

We've been lovers for quite a while, but never slept overnight at either house. Annabelle has a fear of the tabloids writing scurrilous stories about the Detective and the Bishop's Wife, put up to it by her neighbours after seeing me sneak away. Car engines don't know how to be discreet at seven a.m. on frosty mornings, and editors don't care whose lives they ruin, if it sells a few papers. We go away for weekends, or spend rainy afternoons in bed. I've no complaints.

'Right,' I said, vainly trying to suppress a smile. 'In that case, I'd better show you where we keep the cornflakes.'

On the pretext of putting the car away I went outside and rang the nick on my mobile, telling them that Mrs Wilberforce had been found, safe and well. She wouldn't need any protection, tonight. The information was received without comment, but no doubt knowing glances were exchanged at the other end.

We sat talking for a while, and I told Annabelle about the Jaguar and the threats, playing them down as much as I could. Staying here saved me the discomfort of camping in the car at the end of her street. She wasn't afraid – a few Heckley villains were small fry compared with what she'd seen in Biafra – but her recklessness worried me.

At Christmas young Sophie had given me a compilation CD of popular classics – all the good bits from a variety of composers who were too inconsistent to achieve superstar status. When we went to bed I put it on the CD player and left the doors open so that the music infused the house with its melodies. I'll never be able to hear the final movement of Respighi's *Pines of Rome* again without a warm glow creeping through me, a tiny smile creasing the corners of my mouth, and whatever task I'm supposed to be engaged in slipping clean out of my head.

Chapter Twelve

I hadn't expected a lodger, so breakfast was frugal. We'd agreed that Annabelle would stay at my house for the weekend, so we visited the supermarket to stock up. Old habits die hard. I headed straight for the single portions, before the OAPs could hit them, then remembered we were catering for two. It was fun. I could get used to this, I thought. Unfortunately, her friends, Marie and Toby, were coming to stay with her on Monday, so she'd have to go home then. I reluctantly agreed that she'd be safe with them in the house with her.

Nigel told me, when I rang him, that everything was running smoothly. It was a warm autumn day, so after lunch I took Annabelle to the Sculpture Park. The trees were turning colour, their shadows striping the cropped grass as we headed for the first piece.

'Oh, Charles, this is wonderful,' she declared. 'Why haven't you brought me here before?'

'I didn't know it was here until last week,' I fibbed.

'So what is that one? A Henry Moore?' she asked.

'Yeah, that's one of our 'Ennery's famous ones, from his, er, *Industrial* period. It's called . . . oh, *Spindle Piece*, or something, I think. I studied Moore at college, but it was a long time ago.' I turned away, so she couldn't see my facial contortions. Annabelle walked over to read the little plaque, while I stood well back, admiring the view.

'*Spindle Piece*,' she confirmed. 'I'm impressed.'

I got the next one right, too. It was called *Hill Arches*, but I couldn't resist showing off when we reached *2-piece Reclining Figure no. 2*, by telling her the material, number of copies made and the date.

Annabelle came back from reading the nameplate with her lips pursed, casually scanning the sky. As she reached me she said, 'You're a fraud, Priest,' and thumped me in the chest. I fell over backwards, partly from the blow, partly because my legs collapsed with laughter.

We had a look round the shop and bought some postcards, and wandered amongst the temporary exhibits. Most striking of them was a crowd of life-size rough bronze figures, standing to attention. They were all headless. Slowly, subconsciously, I steered us towards the far side of the park, adjacent to where K. Tom Davis's home lay.

'Right, Clever-clogs,' Annabelle said, 'what is that one called?'

It was the last statue between us and the fence, beyond which was Davis's paddock. I remembered it, tall and spiky, with a bicycle wheel on top. It was the first one I'd seen when I climbed over the fence, and I hadn't known about the name tags.

'Er, don't know,' I admitted. 'It's not a Moore. I specialise in Moores.'

'Well, have a guess. What image does it convey to you?'

'Mmm. Long and skinny,' I said. 'Bit like you. Is it called *Mrs Wilberforce, balancing bicycle wheel on her nose*?'

She wandered over to it. I could see the house through the trees, and the garage where I'd hidden. Beyond them, through the gap, was what looked like his Range Rover, but I couldn't be sure. I should have brought the binoculars.

'No, it is not that,' she called back to me.

'Right,' I shouted. 'How about . . . *Tour de Force*?'

'No, but you are close.' She was back with me now.

'*Tour de France*?'

'Ha ha! Well guessed. What are you staring at, Charles?'

'Er, pardon?'

'I just asked you what you were staring at. Something has caught your attention.'

'Yes. I'm sorry. I, er, just remembered something Nigel told me, a few days ago. You see that house, through there.'

She turned and nodded.

'Well, we think it belongs to a villain. If possible, I'd like to watch it for a while, a few minutes, see if I can get a bit closer and read the number of the vehicle.'

Annabelle rolled her eyes in a here-we-go-again expression. I couldn't blame her, and I realised I was lying, breaking my resolution. I knew the number; it was written in my reports. What I'd remembered, coming off Great Gable, was that Nigel said he'd almost left a bullbars poster behind the wipers, but decided it might not be appropriate. Why would he want to do that? When I'd seen the vehicle, a few days earlier, it hadn't been fitted with bullbars.

The park was busy with people enjoying the fine day, Michael Angelo was in jail and I was certain we hadn't been followed. Tailing another car without being noticed in a city centre is fairly straightforward, but it's nigh impossible on country roads. We were safe enough. I put my arm across Annabelle's shoulders. 'Quarter of an hour,' I said. 'It is rather important. You have a coffee, while I sit on that fence and watch for a while.' I gave her the keys to the car. 'I'll see you in fifteen minutes,' I promised. 'Either in the café or the car.' I pecked her cheek and watched her walk away. If she was disappointed she didn't let it show.

I didn't sit on the fence. That's never been one of my failings. I leapt straight over it and crossed the paddock, veering off to the right in case they were having drinky-poos in the conservatory. At the other side I sneaked along the fence until I reached the corner of their garden. They didn't appear to be in there, having a post-prandial swim or sipping piña colada while swatting the odd passing humming bird.

It was definitely the Range Rover. I let myself in through the gate and put the garage between me and the house windows. I listened for a while before peeping round the end of the garage. He might have been washing the cars, or decoking his barbecue, but he wasn't. The Golf – I always thought it a daft name for a car until someone told me it stands for *Goes Like Fuck* – was there, so they were probably both in. Thinking about it, it's a daft name for a game, too.

Fortunately, the big Range Rover was nose-up to the garage. Nigel was right. I squeezed between the front of it and the up-and-over door and ran my fingers over the bullbars that I was certain hadn't been there before. If anyone came out, I'd be caught. 'Just happened to be passing, Mr Davis. Thought I'd pop in to see how you are.' Feeble, but it'd do.

Unless he shot me, and asked questions afterwards. There was a precedent, where a detective had been killed as an intruder, and the householder, a known villain, was unconditionally discharged and given fifty pence from the poor box for the cost of the cartridge. I made a mental note to check if Davis was a shotgun licence holder.

There was something fishy about the bullbars. When I ran my hands over them the feel of the paint was inconsistent. The ends, which curl over the headlamps and are designed to mash the kidneys of any pedestrian who gets in the way, were coated in what felt like enamel, or maybe even some sort of epoxy paint. A good solid finish. What you'd expect on a vehicle of this quality. But the horizontal tubes across the front of the radiator, put there to break femurs, spinal columns or children's skulls, were different. They were just spray-painted with black cellulose. The sort of job you could do yourself with a couple of aerosols from Halfords. I tried to remember if I'd seen any in the garage, and felt that I had.

Trouble was, they were welded in. The ends fitted into vertical pieces, and a seam of welding locked them in place. It wasn't good deep welding, though. It was what my mate Jimmy Hoyle would call chicken shit. I wondered if the insurance company had been to look at the Jaguar yet.

A good shake might have dislodged the tubes, but that would probably trigger the alarm. I picked at the welding with my thumbnail, without success. One time, I never went anywhere without my Swiss Army knife, but they were now considered offensive weapons, so I didn't even have that. I found a two-pence piece in my pocket and attacked the welding with it as best I could.

A big flake fell away, revealing how the tube was

loosely slotted into the uprights. I found the flake on the floor and examined it. Plastic Padding has a thousand uses, and Davis had created another one. It's good stuff. I spat on the piece and fitted it back where it came from, but you could see the join as a white line where the paint had cracked. It'd have to do.

A voice shouted, 'Please your bloody self! I'm washing the car,' and a door slammed. I forgot my rehearsed lines and bolted round the end of the garage. It was Davis. I couldn't see a hosepipe at this end, so I might be safe. He wasn't at the back when I peered round the corner, and when I calculated he was busy I tiptoed down his garden, breaking into a nonchalant stroll as distance gave me confidence. A minute later I was heading across the neat grass of the park, in Annabelle's wake. With luck, he'd dislodge the piece of Plastic Padding with his brush and think he'd not made a good job of it. With a bit more luck, they'd serve apple pie in the café. I deserved a piece.

On Monday morning I returned Annabelle to the Old Vicarage and still made it to the office before Mr Wood did. It was a pleasant way to start the week.

My good mood didn't last long. Gilbert hadn't read a paper or listened to the radio for two weeks, so news of a murder, the rhubarb run and his senior officer on a fizzer came as a succession of shocks to him. After the early morning briefing we deployed the troops and Inspector Adey and myself returned to Gilbert's office for a policy discussion. That meant budgets. While we were there the assistant chief constable rang Mr Wood to say that Bramshill had been delighted with my talk.

'He said it was down to earth and provocative,' Gilbert growled. 'I bet it was.'

'I want some time to concentrate on Lisa Davis's murder,' I told him. 'I'm sure it's tied up with the bullion robbery.'

'I thought you said Superintendent Isles had arrested Mr Watts junior,' he replied.

'He has, but Michael Angelo didn't do it. I'm sure of that.'

'OK. No doubt Sergeant Newley can cope.'

'Just what I thought.'

Mr and Mrs Davis were in when I knocked on their door. The Range Rover was in the garage, so I couldn't see if K. Tom had done a repair job on the Plastic Padding I'd disturbed. He was in his shirt sleeves, spectacles hanging round his neck on a lanyard, and he didn't look pleased to see me. Not many people are.

'DI Priest,' I said. 'Can I have a word?'

They sat me on the same shiny seat as before, after removing a selection of the morning papers. They had mugs of coffee, the real stuff, liberally dosed with brandy from the smell of it, but they didn't offer me one. If this was how the wealthy spent a typical Monday morning, it hardly seemed worth the hassle.

'Your sergeant came to see Ruth on Friday,' K. Tom told me. 'I'd gone for a round of golf, but I can't add anything to what she said.'

'Fair enough. Have you heard from Justin?'

'Yes,' Mrs Davis replied. 'He arrived back on Thursday, and rang me Friday morning.'

'But you haven't seen him?'

'No. He said he was spending some time with Lisa's parents.'

'How did he sound?'

'Shocked. How would you expect him to sound?'

Her hackles were rising. Good. It's always more interesting when there's a note of antagonism in the answers, and it saves a lot of misdirected sympathy. I turned to her husband and said, 'Mr Davis, do you think I could have a word with your wife in private, and then perhaps the same with you?'

He looked perplexed for a few seconds, then shrugged and rose to his feet, saying, 'If it helps. I'll be in the snooker room, when you want me.'

As soon as he'd gone I opened with, 'Why don't Justin and his stepfather get on with each other, Mrs Davis?'

She fingered the material of the mohair cardigan she was wearing. 'They do get on,' she assured me. 'There were a few difficulties a while ago, just, like, growing pains, when Justin resented Tom, but they patched it up. Now Tom follows him all over the place. Helps him in his career. He says he's Justin's number two fan, after . . . after . . .' Her voice trailed off. She looked pale and upset, but I noticed that she'd been reading *Hello!* magazine when I came in. It jarred with her apparent demeanour, but I don't suppose there is a publication called *Grieving Mother-in-Law Monthly*.

I said, 'I believe your husband knew Lisa before Justin did. What exactly was their relationship?'

'You mean did they have an affair?' she snapped.

I waved a hand in assent.

'Of course not,' she retorted. 'Lisa worked for K. Tom for a while as a temp. She had ideas above her station. He helped her start up in business and she repaid him by trying to wreck our marriage, steal him away. She was a gold digger, but Tom wanted none of it. Then she met Justin and changed her target.'

'So you didn't approve of her marrying Justin?'

'That's putting it mildly, Inspector.' She moved the newspapers again, looking for something. Her handbag was alongside her easy chair. She lifted it on to her knee and found a long, gold cigarette case in it. Her hands were shaking as she lit up and puffed clouds of smoke towards the chandelier.

'When did you last see Lisa?' I asked.

'July twenty-third.'

I blinked in surprise. 'That's, er, a very precise answer,' I commented, inviting an explanation.

'It's my birthday. Justin always buys me a present. They called round with it, stayed about ten minutes. Anything else?'

'No, that's all for now,' I said. 'Which way is the snooker room?'

K. Tom was crouched over the table when I walked in. He played a shot without looking up and balls clicked against each other. None went down. The table was probably half-size, and there was a bar in the corner of the room, with a proper hand pump. The walls were lined with high chairs, so his cronies could watch the action.

'Nice room,' I told him, looking round.

'Do you play?' he asked, wandering round, studying the pattern of the balls.

'No.'

'You should try it. It's a good way of relaxing.' He saw whatever he was looking for and played another shot. The black ball cannoned into the cushion alongside a pocket and sped away. The white one trickled towards me and fell into the net bag. Even I knew that this was bad. Maybe the gold bracelet was interfering with his swing. I lifted the ball out and placed it on the baize, at my end of the table, to signify that his little game was over. He straightened his back and placed the cue in the rack.

'Did you have an affair with Lisa?' I asked.

For a second he did not know how to answer. He reached across and started rubbing the muscle of his left arm, a pained expression on his face. 'Who told you that?' he asked.

'I get paid to ask questions.'

'Did Ruth tell you?'

'Did you?'

'No, of course not. What did Ruth say?'

'Same as you.'

'So who told you I'd had an affair with Lisa?'

'She did.'

'Lisa? You knew Lisa?'

Full marks to K. Tom. We were supposing that Lisa told him about me in the second phone call.

'Mmm.'

'So why did she tell you that?'

'Why would she lie? She rang you, twice, the night before she was murdered. What did she want?'

'Just someone to talk to. She was drunk. She said it was about her VAT returns, but that was just a pretext.'

'And the second call?'

'I'd asked her for some figures. She rang me back with them.'

'What were they?'

'I don't remember. I didn't even write them down. I only said it to get her off the phone. Like I said, she was drunk,'

'So late Friday night this drunk woman finds her accounts books, extracts some figures from them to do with her VAT returns and rings you back with them. Sounds unlikely, to me.'

He was rubbing his arm again and looking disgruntled. 'Well, it's the truth,' he declared. In other words, prove otherwise, if you can.

'When did you last see her?'

'Months ago. Sometime in the summer.'

'When exactly?'

He shook his head. 'Can't remember.'

'What was the occasion?'

He picked up a blue ball, rotated it in his fingers and put it down again. 'That's right,' he stated. 'Ruth's birthday. They came round with a present for her. So it would be . . . June . . . or July.'

'And when did you last see Justin?'

'Same time.'

'And you haven't seen him since?'

'No.'

'I thought you were his number two fan, his mechanic, followed him all over the Continent.'

His face turned red and his arm was troubling him again. Some people pull their ear lobes or scratch their heads. He rubbed his upper arm. 'I, er, might as well tell you,' he sighed.

'Go on.'

'All that . . . going over to the Continent, with Justin's bike and some spares. It's just a ruse. I don't go to watch him.'

'So why do you go over there?' I couldn't believe he was going to tell me about smuggling gold. He didn't.

'It's, er, Ruth. We, er, don't have much of a, er, relationship, you know.'

'You mean, sex.'

'That's right. I have a friend, in Amsterdam. I go over to see her as often as I can. You're a man of the world,

Inspector. I'm sure you can imagine how it is.'

Why do they always throw it back at you? I didn't have a bloody clue how it was to have a street full of friends in Amsterdam. Someone once told me that the tour guides always recommend the girl in number 42 as the most beautiful. Presumably she was the one to avoid, unless you fancied catching the Japanese strain of HIV.

It was blowing cold outside, threatening rain. I glanced at the garage as I climbed into my car, and wondered about the bullbars. It would be easy enough to raise a search warrant, and that might tell us if he was smuggling gold inside them but we'd not find the rest of it. So far he didn't know we were interested in the gold, unless Jimmy the Fish or the Wattses had tipped him off. I decided it was best to keep on playing it softly-softly.

The next call was the one I wasn't looking forward to. Normally, I don't hang about when I drive, but everything overtook me as I wound reluctantly up the old back road between Heckley and Oldfield, towards Broadside, home of Justin Davis.

He was digging the garden, working furiously, oblivious to the knife-edged breeze flattening the cottongrass on the moors. I closed the gate and walked towards him as he straightened up. Long hair blew across his face. He was wearing a T-shirt and jeans with ripped knees. I stopped about five yards from him, not sure what to expect. He only stood about five feet six tall, but was wiry with it. Proper muscle, not the false stuff you see on TV freak shows.

'I came to say how sorry I was – about Lisa,' I shouted to him, across the patch of newly dug earth.

He placed his foot on the spade and drove it into the ground. 'Let's go inside,' he suggested, and walked towards the house, leaving the spade standing there as if marking a grave.

'Just give me a minute,' he said, ushering me into the front room. 'Sit down, please.'

The parrot wasn't there. I stood and looked out of the window, down towards the Peak District and what I imagined to be Mam Tor. Big drops of rain dashed on to the glass and slid diagonally away.

'Take a seat,' he told me when he returned. He'd changed into a clean version of the same outfit, but was barefoot. His hair was back in a ponytail and his face freshly washed.

'Thanks.' I sat in silence for a long time, looking at some object on the floor, like a Buddhist monk contemplating a candle flame. 'I rang Lisa, Thursday night,' I began. 'I wanted to ask her about K. Tom – your stepfather. There are certain suspicions about him smuggling. Gold, we think. I wondered if your falling out had anything to do with it, so I made an appointment to talk to Lisa Friday morning. That's why I was here. The papers made it sound . . . They tried to make something out of it. You know what they're like.'

He nodded. His face was white and lined beyond that caused by an unhealthy lifestyle, his eyes bloodshot and twitching. Fifty hours in a jumbo jet wouldn't have helped. Fingers with chewed-down nails drummed on the arms of his chair and his feet beat a rhythmless tattoo on the carpet. He badly needed another fix of whatever kept him going.

'Has the doctor seen you?' I asked.

'Yeah. I think the police must have asked him to call.'

'Did he give you anything?'

He shook his head. 'I don't like pills. Reality is scary enough. The thought of not being in control terrifies me.'

'That's a good philosophy,' I agreed, 'but the odd pill might help you sleep, or something.'

'No, I'm OK.'

'Is anybody calling to see you? Friends, anybody?'

'Team mates, and their wives. One or two. I guess it's awkward for them.'

'You're right. They want to do whatever is best, but don't know what that is.'

We chatted on, me letting him do most of it. He suggested coffee and we drifted into the kitchen.

'When will I be able to ... ?' he began. 'When will they let me ... ?'

'The funeral? When will they let you arrange a funeral?'

'Yes. That's what I meant.'

We perched on high stools round what I supposed was a breakfast bar. 'Usually,' I said, 'in a situation like this – a murder case – we have to leave the body in the mortuary after the post mortem, for the defence to arrange their own PM, if they require it. I can't see that being neces- sary. I'll have a word with the coroner, see what we can do.'

'I'd be very grateful. So would Lisa's parents.'

'I know.'

I asked him if he'd go back to Australia, but he hadn't thought about it. Said he might eventually settle over there, make a fresh start.

'Where's the bird – Joey?' I wondered. 'He'd be some company for you.'

'Lisa's parents are looking after him. I'll have a ride over to collect him, this afternoon.'

'I should. He, er, was on the floor, near the front door when I came. I picked him up. It was the bravest thing I've ever done in my life.'

Justin gave the briefest of smiles. 'He was probably scared. He wouldn't hurt you.' He looked in his coffee mug, realised it was empty and reached out for mine. 'Another coffee?'

'Please.'

With his back to me, as he waited for the kettle to boil again, he said, 'Lisa loved Joey. And he loved her. He was a present for her tenth birthday. She used to take Joey in the bath with her. He'd stand on the taps, and after she'd rinsed her hair with the attachment she'd give him a shower. He enjoyed that.'

'He did look a bit straggly,' I said.

He slid the full mug across to me and climbed on to his stool. 'Did Lisa suffer, Charlie? That's the question I need answering, most of all.'

I finished stirring in a couple of spoonfuls of sugar, touched the tip of the spoon on the surface of the coffee to remove the last droplet and deliberately placed the spoon alongside my mug, equidistant from it and two edges of the tabletop. 'It was quick,' I told him. 'And she didn't struggle. She had no time to struggle. That's all I know, but that much, I guarantee.'

'I appreciate what you say. Will you catch . . . whoever it was?'

'I'll catch 'em, Justin. That I vow.'

The visit I'd been scared of making lasted two and a half hours. I promised to call again and told him he could ring me any time, night or day. At the door I said, 'Sooner or later, Justin, it's going to occur to you that if I hadn't been nosing into various people's affairs, this might not have happened. I'm aware of it, and it bothers me.'

He shook his head, saying, 'No. You were only doing your job. Two years ago a rider crashed while trying to get past me. He's in a wheelchair, now. If I hadn't been so determined not to let him through he'd still be walking about. I won an extra point and twenty quid. He got that.'

The car was facing in the wrong direction, but I didn't bother turning it around. I drove to the highest place on the moors and just sat there for half an hour, safe and warm, with the wind buffeting the car and the view slowly turning to a khaki smudge as a wall of bad weather blew in from the west and the first sleet of the season built up on the windscreen.

I knew Gilbert wouldn't be in, so I used the back stairs and sat in his office while I rang Superintendent Isles. He couldn't see any reason why Lisa's body shouldn't be released. Sometimes, with cut throats, great weight is put on the angle of the attack, and whether it was done by a left- or right-handed assailant, but we'd made no conclusions about this. He promised to have a word with the coroner. After that I waited in the gathering gloom until it was time to go home.

I wasn't hungry, so instead of tea I settled for listening to a Joan Baez CD. The first song on it was 'Diamonds and Rust', straight out of my desert island selection. After that I typed my ethics paper.

At eight o'clock I rang Annabelle. 'Have you finished eating?' I asked, when she answered.

'Yes, thank you. I wish you'd been able to be with us.'

'I, er, thought I might be working late. Did your friends find you OK?'

'Yes, but . . .' She lowered her voice to a whisper. 'I think they expected you to be here, too.'

'You mean, living with you?'

'Yes.'

'I'm open to offers.'

After a pause she said, 'Maybe that is something to discuss another time.'

'Right,' I replied. I liked the way this was going. 'Have you been anywhere?'

'Yes,' she answered, brightly. 'Marie and Toby didn't arrive until nearly two, so we couldn't go too far. Would you believe I took them to the Sculpture Park? They enjoyed it immensely.'

'Good. I bet they didn't guess as many as I did.'

'Well, they wouldn't, would they, never having been before?'

'I'd never been before,' I protested in my hurt voice.

'Ha, I'll believe you. They didn't even make a passable attempt at poor old St Sebastian.'

'At who!' I exclaimed, sitting up.

'St Sebastian. Surely you remember him.'

'No, you've lost me.'

'The tall one, with the bicycle wheel on his head. That is his halo. He was martyred by being shot with arrows, hence the spiky bits. Didn't I tell you who he was?'

'No,' I mumbled. 'You never mentioned it.'

'Well, now you know. Are you coming for supper, tomorrow?'

'Er, yes, I'd like that.'

'Good. Any requests?'

'No, er, Annabelle, I, er, won't keep you from your guests any longer. See you tomorrow, eh?'

We said our goodbyes and I rolled on the floor, holding my head. The martyrdom of St Sebastian. Five yards in, at five yard intervals. That's where the gold was buried, just over the fence from Davis's paddock.

Sparky was at home when I rang. 'Does Daniel own a metal detector?' I asked him.

'No. Why?'

I explained.

'Task force have them,' he said when I'd finished. 'I could collect one from HQ and meet you there.'

'What, now?'

'Why not? If we did a search in daylight we'd end up with every gold-hungry nut in the country converging on the place. I could meet you there in less than an hour.'

'Right,' I agreed. 'Pay and display car park. I'll take a spade. See you there, quick as you can.'

I'm not sure what the courting couple thought when these two dark-clad figures unloaded their cars and set off across the park, but nobody rang the police. Maybe their attention was elsewhere. I led the way across the big field, hoping to find a short cut through the temporary exhibits.

'Waaah!' Sparky yelled, dropping the detector and throwing his arms around my neck. We'd reached the crowd of headless men.

'Be quiet,' I hissed. 'Security will hear you. They're only statues.'

'Scared the living daylights out of me,' he gasped.

The short cut wasn't such a good idea and we had to retrace our steps.

'What's that one supposed to be?' he hissed.

'It's called *Spindle Piece*, by Henry Moore.'

'What's it worth?'

'Oh, about half a million.'

'Jesus. We're looking for the wrong guy.'

'You're a Philistine.'

There were no lights coming from the direction of Davis's house. 'This is the one we're looking for,' I whispered. 'It's St Sebastian.'

'Could've fooled me.'

'And the fence is about fifty yards that way. I'm presuming they mean five yards in from that.'

'Makes sense.' He lowered the metal detector to the ground, placed the headphones over his ears and shone a little torch on the controls.

'Do you know how it works?' I asked.

'They gave me a crash course. It's set to detect anything metallic, so if I get a buzz in the headphones, you have to dig it up.'

'OK. Let's go.'

I paced five yards in from the fence and Sparky wandered away, skimming the head of the machine from side to side, just above the ground.

Nothing.

'Maybe it doesn't work,' I suggested.

'Well, let's try it on something.'

I took a coin from my pocket and dropped it on the grass. Sparky found it straight away.

'Did it make a buzz?'

'Mmm. Loud and clear.'

'What's it like with something bigger?' I asked, pushing the head of the spade under the business end. He jumped about a foot in the air.

We tried again, in the opposite direction. Nothing. Then we climbed the fence and tried five yards that side of it, in Davis's paddock. We found two ring pulls from drinks cans, from the days when they came away in your fingers, an old key and a horse shoe.

'This is fun,' Sparky confessed. 'I might convince Daniel that he ought to have one.'

'Why?' I asked. 'Have you tired of his train set, and the radio-controlled aeroplane, and the fishing rod and the mountain bikes and the . . .'

'OK! I get the message. It's just that – Charlie! There's something here! Something big! I think we've found it!'

'Where!'

'There! It's nearly blowing my head off.'

He pinpointed the spot and I started digging. I removed a square of turf and waved him to have another go.

'It's still down there,' he said.

The world started to revolve around me, as if seen from a carousel.

'They're back!' Sparky hissed.

I turned as the headlights of the Range Rover swung across the paddock, sweeping the shadows of trees and fence before them.

'They can't see us,' I said.

A security light came on, headlights were extinguished, doors slammed. We sat on our heels until all was dark again. 'Right, where were we?' I wondered.

I dug deeper and Sparky checked the hole again. Still there. I widened it and removed several more spadefuls of soil.

'It's still down there.'

'I'm not happy with this division of labour,' I puffed as I pushed the spade further down. It came to an abrupt stop.

'I've hit something!' I exclaimed.

And it was metallic, I quickly discovered, as the spade scraped across it. I removed soil with my hands, revealing a square object, exactly the size I imagined we were looking for. The spade down the side and some applied leverage eventually freed it from its hiding-place. I rose to my feet, holding the heavy metal block as if it were a piece of the true cross.

'Shine the torch on it,' I suggested.

'I've been trying. It's duff.'

'There's something embossed on the side.'

'You'd expect that, wouldn't you?'

'Yeah, and it's heavy enough. Bring the stuff, young Jim, lad; we could be in business. Let's get back to the cars.'

Chapter Thirteen

The doubts started on the way back. 'It's not gold,' I decided. 'It's more like a tin box. You know – a cash box.'

'Maybe it's a cash box full of gold.'

'Mmm. Perhaps.'

'Well let's see, shall we?'

He switched his headlights on and we crouched in front of them, examining our find. When I realised what it was I gave it a hard bang on the Tarmac and a wad of clay came out in a large loaf-sized lump. Exactly loaf-sized. The word embossed on the side of the box said: BREAD.

Sparky placed his hands over his head, sitting on the floor, and rocked backwards and forwards, making gurgling noises. I hurled the tin over the hedge, far into a copse. It clattered through the branches before falling to earth.

'I think you and I ought to come to some agreement about this,' I declared.

He looked up at me, his nose casting a horizontal shadow in the glare of the headlights, the tears from the eye at the illuminated side glistening on his cheek.

'Agreed,' he replied, nodding and sniffing. 'I won't say a word to anyone about tonight . . . if you promise not to ever mention line dancing again.'

'You got it.'

We cleaned up as best we could and put everything in his boot. Any disappointment at not striking gold was tempered by the fact that we were enjoying ourselves. My appetite had returned. 'God, I hope there's a fish and chip shop still open, somewhere,' I said.

Sparky waved an arm in a northerly direction. 'There's a good one next junction up. Little restaurant attached.'

'Great! Fancy some?'

'Nah. I had a big tea. I'll come and let you buy me a cuppa, though. I think I deserve it.'

He led the way. It was busy with the trade from the pubs, but they found us a little table in a corner. A young waitress gave us two menus and returned for our order after a few seconds. There were no big decisions to be made.

'Haddock, chips and peas,' I told her. 'That's just for one. And could we have a pot of tea for two, please?'

She scribbled on her pad. 'So that's haddock, chips and peas for one, and tea for two?'

'Yes, please.'

'And would you like bread and butter?'

The poor girl blushed to the roots of her hair, wondering what she had said, as two grown men broke down and giggled like imbeciles.

Sparky left me to it, and I took my time, asking for more hot water for the tea. I felt a lot better with something inside me. When I got back in the car I took the mobile phone from my pocket and placed it on the dash. I don't remember switching it back on, but I must have done. Otherwise, it wouldn't have started ringing before I was a quarter of the way home. The road was quiet, so I pulled in to the side.

'Priest,' I said.

'Charlie, it's Dave. Where are you?'

'I've only been driving five minutes. Why?'

'When I arrived home Shirley said Nigel had been trying to contact us, so I rang him. He said that the APW he put out on K. Tom Davis has borne fruit. Apparently Davis rang Le Shuttle at Folkestone to ask if they could accommodate a Range Rover. They sold him a ticket and he's supposed to be there at eleven a.m. tomorrow.'

'You mean – the Channel Tunnel?'

'That's right.'

'Hey, that's great.'

'So what do you want us to do?'

Good question. 'Let's have a think,' I said. 'If he's booked on for eleven, he'll have to leave home, what, about six hours earlier?'

'At least. And presumably you have to be there an hour before take-off, or whatever, for loading, but apparently you don't book a place, so he could still go anytime.'

'Could he? But he specifically asked about tomorrow?'

'That's what they said.'

'Right. It looks as if the time has come to have Mr Davis's vehicle reduced to its component parts. That'll please him. OK, my faithful friend, thanks for telling me.'

'So, what are we doing?'

'Oh, I can manage.'

'What are you going to do?' he demanded.

'I might just go back and hang around. Maybe he still has to fit the bullbars, or something. If I see him leave I can follow him and rustle up some muscle to stop him. I'd like to be there to see his face. And I want to talk to him about Lisa, while his defences are low.'

Sparky said, 'Right. Where shall I see you?'

'You don't have to come all this way back,' I told him.

'I bloody well want to,' he argued. 'Why should you have all the fun?'

I didn't mind. It might be a long cold wait, so some company would be welcome. 'Fair enough,' I said. 'Where shall we meet?'

'And Nigel said he wants to come, too.'

'Nigel? Where is he now?'

'At the nick, awaiting further instructions.'

'OK,' I said. 'Sounds as if you two have it all worked out, so let's make it a Heckley special. We'll lift K. Tom ourselves, as soon as he leaves home. You get back here pronto, meet me, oh, remember the sculpture called *Spindle Piece*?'

'Yep.'

'Meet me there. We might be able to see any lights at K. Tom's from there and we'll be able to get back to the cars quick to catch up with him on the motorway. Have you a radio?'

'No.'

'We'll have to use mobiles, then. Nigel won't know where we mean. Tell him to keep observation at the end of Davis's lane. Ring us when he's there. OK?'

'Fine. See you shortly.'

I spun the car round and headed back to the pay and display. Fortunately, they don't charge after five o'clock. Different cars with steamed-up windows were parked in the darker corners. There's a lot of it going off.

The moon had risen, but spent most of its time hiding behind high cloud. I trudged across the grass for the second time that night, wishing I'd heeded my mother's constant advice and worn something warmer. An animal, a long way off, gave a blood-curdling scream. Probably a rabbit, meeting its end in the jaws of a fox or a weasel. I made a detour round a flock of grazing Canadian geese, and hoped Sparky wouldn't blunder straight into them and be pecked to pieces. On second thoughts, I hoped he would.

It was a privilege to be there. Scattered around me were some of – arguably – the finest works of art in the world, and I had them all to myself. I wandered around, like a visitor to a new, benign planet, as the moon drifted in and out of the clouds. Lighting by God, I thought, putting on a show just for me. I witnessed a little magic, that night, in that park.

Davis's house was in darkness. I watched it for a while from across his paddock, wondering if that would have been a better place to meet Sparky. But then we'd have been a long way from the cars.

He should be nearly here, so I strolled back to our meeting place. 'Serves you right,' I told St Sebastian as I passed his contorted outline. *Spindle Piece* is on a concrete plinth, but it was almost as cold as the bronze. I sat on it for a few seconds before jumping to my feet and doing some exercises to try keeping warm. *Interlocking Pieces* was about two hundred yards away, up the hill. I sprinted across to it, my legs turning to rubber before halfway, and walked slowly back. Now I felt tired and cold.

I was sitting on my heels, like an aborigine, when I heard the footsteps. The sculptures are hollow, and I'd thought about hiding inside one and scaring the shit out of Sparky, but even I know when the fooling has to cease. Well, sometimes. I was peering in the direction I expected him to approach from, waiting for the moon, when I realised the steps were a lot nearer than I expected, and behind me. I turned, slowly lowering myself to the ground.

The bulky outline that approached wasn't unmistakable as K. Tom, but I was certain it was him, even though his shape was distorted by the long bundle he carried, remarkably similar to the one Sparky had lugged back to the car two hours earlier. A spade and a metal detector, at a guess. He came straight up to the sculpture, the cold night air rasping in his throat as I held my breath, barely ten feet away, with only the Henry Moore between us. I dared to lift my face heavenwards and saw that the moon was well hidden, for the moment.

K. Tom took about fifteen deliberate strides away from me, heading towards the lights of the television mast on the skyline, and lowered his bundle to the ground. The crafty bastard, I thought. He's moved the gold.

He was almost lost against the trees, but I saw what I took to be the swinging motion of the detector. He paused, removed the headphones and reached down for the spade.

We both heard Sparky's footsteps at the same instant. Big men are supposed to be light on their feet, but Dave was the exception. He was as graceful as a hippo with bunions. The line dancers probably suffered heavy casualties the night he went along. Davis was stationary, poised in a crouched position. It looked as if we'd have to arrest him, there and then, and finish looking for the gold ourselves. This time I'd bags the metal detector.

The sickening noise of a pump action shotgun being cocked shattered my equilibrium.

Shit, I thought, not even a double-barrelled number. He had seven shots. And, just to make it easier for him, the moon came out to have a look, bathing the park in frail light, as if to give the big lighting man in the sky a better view of the drama.

Sparky was hunched up, hands deep in pockets, his head moving from side to side as if he were whistling or humming to himself. I looked from one to the other, praying that Dave would raise his head and see K. Tom. When the range was less than thirty yards Davis lifted the gun.

'DAVE!' I screamed. 'SHOTGUN!'

K. Tom whirled and loosed a blast off in my direction. The pellets hit *Spindle Piece* and buzzed off into the night as I dived to the ground. He'd missed me. I jumped up and skipped sideways as he re-cocked the gun, trying to keep one of Henry Moore's finest between us. I risked a quick glance in Sparky's direction, but he'd vanished.

That's when I realised that Henry Moore's most famous characteristic was also his big failing. All his works have bloody great holes through the middle. They're useless for hiding behind from mad gunmen. I dodged one way and then the other as soon as I glimpsed K. Tom to the right or left of the sculpture, or through the middle, and all the time I was retreating, up the hill, putting precious yards between us.

But that was another mistake, and K. Tom realised it at exactly the same instant as I did. The further I moved back, the more I had to move sideways to keep that great shapeless useless mass of bronze between us. Suddenly, I'd gone off *Spindle Piece*.

K. Tom calmly walked round it and levelled the gun at me.

Three explosions burst into the left side of my head. I hit the ground and rolled over, my brain filled with a muffled, screaming silence, and looked for my new adversary.

Nigel was standing there, as immobile as anything in that park. His arms were reaching forward, the hands clasping a big, beautiful, police-issue Smith and Wesson ·38 revolver, silhouetted against a pall of white smoke that drifted off into the darkness.

I rolled on to my knees. K. Tom was on the ground, with Sparky running towards him, then toeing the shotgun away from his body. I stood up and turned to Nigel. He hadn't moved.

'Easy, young feller,' I panted, reaching for the gun. I grasped it by the barrel and pointed it skywards, prising his fingers open. The barrel was warm, and the smell of cordite burned my nostrils, pungent in the cold air. He suddenly released it and lowered his arms, but remained staring in the direction of the fallen body.

'You did well,' I told him. 'You did well. Come over here.'

I led him by the arm and sat him on the plinth of the sculpture. 'Just sit there,' I said and turned to Sparky. 'How is he?'

'Not sure, but he's breathing.'

'I'll ring for assistance.'

When I'd finished, Sparky said it was only a shoulder wound, and the patient was conscious. Two bullets had missed. If I'd been there alone I'd have been sorely tempted to finish the job, once and for all.

The adrenaline rush faded with the danger, and reality returned. I had a police ·38 in my pocket, with three spent chambers, and a wounded prisoner. I unloaded the gun and walked back to where Nigel was sitting.

'You OK?' I asked.

He nodded. 'Will he live?'

'It looks like it. Come for a little walk. I want a word.'

I led him up the hill until we were out of K. Tom's earshot. 'Nigel,' I began. 'How come you had a gun?'

'What's it like when you kill a man, Charlie?' he asked.

'You haven't killed anyone,' I reminded him.

'He might die.'

'OK. It's not very nice. You have to convince yourself that you had no other option, and learn to live with it. K. Tom might die, but if you hadn't fired when you did, you'd be going to two funerals next week. Never forget that. Some of us are very grateful you were here, tonight, and did what you did. Now answer my question, Nigel. This is important. Why did you have a gun and where did you get it?'

He brushed his hair out of his eyes. 'I was waiting in the nick,' he replied, 'for Sparky – Dave – to ring me back. I decided to check if Davis is licensed to hold a shotgun. He is. It occurred to me that he might have it with him, so I drew the thirty-eight from the armoury.'

'How, Nigel?' I insisted. 'How did you withdraw it?'

'Inspector Adey was on duty. He signed it out for me.'

'Off his own bat?'

'No. He rang Force Control. The officer in charge sanctioned it.'

'You're sure about that?'

'Yes. It's all right, Charlie. We did it by the book.'

'Thank Christ for that,' I sighed. Good old Nigel had played it by the book. I should have known better than to imagine he'd do it any other way. Suddenly, I felt weary. I sat down on the grass and stretched out, lying on my back staring at the moon. I could have lain there all night, except the revolver was sticking in my kidneys, and the helicopter was chomping in over the treetops, flashing and banking like something out of *Close Encounters of the Third Kind*.

K. Tom survived. Considering the range, and the bad light, it was good shooting by Nigel, but outside the normal parameters for taking out an armed assailant. By the rules of the game Davis should have been dead. I spent Tuesday morning giving evidence to the investigating officer brought in from another division to look into the shooting. He shook his head once or twice, but nothing worse.

After that I needed a cup of tea and a pork pie, badly. I was running down the stairs when I met Inspector Adey.

'Hi, Gareth,' I said as I passed him.

'Everything OK, Charlie?' he called after me, concerned.

'I think so,' I shouted back over my shoulder.

'Charlie!' he yelled.

I stopped and looked up at him.

'Thought you might like some good news,' he said.

'That would be most welcome. What is it?'

'This morning Fingerprints rang us about a match they'd made. We've just arrested a youth for killing the swans in the park, thanks to that beer can you found there.'

'Hey, that's great. Is it anybody we know?'

'We don't know him,' he replied, 'but apparently he's an old friend of yours.'

'Oh,' I said, taking a step back up towards him. 'I think you'd better tell me all about it.'

In the afternoon Superintendent Les Isles and I held a case review meeting in his office. Makinson was with us, too, but he didn't have much to contribute. K. Tom Davis was in Heckley General, under armed guard. He was sitting up and had been charged with attempted murder.

'First of all,' Les began, 'let me tell you about Michael Angelo Watts. I have a miracle to report – his memory has returned. We fed it to him that Davis had been arrested

and the remainder of the gold recovered, and he decided
that it might be helpful to us if he made a statement. The
gist of it is that he'd left his portable telephone – more
correctly, his father's telephone – at K. Tom Davis's
house on the Wednesday before Lisa was killed. I asked
him if there was anybody who could corroborate that and
he suggested Mrs Davis. I told him that was a no-no. She
denied ever seeing the phone, and he looked uncharacter-
istically glum. He brightened a little when I disclosed that
I had a witness who might help him.'

'Me,' I said.

'Mmm,' Les continued. 'I told Watts that you had made
a statement saying how you saw him visit Davis at the
appropriate time, and suggesting that his behaviour indicated that he had taken the wrong phone with him. In
other words, you'd got him off a murder rap.'

'Did he express his gratitude?'

'Not exactly – don't forget you had helped put him
behind bars for dealing. I made it plain that we'd been fair
with him, and that making threats against your girlfriend
was bang out of order. I'd be lying if I said he looked
sheepish, Charlie, but I think he took it onboard.'

'Great,' I said. 'That's good news. It was worrying me.'

'I'll bet it was. Now let's have a look at Davis. I'm afraid
the outlook is not so rosy from now on. We've only
recovered the one bar of gold, for a start. Either he spread
it around, or that's all there is left.'

'Twenty kilograms, or one hundred and twenty-five
thousand pounds' worth, out of ten million quid. That's
not bad going.'

'These drugs barons have expensive tastes. Mr and Mrs
Davis – K. Tom and the desirable Ruth – have had sudden
pangs of remorse, too, and they have both decided to fully

cooperate with us. Their tales, sadly, differ in one important area. He says that he stayed in on the night Lisa was killed, but that she stormed out in a paddy. Ruth Davis says more or less the opposite.'

'What are the stories?' I asked.

'Well, according to K. Tom, Lisa rang him about her business, as previously stated. Ruth was insanely jealous, he claims, convinced they were having an affair. After the second call she dashed out of the house, saying she would settle things – wait for it – "once and for all."'

I said, 'Gosh, well, that proves it. Did he mention the phone?'

'Reckons he never saw it. She must have found it and planned the whole thing to put the blame on poor old Watts.'

'So he claims that her motive was jealousy, and the desire to protect her loveless marriage.'

'Cor-rect.'

'And what's her story?'

'Ah. Mrs Davis wants to eat her cake and have it. Her tune has changed since she learned that, whatever happens, she keeps the conservatory. She claims she was in bed with migraine . . .'

I chipped in with 'Not DC Migraine from Huddersfield?'

Makinson scowled while Les smiled and went on. 'That's the one. Her loving husband brought her a cup of tea and two aspirin, at about ten thirty, and said he was popping out for the last half hour in the pub.'

'The woman's a living lie,' I stated. 'Can't accept that they hate each other's guts. They're held together by mutual greed. You said she hadn't seen the phone, either.'

'That's right. Says he must have found it and planned the whole thing ...'

I finished it off for him. 'To incriminate poor old Michael.'

'That's right. And then there's the problem of motive. We believe he killed Lisa to stop her spilling the beans about the gold, but we've only your word about that, Charlie.'

Makinson shuffled in his seat and was about to speak when a PC came backwards through the doorway, carrying a tray with coffee and biscuits.

'About time,' Les said, jovially, pushing papers aside to make room on his desk.

We shouted our thanks after the departing uniform and I looked for the sugar. There wasn't any. I took a sip. It was like drinking neat creosote.

When we were ready again Les asked Makinson what he'd been about to say. He was called Tim. He wiped a crumb of chocolate digestive from his chin and sat back. 'I was just about to make an observation,' he mumbled. 'As I see it, we have two suspects, and one of them almost certainly killed Lisa Davis. Unfortunately, we can't present them both to the court and say, "Take your pick." We have to decide which case is the stronger, and go with that. The evidence against him is minimal. She has the stronger motive, but would come across as a harmless housewife. Taking them individually, I'd say we didn't stand a chance of a conviction.'

'Mmm. What do you think, Charlie?' Isles asked.

I lifted the cup to my lips and decided I didn't really need it that badly, so I lowered it again. 'I'd say that Tim has just made a very fair assessment of the situation,' I admitted. 'But I'm not leaving it at that. K. Tom Davis might be going away for a long time, but that doesn't help Justin Davis. He wants a conviction. He needs someone to blame, to focus his hate on. He needs to make sense of what happened to his wife. If this goes to court on a not guilty plea, Lisa's reputation will be dragged through the mire, laid open for the vultures to pick over. How's that gonna make her husband feel?'

'Not to mention,' Les added, 'the suspicion that his mother killed his wife. It's like bloody King Lear.' His Shakespeare was worse than mine but I know what he meant. After a sip of coffee he dunked a biscuit, saying, 'Aah. It's taken a long time, but I've got them making it just how I like it.'

'So Forensic haven't come up with anything?' I asked, forlornly, already knowing the answer.

'Some tyre tracks,' Makinson informed me. 'Small sample of the same type as on Davis's Range Rover, but nowhere near enough to be conclusive. Oh, and some really good ones that are a perfect match with your Cavalier.' He enjoyed telling me that.

I stood up and turned to Les. 'Is it all right if I have a go at K. Tom?'

He looked at Makinson, who shrugged his shoulders. 'Be our guest,' he replied.

'Cheers. Maybe I can appeal to his better nature, convince him that a confession would be in order.' Winking at Isles, I added, 'Failing that, I'll kick the shit out of him.'

I could have done it, I know that. Last night, in the Sculpture Park, I coud have put the gun to Davis's head and blown his brains out. And in the years afterwards, whenever I woke in the night filled with doubts about what I'd done, I'd have conjured up that image of Lisa, lying in the bath of blood, and fallen back to sleep again.

I went down to the canteen for a mug of sweet tea, and succumbed to a vanilla slice while thinking about how to handle K. Tom. I decided to cause him as much grief as I could. That way, there'd be no need for acting.

The hospital is only a couple of streets away from headquarters, and parking spaces there are auctioned by Sotheby's since they sold most of their land for office developments, so I walked. The afternoon visitors had left and meal trolleys were monopolising the lifts, so I climbed three floors rather than wait. My, I was catching up on my exercise today.

The PC on guard duty was sitting outside Davis's private little room. 'They're changing his dressings,' he told me, after I showed him my ID.

'Has he much to say?' I asked.

'Not to us, sir, but he's plenty of chat with the nurses. Has them eating out of his 'ands, running about, doing favours for him. Sometimes I feel as if I'm the villain. Takes me all my time to get someone to fetch me a cup o' tea from the machine.'

'Right. We'll see about that,' I said, pushing the door open.

Three figures turned to me, two of them wearing nurses' uniforms and the third an expression of loathing.

'Detective Inspector Priest,' I announced, showing my card.

'Sorry, Inspector,' the older nurse said, straightening up, 'we're just changing Mr Davis's dressings. I shall have to insist that you leave.'

'That's all right,' I replied, looking at him. 'I don't faint at the sight of other people's blood. Neither do you, eh, Tom?'

'What do you want?' he hissed.

'I came to see where you were shot. The officer who fired at you has a certificate for marksmanship – I'm thinking of revoking it.'

The older nurse came to the foot of his bed as I positioned myself at the other side. He was propped up on several pillows, bare chested except for the bandages on his right shoulder. His right arm was across his body, rubbing the top of his other arm, the way he'd done in the snooker room.

Boss nurse said, 'This is highly irregular, Inspector. It isn't a matter of you fainting. We have to consider the patient's privacy and the risk of infection. I'd be . . .'

'Look,' I interrupted, 'from now on, he has no privacy. As for infection, I've had all my jabs. I'm staying, so why don't you just get on with it?'

She made a few tutting noises and muttered threats about taking it further, but went back to the task of snipping away the old bandages. The young nurse, who was only a green belt, noticed Davis massaging his arm and said, 'Is that still bothering you? Would you like the doctor to look at it?'

'N-No. It's n-nothing,' he stuttered, holding his hand still but not removing it.

'Have a look at what?' I demanded, grabbing his wrist and yanking it away.

'How did you get that?' I asked, as he pulled his hand free from my grasp and placed it back over the mark on his upper arm.

He glowered at the young nurse and the older one took a step backwards, holding a pair of scissors towards me. Davis hyperventilated, his face reddening alarmingly, and his body jerked backwards and forwards.

'I asked you a question, Davis,' I yelled at him. 'How did you get the mark on your arm?'

He took a long slow breath, staring at the pattern on the quilt over his legs. 'I banged it,' he replied. 'In the garage. I banged it.'

The PC outside had managed to find himself a cup of coffee. 'You haven't time for that,' I told him, holding the door to Davis's room open so I didn't lose sight of him for a second. 'Radio HQ straight away. Tell them to get a photographer here, as soon as possible. Then find out where Superintendent Isles is and tell him Charlie Priest wants a word, urgent.'

He dashed off to a window, where the reception was better, and I went back inside. It wasn't necessary – he was already under arrest for attempted murder – but I did it just the same. I wanted to see their faces. I said, 'K. Tom Davis, I am arresting you for the murder of Lisa Davis. You do not have to say anything, but it may harm your defence if you do not mention, when questioned, something which you later rely on in court. Anything you do say may be taken down and used in evidence.'

There was a chair for a visitor in the corner. I sat on it, hoping the photographer wouldn't be long. The marks had been on Davis's arm for twelve days but I didn't want my case thwarted by a miracle recovery. I rocked back on two legs, leaning against the wall at an impossible angle, watching him, wondering if I'd still be able to make it to Annabelle's for supper. I wanted to – I deserved it – but there was work to do, and people to talk to. Happy, happy happy happy talk.

Chapter Fourteen

The waiter slid Annabelle's chair underneath her and, when she was settled, lowered the huge leather-bound menu into her hands. She was wearing her purple suit, no make-up, no blouse visible, no jewellery. If the architecture is right, you don't need decoration. Her hair had grown longer, and she'd tied it up on the top of her head. I dragged my eyes away to study the menu the waiter was manoeuvring into my grasp.

It could have been *The Book of Kells*, hand illuminated, written with the imagination of a Stephen King, but it was only a menu. I studied it for key words, like chicken, or steak.

Annabelle leaned across and whispered, 'Can we afford this, Charles? There are no prices in my menu.'

I smiled at her, saying, 'Don't worry about it. I think the prices in mine are for two.'

'Ho ho,' she laughed. 'You will be lucky.'

The wine waiter brought the bottle we'd ordered earlier and went through the usual ritual. I waved a hand for him just to pour it. When he'd gone, Annabelle said, 'You were telling me about K. Tom Davis. So how did you prove it was him?'

'Right,' I replied. 'It was all down to highly skilled detective work.'

'Well, of course.'

'Absolutely. I took a SOCO round to Broadside – Justin's house – and he cut a slice of apple that was just the right thickness. Don't ask me how he worked that out. Justin offered it to the parrot – Joey – who promptly bit straight through it and ate the piece. So he tried again, this time with a piece of turnip. Joey sank his beak into that and either didn't like it or it was too tough for him, so he let go. SOCO sliced into the turnip and unfolded it, and *voilà*! A perfect imprint of Joey's beak. Have you ever studied a parrot's beak?'

'No, not at close range.'

'They're amazing. Incredibly powerful, yet they can be so gentle. When they bite, the top part makes a puncture wound, but the lower mandible leaves two incisions, so you receive three bites for the price of one. Justin says it's the most excruciating pain imaginable, and he should know – he's broken most of his bones at various times.'

'And the imprint of Joey's beak matched the mark on K. Tom Davis's arm?'

'Mmm. Exactly. We couldn't prove it was Joey, but he's certainly been bitten by a macaw. According to Justin, it's a wonder he didn't mark K. Tom for life. Any idea what you're having?'

'So Joey was in the bathroom with poor Lisa?'

'That's right. They were inseparable.'

'In a way, I suppose he did, bless him.'

'Did what?'

'Mark K. Tom for life.'

I folded the menu, being careful not to swipe everything off the table, and gazed across at her. She looked sad. I wanted to hold her hand, but she was too far away.

'I've decided,' I announced. 'It's either the flamingo's

kneecaps, on a bed of lily petals in a cage of baby asparagus stems, or – wait for it – the Beef Wellington.'

'I knew you would have the beef,' Annabelle declared.

'Am I so depressingly predictable?'

'Not at all. It's probably the best thing they do. I think I will have the salmon. So how much gold did you recover?'

'Just the one bar, unless Sparky concealed half a dozen in his car boot.'

'Good gracious. Where did it all go?'

I shook my head. 'No idea. Somewhere on the Continent, we presume, concealed inside K. Tom's bullbar. We think that part of the deal was that he deliver the gold over there, to work off his debts to Michael Angelo Watts.'

'Because of the diamonds failure?'

'That's right. And for madam's starter?'

'Umm, the duck pâté, I think. Yes, the duck pâté.'

'Ah!' I exclaimed.

'Ah? Why "Ah"?'

'Oh, er, nothing. A wise choice if I might say so.' I reached across and she gave me her menu. The waiter ceased to hover and went into a dive, pulling out alongside me with inches to spare. When he'd gone, taking our orders to the kitchen and the menus back to their air-conditioned vault in the Bodleian, Annabelle repeated, 'Why "Ah"? What do you know about the duck pâté?'

I sighed and unfolded my napkin, draping it over my knees like a travel rug. 'I'd, er, rather not say,' I told her.

'Now you are being infuriating, Charles,' she insisted, in her pretend-school-ma'am voice.

'Well, this involves my eating humble pie, and it will ruin my appetite.'

'Gosh. The great detective having to admit he was wrong. Tell me all about it.'

I took a sip of wine. 'This is nice,' I said, turning the glass in my fingers.

'Tell me!'

'OK! OK! We, er, caught someone for killing the swans in the park.'

A smile crept over her face. 'You mean – poor Donald is no longer a suspect. What's the phrase? He's not ... *in the frame*, any more?'

I pulled my best grimace. 'For the time being,' I growled, 'but I'll have him, one day.'

'You can't win 'em all, Charlie boy,' Annabelle smirked, tipping me a wink. The waiter returned to give us the appropriate cutlery.

'It's a sad story,' I told her. 'Young man, only twenty-one. Lots of problems, into drugs and anything else he could find or steal, probably schizophrenic. Another one let down by the care in the community system. I actually arrested him, later that day, but we never thought to associate him with the swans.'

'Poor chap. What had he done?'

'Tried to break into a flat. He was up a ladder, threatening to throw a dog down. I managed to talk him out of it.'

'Donald wouldn't do anything like that,' Annabelle assured me.

'No. Maybe I owe him an apology. No I don't. What am I saying? He comes and digs your garden, has morning coffee with you, and I'm jealous. I'll get him, one day.'

'That reminds me!' she exclaimed. 'I am the one you owe an apology. Thanks to you, Donald now charges me four pounds an hour. He says you told him to!'

'He's worth every penny,' I countered. 'You were exploiting him.'

The first courses arrived, arranged on the plates to look like something knocked up by Paul Klee. I was selecting the correct implements when a thought occurred. 'Wait a minute,' I said, 'wait a minute.'

Annabelle looked up from her work of art.

'This money you pay Donald,' I continued. 'I don't suppose you know if he declares it to the Inland Revenue, do you?'

Annabelle placed her knife and fork back on the table.

'Oh, Charles,' she giggled. 'You are impossible,' and her nose wrinkled the way it does when the happiness takes over, and any hunger I had for food went flying right out of the window.